SWEDES'
FERRY

ALLAN SAFARIK

COTEAU BOOKS

10 9 8 7 6 5 4 3 2 1

Edited by Terry Jordan
Designed by Tania Craan
Typeset by Susan Buck
Cover art: *The Cowboy*, Frederic Remington
Printed and bound in Canada at Gauvin Press

Library and Archives Canada Cataloguing in Publication
Safarik, Allan, 1948-, author
        Swedes' ferry / Allan Safarik.

Issued in print and electronic formats.
ISBN 978-1-55050-561-0 (pbk.).--ISBN 978-1-55050-562-7 (pdf).--
ISBN 978-1-55050-746-1 (epub).--ISBN 978-1-55050-747-8 (mobi)

        I. Title.

PS8587.A245S93 2013   C813'.54   C2013-904969-X
                                           C2013-904970-3

2517 Victoria Avenue
Regina, Saskatchewan
Canada S4P 0T2
www.coteaubooks.com

Available in Canada from:
Publishers Group Canada
2440 Viking Way
Richmond, British Columbia
Canada V6V 1N2

Coteau Books gratefully acknowledges the financial support of its publishing
program by: the Saskatchewan Arts Board, The Canada Council for the Arts,
the Government of Canada through the Canada Book Fund and the
Government of Saskatchewan through the Creative Industry Growth and
Sustainability program of the Ministry of Parks, Culture and Sport.

for Dolores

1

May, 1894
Province of Manitoba, Canada

He came into the country on a stolen horse. Ridden hard and lathered up. The sun seemed to shine from its foaming mouth.

The old man, Bud Quigley, walked out from his dirt floor cabin and spat brown juice into the dust. He looked at the horse and shook his head.

"Bugger's been pushed to the edge."

Heat from the sun was intense in the middle of the afternoon. Sweat stained the saddle leather. The lanky young rider the old man had named Tall Bob when he first arrived in these parts a couple of weeks earlier, dismounted, handing the reins to the old man while he dipped a ladle into the rain barrel and sucked in as much water as he could handle. The clothes on his body were crusted with salt and faded by the weather.

The old man ran his finger down the long, raw wound on the horse's rump while the young man stood squinting in the sun. The rider's mind was on other matters – a gunshot in the street, a bank manager lying dead in the doorway having made the mistake of sounding the alarm, the result being that he caught a bullet in the fat part of his balding forehead. Like the dot below an exclamation point. The very nature of that punctuation had torn him apart – a red dot in the middle of his wrinkled brow, a bullet rattling around making soup of the brain in his skull.

"I'd have a drink if there was something stronger than rain water."

"Be my guest," Bud said when he returned from his cabin with a bottle of whisky. Tall Bob pulled on the bottle with a long slow swig that made the sun swoon in the absolute purity of the sky. The old man, waiting for his turn, licked the dust from his lips.

"You're doing a pretty good job on that bottle for a man who don't drink."

"Changed my ways," the young man answered.

Bud polished the bottle's neck under his armpit before he half-filled a tin cup with whisky for himself. The tall man took back the bottle, arched his back and drained another couple of inches. The burning liquid gurgled down his throat. He smacked his lips and wiped his mouth on his ragged sleeves.

The horse sat on its haunches in the dust, lathered up on its withers. The oily chestnut hide shining under an eighth of an inch of sweat. Flies settled on the injury like a black scourge. Tall Bob poured some of the whisky onto the open wound, scattering the flies into the wind until the liquor evaporated. Soon the hovering winged horde landed back on the raw furrow.

Bud took a good look at the figure vibrating in front of him. There was a dramatic change in the serious young man who had come to him in search of a horse and the gear for an adventure south of the border. Clear-eyed, a self-proclaimed abstainer with few words and a calm emptiness that seemed to haunt him. He needed a horse that could outrun the devil on his best day. An unruffled animal that could handle panic and loud noises and stay composed under intense pressure. When the old man took him to the pasture to look at his horses, he realized the kid was a natural. A cool customer who rode like the jockeys he'd seen riding in match races at summer fairs. When Tall Bob talked to the horses they crowded around as if they understood his lingo. Now he was standing in Bud's yard calming an unfamiliar horse that had given its all for the stranger on its back. The young man's eyes staring out from his sunburnt face and peeling nose had grown intense and hawk-like, as if they had witnessed some cruelty or experienced a measure of pain somewhere on the trail.

The old man loosened the belly strap and slid the saddle from the horse's back. He looked at the cruel bit in the broken mouth. He saw the bloody signs of a hard-mouthed ride that must have seemed like a trip through eternity. Bud filled up a bucket with the bitter mineral-tainted water from the well and threw it over the horse's head. Fetching another half-dozen pailsfull, he poured them over the horse's back until the chestnut colour turned a glistening, deep shade of maple syrup brown.

Eventually, the gelding lurched back to its feet as if fate had decided it was time to rise or die on the cricket-laden dirt under the open sky. The old man was exhausted from pulling so many pails of water from the depths. Panting like a dog, he felt a sudden loss of breath so he sat on the chopping block beside the wood pile. He rested until the colour came back into his face and the dizziness subsided.

The chestnut was up, shivering under the light from the sun. The old man considered its condition for a moment and impulsively decided against the gun.

"Poor thing might make it yet," he muttered, "I could shoot him now or shoot him later. I guess he's suffering, but Christ so are the rest of us." He took another furtive swig from the cup. The whisky burned his lips like hot fat before he gulped it down with a strange, airy, after-burp.

Tall Bob tipped back the bottle and drained two inches of it in one pull. His spurs glinted when he walked over to the desolate creature standing transfixed under the buzz of the worrying flies. The horse's big round eyes stared out from its head like brown jewels. Occasionally its flanks flinched in a kind of semi-complicated movement. The light ran off its hide like water sliding down a slicker.

"No use letting the poor beast die here."

The old man agreed. "Yep, be like having a big stinking advertisement for bank robbery on the premises."

Tall Bob laughed hard and sputtered as he coughed at the same time.

"Premises you say? That's a bit of a stretch, don't ya think?"

Bud led the chestnut past the rough chicken coop. He let it go in the split-rail corral that was partially shaded by a grove of aspen trees. A dozen rusty-coloured chickens ran about pecking at the sand or squawking when the rooster stalked one of them. The old man owned an ever-changing herd of horses that usually numbered around twenty depending how active he was in wheeling and dealing. A knot-headed stud, eight mares and a half-dozen foals were turned out in the fenced pasture about four miles away. A bay saddle horse, the Belgian-Clyde cross he used for pulling the plough, and Suzy, the mare he rode to town on, were hobbled in the bush beside the creek in the coulee bottom, about a mile from the cabin.

"Look," said the old man, squinting his yellow eyes, "I have another good runner in my pasture. In the morning I'll ride up and fetch Red Ned and bring him over here. He'll carry you back home. That is, if you have any money to spend. If you encounter any trouble, Ned will give you a run for it. I'll give you a bill of sale and you can dispose of him when you feel like it. So at least nobody will accuse you of being a horse thief."

Tall Bob, a man of few burnished words, took it all in without comment.

"I recommend you pound out a couple of hundred miles before you stop to enjoy yourself. Wait a long time before you come back in this direction. I'll ride the mare and take your chestnut out into the country and drop him in a thicket somewhere. The coyotes will have a big feed for a week. The only evidence left will be a pile of bones that won't be of any use, even to a raven."

When the stars came out, Bud dug out the bean pot from a smouldering hole in the ground and announced that supper was served. They sat in the glow of the fire and forked in beans, then cleaned up with the bannock Bud cooked over the fire on a stick. They washed it down with the coffee from the blackened coffee pot that percolated like a pulse in somebody's neck.

Tall Bob stood up after eating and stretched his long legs. Then he sat down on the chopping block and asked Bud to pull off his scuffed boots.

"These are on real tight," Bud grunted as the first boot was finally separated from its owner. "Holy mackerel, your boot's full of cash!"

"So's the other one."

"Put your clothes on the fire. I have some duds that'll kind of fit you. At least you'll look different from when you arrived here."

Tall Bob was up on his feet stripping off his dusty, torn clothing. He ripped the shirt into tatters and threw it into the fire along with the shiny-seated, worn-out pants that had seen a thousand or more hard miles on the back of a four-legged ride. He picked up his hat and duck coat and added them to the fire, then stood in his stinking underwear suit directly under the handle of the Big Dipper. He opened the buttons in the front and pulled out a flattened oilskin bag.

"Here's the rest of it," he muttered, dropping it in front of Bud, who was counting up the cash from Tall Bob's boots.

"Jumping toads, that's eight hundred dollars."

There was three thousand six hundred more in the oilskin packet that smelled intensely of Tall Bob's body odour.

"Suppose there's no use asking about Foxy?"

"He's pushing up posies somewhere the other side of Bottineau, North Dakota."

"Hand-raised that character myself with a bottle when his mother died. Taught him everything he knew."

"Well you did a fair-to-middling job. A good, solid ride with a big heart, but he didn't see the badger hole he stepped into. Threw me right onto a rock pile on my way into Minot. Broke his leg near clean off. Shot him on the spot. I rode that packhorse you sold me until I had a chance to steal some real horse flesh from a wrangler's herd. Didn't take me long to figure out the chestnut. Gunshots don't bother him and he can run like a jackrabbit. Too bad he gets spooked by little dogs. But now he too has reached the end of the line."

"Yes sir, that's a fact," Bud answered.

"Now, let's talk less and settle up," Tall Bob said.

"Okay, let's see, you owe me sixty bucks for Foxy. That was a good horse, one of the best I ever had. And ten more for that reliable but long-in-the-tooth packhorse I sold you. I hope you put him out of his misery when you had no further use for his services. I'm relieved I don't have to feed him for another winter. Then there's another ten for your new wardrobe and, say about three hundred more for using my place as a base. That roan you came here on is no more. You need a horse to ride out of here on. I'll tell you what. I'll throw in Red Ned for another forty bucks. Not as good as Foxy, but a pretty good traveller all the same. He'll take you a fair piece of distance in a hurry if you've a mind. That makes a tidy sum of four hundred and twenty dollars for me to bury under a tree and hallelujah, I'm a rich man!"

"Problem is, there's a fly in the ointment, Bud."

"What kind of fly?" Bud said, lifting his sad eyes and staring nebulously at Tall Bob. He felt his throat tighten. The tendons in his fingers tugged at his hands as if something unexpected was about to happen.

Leaning forward from his perch, Tall Bob began to count out the cash.

"Fly in the ointment is I left a dead man in the doorway of that damn bank."

"Jeezus loves me." Bud was nearly speechless for a long while after.

6

"You know what that means," Tall Bob said, looking forlorn in his baggy red long johns. "Then, out on the edge of town, a damn kid with an ancient rifle taller than he stands, walks out and lets the chestnut have it. Lucky the ball only nicked him a little or I'd already be in the iron gate cafe waiting for the hangman."

"They'll be coming after you," the old man answered.

"Do you think crossing the border will make a difference?"

"Might slow 'em down but if they're a big posse they'll be all liquored up and they'll just keep coming."

"Yeah, like a pack of hounds. I'll rest up here tomorrow and then leave early the next morning. So here's the deal, Bud. I give you the four hundred and twenty bucks plus a thousand more. You dispose of the chestnut first thing and then clam right up. The thousand bucks is a bonus for my bringing down the wrath of the law upon our heads. You're a clever old bastard, I reckon you're smart enough to bury the cash for a long time. And you, my friend, have the gift of the gab so, if by chance the law travels up to Bottineau and starts asking questions, you stay composed and mum and it'll be okay. Especially with you knowing you're a rich man with your cash buried somewhere safe."

"Never had this kind of money before," Bud answered, looking away into the distance. "I'll shoot that sucker first thing after you leave. You've made a deal."

"Let's shake on it," Tall Bob said, holding out his right hand.

"Why sure enough," Bud replied, sticking out his own right arm and giving Tall Bob the dead-fish-at-the-end-of-the rainbow handshake.

In the morning, when the sun was a bloodshot grapefruit on the wistful horizon, Bud was up and out the door, headed on foot west into the coulee to fetch the bay. Tall Bob walked to the creek behind the cabin, jumped in and scrubbed himself with some of Bud's caustic soap. *It's like starting life all over again*, he thought as he scrubbed off the miles of dust and grime that had settled into his pores. He put on the clean suit of Bud's underwear, an old pair of overalls and a flannel shirt Bud had hanging on the back of the cabin door. Both were a little short in length but they worked well enough. Then he put on a moth-eaten overcoat and well-worn grey hat that Bud had also produced. He looked into the cracked mirror on the cabin wall at his own image and decided he felt like a new man, even though the memory of the bullet entering the bank manager's forehead would never stray far from his thoughts.

Bud returned, riding bareback on the mare he called Suzy, towing Red Ned. He and Tall Bob settled in at the fire he had started before he left, drank another pot of coffee and ate a plate of leftover beans with eggs that he rustled from his chicken house.

Then Bud set off down the trail with Suzy and his telescope. He told Tall Bob that he would go to higher ground and eyeball the back trail to see if anybody was approaching. He warned that if Tall Bob heard a shot it would be a warning and that he better load up, mount Ned and hit the trail because trouble was on the horizon. Near the end of the day, when the light was leaving, Bud came back pretty confident there was nobody following Tall Bob.

"You headed north?" Bud asked at the next dawn, as they were drinking their morning coffee.

Tall Bob was in no mood for conversation, especially about his travel plans.

"I understand," Bud answered, talking to himself since there had been no response to his question.

"It's just that I have a cousin near Moose Jaw you might consider looking up if you need a place to hang out."

"Not going north."

"Well, that's that then," Bud said, backing out of the conversation.

"Not going south either, not going east, not going west. Just going."

"Well if you ever return this way, you're welcome anytime."

"Won't be back in this direction, likely ever."

They finished their breakfast in silence. There didn't seem to be anything more to talk about. After breakfast, Bud threw Tall Bob's saddle up on Red Ned's back.

"I'm hitting the trail. Now Bud old boy, you remember our deal. You take the chestnut five miles from here to some wild place and put a bullet between his eyes. You hear me? Do it today!"

"I hear you, boss," Bud answered, as he turned his yellow eyes up at the sky. He glimpsed Tall Bob's silhouette against the clouds. "Done before noon, you can count on me."

2

LATER IN THE MORNING, BUD WENT OUT to the corral to have a close look at the chestnut, half-expecting to find it broken down. To his surprise, the horse had already nearly recovered from his long ordeal. He was bright-eyed and full of vinegar, whinnying at the mare, standing beside her like a long-lost friend. Bud looked at the wound on the gelding's rump and noticed that, while it was raw and angry, there was no sign of infection.

This horse is from good stock, well-mannered, solid on his feet, with a good build and the constitution of an iceman, he thought. *A handsome chestnut gelding with three white stockings on his legs. The man who owned this horse must be some riled up at losing him to a thief in the night. Two hundred and twenty miles as the crow flies, countless more miles on the journey across tough country with a maniac on his back. He looks ready to go again after a night of rest in a thicket, a couple of pails of water and a fork full of hay.*

Bud saddled up the mare, put his gear and some food in the saddle bags, dropped his rope over the chestnut and set out on the trail to the fenced meadow where he pastured his main herd. He'd stop in a thicket along the way and keep his end of his bargain with Tall Bob. Then he figured he'd check out his herd and take the ride to Bottineau. From there, he could touch base with the townies and he'd hear all the goings-on in the region. A few drinks in the saloon at Bottineau was as good as reading the newspaper. He figured it would give him notice if the hounds were sniffing around. Maybe he could head them off if they were planning a trip up his way. Besides, he never could tell when he could make a trade or pick up some horse flesh he could recondition and sell to one of the local ranchers.

After a few miles along the trail he started thinking things he should not have entertained for even a moment. When he looked at the chestnut he saw a beautiful animal deserving of a better fate than a two cent bullet and being turned into a feast for coyotes.

Bud soon figured that, with a little imagination and some doctoring, he could alter the chestnut and sell it for a good profit to some buyer who was headed toward the other side of the continent. He already had a good business from wagon men who were directed up to his place to trade in their worn-out nags for fresh stock. The little voice in his brain kept telling him it was time to stop and shoot the chestnut, just as he promised. *On the other hand,* he thought, *maybe that is too harsh a punishment for the nag and a bad decision for a businessman like myself. Hell, I might as well hide this fellow out for a while, disguise him and pawn him off for cash to some do-gooder headed for the Promised Land rather than waste him with a slug and spoil a perfectly good afternoon.*

Talking out loud to himself again. Bud figured that wasn't too good a practice, even though the Bohunk down at the Bottineau saloon said it was okay to talk out loud to yourself as long as you didn't answer. He left the chestnut in the pasture, turned Suzy around and headed off to town.

Bottineau was really only a tin-pot village with a general store and a saloon with six tables and a fifteen-foot-long bar on top of a dirt floor. The saloon owner was also the proprietor of a bunkhouse. He rented beds for ten cents per night. There was a stable with corral, two dozen log houses and another twenty or more sod houses. The government building housed the post office and a jail that consisted of a small office and two cells built below ground level. The staircase down to them was guarded by a stout metal grate. At one end of town there was an enormous pile of lumber which had been shipped by train to Devil's Lake, then overland by horse and wagon, eighty-six miles to Bottineau. Some rich promoters, anticipating that a new railway line would soon be coming to town, were planning a swank hotel and saloon with proper rooms and comfortable furnishings. It was rumoured that the men behind this operation were eager to start a gambling emporium and brothel. But five years had already passed with nothing changed except that the pile of lumber grew warped and grey under the weather.

Bud stayed for free in the log bunkhouse because he frequently did business with the owner. He received free drinks at the saloon because he had sold the Bohunk a side of beef the previous winter and had barely touched his credit at the bar. Since food was free for those who drank, he was settling in for a couple of cheap days taking advantage of all that Bottineau had to offer. He wasn't in the bar for more than an hour, in the middle of downing his second pint of beer, when in walked Gerry, the town's constable. Wearing a pair of bedroom slippers and looking like he had just crawled out from under a wagon train, the constable was just back from his weekly session with Widow Murphy, who was old but took her time on all the men in town who were pining for love.

"Damn, she may be ancient, but she's golden in all the ways a man cares about," Gerry said. He bought himself a beer on his tab and sat down on a chair beside Bud.

"Well how's it going?" he asked.

"Going about as well as always," Bud answered, wiping the suds off his handlebar. "The horses are all happy enough. The chickens are laying. I have everything I want but a woman, and having one of those would be impossible."

"Bud, I recommend you try the Widow Murphy. No commitments and a real wild ride!"

"At my age I'm thinking along the lines of falling in love. You know, finding someone to pretty up the place and maybe cook me a good meal once in a while."

"You've been out in the sun too long."

"So what's the news around here? Any word about the railroad coming this way?"

"Afraid that seems to be dead in the water for now. The store did a big business when some Assiniboines passed through here last month. Before they left they came over to the jail and gave me three bucks for being good to them. I told them, think nothing of it, any time. It's been a pretty slow season. Even the drunks around here are polite and easy to manage. Once in a while I get a workout when cow punchers come to town."

"Been pretty quiet up my way, too. With the exception of a couple of travellers who stopped by and camped for a night, I haven't seen a soul. Gerry, can I buy you a beer? Hey Bohunk, bring us a couple of pints and two shots of your best firewater. I want the home-made stuff you make from potatoes."

"Which reminds me, Bud. I did hear from the U.S. Marshal's office. The bank in Bismarck was knocked over by a lone gunman who got away with a substantial amount of cash and put a big hole in the manager. So it's bank robbery complicated by murder. There are a number of riders out in various districts, lookin' for the culprit. I've been warned to be on the lookout up here, but I don't have time unless he lands in town and starts handing out wads of cash."

"I suppose they know who done it," Bud said, draining his whisky.

"Naw, it's just a description. A tall man riding a chestnut horse. They figure maybe the horse was packing a bullet when he left Bismarck."

"Well, that could be just about anybody in this country."

"No, I don't think that's right," said Gerry with a snicker.

"What do you mean?"

"Well, it couldn't be an old codger like you riding Suzy, the little mare, now could it?" he said, laughing as if he had heard the world's funniest joke.

"You're right about that," Bud answered, feeling his neck turn red.

"Now Bud, you keep an eye out and if you see anybody around your place of that description, you wait until dark and fire off a flaming arrow and I'll come running."

Even the Bohunk was laughing at Gerry's feeble humour.

After two days of gabbing with the folks in Bottineau, Bud was ready to go home. He had found out exactly what he needed to know. On his way out of town he hitched Suzy in front of the general store and entered the establishment.

"Well, if it isn't Bud, the hermit from horse heaven," chimed a ruddy-faced man with a Scot's accent.

"How you doing Mac? I bet you still miss the Hebrides."

A year back, Bud had sold MacGregor, the general store operator, a pair of docile wagon horses that made all his deliveries and provided him and his wife with respectable transportation when they took excursions in their buggy. By now he had hardly touched the total of his credit on MacGregor's books.

"Let's see," he said. "Mac, it's time I spruced myself up a mite. I'd like a new shirt, a suit of long johns and these overalls. I'll take this blanket and this sewing kit and that jar of boot polish. Better give me two. I have an old pair of boots I want to dress up. Let me see, oh yes, give me a pound of that plug tobacco and a handful of the hard candy with the green and red stripes. That's about it."

While Mac was bundling up his goods, Bud took a look in the glass case that sat on top of one corner of the general store counter. It was a box with a clear top that contained a number of handguns, including a derringer. On a whim, Bud suddenly blurted out words he barely recognized himself saying.

"Mac, I want that silly little gun in that glass case. And give

14

me three boxes of cartridges."

"Certainly," MacGregor answered. "Three boxes of .41 calibre rim fires to go with the Remington Model 95 over-under derringer. Will that be all, then."

"Yeah, that will do," Bud said, holding the pistol in the palm of his hand.

"Rats in the cabin are bad this time of year. This here banger ought to help me sort 'em out."

Before he made the journey home, Bud decided to head south to visit with his friends, two Swedish brothers who operated a ferry station on the Mouse River. On the way, he stopped by the trail and rested beside a patch of birch trees. He carved a circle about as big as a man's head with his knife on the paper of one of the trees. He marched off ten paces, held out the derringer at arm's length and pointed it at the target. When he gently squeezed the trigger the little gun made a sharp report, more like the yap of a dog rather than the full bark. He walked up and put his finger on the tiny slug embedded in the centre of the target.

By midmorning he had reached the ferry station and was drinking a cup of ferocious brew with the twins, who were happy to see him. The throat of dancing river water caught the sun in its riffles. It made the whole country seem alive. He said the same things he always said, telling the Swedes he appreciated their hard work keeping the heavy, awkward river craft operating. They charged one buck for a one-way ferry trip. Bud didn't have to pay. Long ago he had sold the boys a pair of mules he obtained in trade from a prospector. Part of the deal was that Bud received free ferry rides both ways across the river as long as the twins were in charge. The boys never said a word about riders out hunting for a bank robber. In fact, just the opposite, business had been lousy since the day they transported a band of Indians and their gear to the opposite bank.

"Don't that beat all," Bud said, sucking on a long straw he plucked out of the sand. "Glad to hear the mules are working out for you fellows."

The boys told him the mules were tough as nails. They easily powered the ferry that had formerly been fuelled by their own broad Swedish backs.

"That's progress, boys!" Bud said.

"Ya, ya," they agreed. "Better."

Bud spent the night beside the river with the Swedes. He asked them to do him a favour – the next time those Indians showed up he wanted the Swedes to send them his way.

"You tell the headman that I'm eager to trade for some of their horses if they're the ones that are spotted. I've got some fat cows that could use butchering. Can you remember that?"

"Ya, I 'a know the ones, you 'a want. You 'a want 'a the horses with spots on 'a their asses."

"Well, that's one way of looking at it," Bud answered.

On the long stretch home, just about the time he was thinking about making camp, Bud met a pair of cowboys on the trail. They worked for the Manson ranch way up on the sea of grass that stretched to the east for miles. Bud decided to join them and camp for the night. They had been out for a few days looking for some missing cattle and now were wondering out loud if maybe the Indians who passed through a few weeks before might have had a hankering for beefsteak.

Bud thought about it a while and then did his best to dispel their gloomy prediction.

"Nah, them Indians are store-bought. They wouldn't risk butchering your cattle. Besides if they did you would have seen signs of it. I reckon you keep looking, you'll find 'em. Probably an old cow took off and the rest of 'em couldn't resist going along for the ride. I'd say look further west of here, maybe they went to find salt."

They figured he might be right and the conversation took a turn. When the light was leaving, just before the full blanket of stars was displayed overhead, they sat drinking harsh black coffee, leaning against their saddles talking about all the horse flesh they had ever encountered. In Bud's experience, that's what range riders did in the evening before they turned in. Even if the conversation started with women, it always finished with an exhaustive discussion about the merits of this or that nag. It was really the only thing cowboys were verbal about.

By the time dawn started eating the treetops, Bud was back on Suzy, headed toward home on the trail through grass country. He always felt the tranquility settle around him on this last twenty-mile stretch. His natural inclination was to be reflective and quiet but the necessities of survival forced him to become a loquacious horse trader when the occasion required it. He was the one who filled the dead air in most of the conversations he had in that country. His trips to town were infrequent, but necessary, to fuel the modest business aspirations which kept him going. He raised a few cattle and chickens and he looked after his horses. Now, he was back to dealing with himself and nobody else until the next horse trader came over the horizon. He plodded along, mile after mile, on Suzy, thinking about all the things in his life that he needed to look after. First on the list was to figure out how to deal with the fallout that might ensue from his last horse trade.

Men like Tall Bob came into his life now and then. Men who were looking to trade a horse or acquire one and *maybe* had money. He could tell if they were good or bad. That wasn't a question he had much trouble with because Bud was as shrewd about human flesh as he was about the horse kind. He judged a man in a different way than most. He figured everybody in this godforsaken land was running away from an unreasonable past or had something to hide. Take Tall Bob. Bud had sold him Foxy, a good ride, and a packhorse on spec. While he didn't exactly know Tall Bob's business, he had a pretty good idea it was going to be risky. The roan Tall Bob rode when he first showed up was already a wreck on arrival, from being pushed too hard. It dropped dead a week later.

How could anybody like a man who could do that to a horse? he thought. He had aimed his yellow eyes at Tall Bob and asked him that very question. Took Tall Bob a while to answer.

"Damn roan had no bottom. I was testing him to see if he had the long ride in his legs. Guy who sold him to me told me he was from a long line of runners. Barely put him through his paces when I felt him dying under my knees. An also-ran sprinter with no heart. The underground telegram from far away sent me to hell and over here to see you, 'Bud the pud, man with the fifty dollar stud'. Listen old man, I'll make you rich if you put me on the right nag."

Yet Bud did take a liking to Tall Bob. He saw the good side of him and figured him for a straight shooter who would go out of his way to pay his debts, even if he was a risk-taker who had danger written all over him just by the way he walked. High risk, high reward, Bud knew that the minute he decided to put him up on Foxy. When he came back on the wrung-out chestnut, Bud knew the deal was real and he was about to be paid with more than he had bargained for.

Home was where there were no people. He put Tall Bob out of his mind and he rode along, listening to the birds, stopping now and then to give Suzy a break, happy to be alive with money in his pocket. He was pretty sure he was past all the conversations he needed to have with his own kind for the next few months.

3

IT WAS EASY TO FIND THE CHESTNUT GELDING when Bud rode
Suzy up to the pasture. The horse, grazing on a far end of the
meadow beside the bush line, walked right over to them when
they got close. Bud put a loop over its head and another over the
sorrel wagon horse that he had acquired from a passing caravan.
The sorrel had gone lame but it was only a matter of rest and attention before it was ready to work. Bud led them down the winding
four-mile trail to the cabin and into the corral with Suzy.

He walked into the cabin and brought out the shoe polish he
had purchased at the Bottineau general store. He tethered the
chestnut to the corral and began rubbing polish into the stockings on the back two legs and above the right front hoof. Bud
combed out and clipped the horse's shaggy mane. He looked at
the wound on the chestnut's rump. He painted it with some
medicine that he mixed up from an ancient recipe he got from
an old-timer.

For two weeks, he kept the gelding in the corral. Every morning he furiously rubbed shoe polish into the white socks until
they merged into the same chestnut colour as the rest of the
horse. In the afternoons he hooked the sorrel and chestnut up in
tandem to pull his wagon. He spent a considerable time training
the chestnut for what was about to become its new occupation:

wagon horse to the first sucker who stopped by looking for a nag to help him find his way to Nirvana.

When the chestnut was finally content to pull the wagon, Bud decided it was time to take him back up to the meadow with the other horses. He turned the gelding loose and let him merge into the crowd.

When the chestnut's wound was healed over, Bud travelled up to the meadow and stayed a few days, camping out beside the creek. He caught the chestnut and rubbed a rag with shoe polish against the white hairs that had grown over the scarred area on its rump.

Two months had gone by since Tall Bob had ridden away and not much had changed. It was the middle of summer. He was sawing wood, putting hay up for the winter and looking after his garden. Bud required at least five hundred pounds of spuds to trade with travellers and last him through the winter, as well as providing seed stock for the following spring. A real good crop would give him ten or more sacks to sell door-to-door in Bottineau. Bud ploughed his garden and made hay with the Belgian-Clyde. He grew a crop of oats on the good field where he spread the manure from his horses. He needed the garden so the chickens could scratch and eat in the summer. He fed the oats to the chickens and horses in the bitter months.

A man can live a long time on spuds, especially if he has eggs and meat, and maybe some onions and turnips, put away for the winter. Bud's potato crop was his life insurance in case of a bad year. He could count on potatoes for every meal if game was scarce. When it turned cold he would try and bag a deer or maybe something bigger, like an elk or a moose. A big animal would be worth a wagon trip to town because the Bohunk would be overjoyed. When the ground froze he'd kill a dry cow or a steer and keep a quarter while hauling the rest into Bottineau. To keep wild animals off he kept his meat hanging in a tall shed that he made from logs.

In the depths of winter he would cut a piece off his hanging supply and cook it in the cast iron frying pan he kept on the stove. Sometimes, he made a pot of stew that he could eat from for a week, storing it outside, covered with a large, flat rock to keep the varmints from getting at it. The rest of the year, he cooked outdoors in order to minimize the chance of burning his cabin down. His one indulgence was coffee. He made sure the haggis-puncher ordered him a sack of the best beans he could find and had them shipped in. He brewed his coffee with the rain barrel water because the water that came from the well stank of minerals and was undrinkable.

Bud was frying some eggs and thinking about the possibility of acquiring a couple of pigs when he noticed a wagon in the distance. *Good thing I built on high ground*, he thought. He had time before it arrived to straighten up his yard and put on the ultra-large coffee pot that he ordered out of the hotel cookery manual the Bohunk had shown him.

Bud kept a sharp eye out for visitors. He thought himself adept at figuring who might be approaching from the kind of display they made coming across the grass. Maybe an erstwhile homesteader looking for a place to grab a piece of the action, or some pilgrim looking for the promised land. The slow movement of the wagon and its precarious journey over the prairie made Bud think it was the latter. The poor sot lost track of the trail and veered onto a rough section of the field. Now the wagon was lurching toward Bud's cabin like a boat floundering in the waves.

When it arrived at the yard, a man in a dusty black suit wearing a black Boss of the Plains Stetson climbed down from the box.

"Sir! Jeremiah Bigalow, that is, Reverend Jeremiah Bigalow, travelling with my wife Minnibelle and her sister Rebecca Jane. I have been recommended to you, good sir, by the graces of the good folks in Bottineau, who said I might stop at your fine equine establishment and refresh our weary wagon-pullers, who have given us yeoman's service over the past months."

"Bud Quigley, at your service. You have arrived at the right place if you're in search of new blood to haul your worldly goods. The ladies are welcome to come over here beside my stone hearth. Pour yourself a good cup of coffee to fortify your spirits while I unhook that unsightly team you're driving and give the poor creatures a drink. Reverend, you say? These horses have been treated no better than slaves. Skin and bones both and near death in the harness."

"Sir, it is true I am no horseman. I have done my best but my talent lies elsewhere in the realm of the spiritual world."

Bud led the wagon horses into the corral. He instructed the reverend to water them by filling up the trough with buckets from the well while he went back to tending his fire.

"Ladies, may I serve you some beef jerky and a plate of eggs? An offering from my flock. How about you, Reverend? Care to put the feed bag on?"

Bud was already wrestling the cast iron frying pan onto the fire and pouring cups of coffee from the miraculous coffee-making machine.

After his exertions watering the horses, Reverend Bigalow sat down beside the women, mopping his red face with one of their lace hankies.

"How's things in Bottineau?" Bud asked.

"A rustic place," the reverend replied. "I heard tell while I was there that some railway officials had come to town and were starting to buy up land in the region."

"That so?" Bud said.

"Yes, won't be long before somebody decides to build a church there. That's what happens when prosperity approaches. Won't be me, though. I have a mission to deliver bibles and minister to folks five hundred miles yonder from here."

"That what you have in the wagon?"

"Mostly bibles and our personal goods and food supply."

Minnibelle, a striking woman with a head of blonde curls

tucked under a respectable bonnet and wearing a long-sleeved apron dress, spoke up.

"We have had the Lord on our side ever since we left home. Why, all along the route from town to town, local congregations have given us donations of goods and food. So many good folk have helped us immeasurably in travelling this far."

"I wouldn't say God has been very loving to your horses, ma'am."

"Course, there are no churches in Bottineau," the reverend interrupted.

"None up here either," Bud answered.

"Sir, you must not blame the ladies for the condition of the horses. I am responsible. I alone will accept your criticism and apologize sincerely for my transgressions toward those poor, dumb beasts. I guess, in my enthusiasm to reach my destination as quickly as possible, I have transgressed. I assure you I have not done it intentionally. As a man of the cloth, I am given to loving all God's creatures."

"Well Reverend, what is it I can do for you? Let me guess, you want me to replace your bagged horses with a fresh pair of my own wagon stock? Is that the gist of it?"

"I believe you have it in a nutshell," the reverend answered before taking another big slurp of his coffee. "This is very good!"

"Let's cut to the chase, reverend. Your horses in this condition are worth nothing. Could be I trade for them and in a couple of days they drop dead on my lot from being used up. Even if they do survive, about all they'll be good for is to sell dirt cheap to some angry rancher who wants to bait a grizzly bear. Let's see what I can do for you if you have cash or something worthwhile I might be interested in trading for. Consider my team of horses, a pretty pair indeed, are available for forty dollars or the equivalent in goods or services."

"You strike a hard bargain, sir. We have no money to speak of. I came this way when a foreign man in Bottineau told me you would take our horses at least partially in trade."

"Not this pair of dead ducks."

"I implore you, sir, to raise your price and take my IOU as collateral for the purchase. When I reach my destination and I'm settled, I'll send the money to you."

"Sorry Reverend, I don't take IOUs from men who are on their way to Paradise. Even if it is a respectable town out there somewhere."

They sat in front of the fire drinking coffee. Both the ladies, Minnibelle and her comely, darker sister Rebecca Jane, handled themselves gracefully. Both complimented Bud on his coffee. The reverend mostly made conversation about his duty to save souls and the ungodly element that was polluting small towns, making them unfit for decent citizens who wanted to settle and raise a family. Bud, growing tired of the lecture, allowed he would stake them all to a good dinner if the ladies would help in the preparation. He sent the good reverend back to the well to draw more water for the corral and asked him to put some water on the garden.

In the evening, when the bean pot came out of its hole in the ground, Bud threw steaks into the frying pan and started a batch of bannock. The ladies peeled and boiled a pot of potatoes. Minnibelle brought out a jar of preserves from the back of the wagon. When the food was ready to eat the ladies proclaimed that they hadn't dined this well for quite some time. Reverend Bigalow was stowing the grub like a starving man having his final meal.

"Reverend," Bud said, "you wouldn't happen to have a bottle of hootch in that wagon, would ya?"

Burping loudly, Bigalow followed the direction of Bud's yellow eyes and answered in a garbled manner that he had no liquor.

"That's too bad. All things with moderation of course, but I do like to have a drink to seal a bargain when I am in a horse-trading mood."

"I see," said the reverend. "Well, I do have one bottle of spirits to be used for medicinal purposes. Perhaps, I could satisfy your tradition with that."

"Depends if it's good or not. I hate drinking rotgut."

"Let me fetch it and you can find out," answered Bigalow, climbing into his wagon and rooting around under the floor boards.

"A jumbo bottle! Good job, Reverend. I like it already."

Bud pulled the cork and poured three fingers of whisky into his telescopic-folding tin cup.

"I won't insult you with a shot, Reverend."

"Feel free to insult me," Bigalow said as he held out his empty coffee cup."

"How about it, ladies? Would you each care for a libation?"

"Now really, Mr. Quigley, this is going a bit far. The ladies are not imbibers of spirits."

"Yes we are," said Minnibelle, reaching for the bottle and pouring double shots into her and Rebecca Jane's coffee mugs.

They sat in the silence for a while, topping up their cups once or twice before Bud stood up and fidgeted with the fire.

"So, what have you for trade?" Bud asked. "Don't tell me all you have in that wagon is bibles and such. Bigalow, I figure you for something other than a reverend. What else have you hidden in the bottom of the wagon? A roulette wheel, maybe a folding card game set-up, or how about a few dozen rifles and a supply of ammunition? Maybe a few cases of this good whisky? You have something in there under your shallow layer of bibles. I'm betting on it. Those two wheezing nags you have over in my corral will most likely be dead by tomorrow afternoon. You and the ladies will have to hitch yourselves up and pull your own wagon to Paradise unless you come up with the scratch or a better idea. To be a sport I'll give you a five dollar credit on each of those two mouth breathers you trashed in your pilgrimage across the big side of grass. Throw in your fancy hat and I'll knock another five bucks off. You can't do better than a Boss of the Plains."

"It's yours," said the reverend. "Try it on."

He carefully placed the Stetson on Bud's head. They could all see it was too big for him.

"If you grow your hair a little longer, it will be a perfect fit," Rebecca Jean gushed, a little tipsy from the whisky.

"I'll give you another five dollars credit for that Parker coach gun you have in the boot. Dandy twelve-gauge, side-by-side with eighteen-inch barrels. Just what I need if I am ever held up on the trail."

Bud already figured he'd swap the Parker with the Swedes or maybe trade it to Gerry, who might like having a Parker for a pal when the trail-drifters hit town and started acting up in the bar. Definitely a conversation piece for anyone with a confrontational nature. He also thought it might be good medicine if that dang bear came to tear up his cabin again when he was in bed.

"Have the gun by all means. We trust in the Lord most of the time. Besides I have an old Spencer rifle that is adequate for our use."

"Rev, you're half way there. You own one first rate wagon puller. Now, what are we going to do about you acquiring the other? I mean they do come in pairs. You have bought yourself a useful sorrel that can pull all day if you treat him right. Now, what's your solution for partnering him up with his chestnut mate. Any idea how you're going to pull that off?"

"Have another drink, sir," the reverend said, sloshing more whisky into Bud's cup.

The stars were out overhead like a living canopy of glittering bugs crawling across the breadth of the sky. The ladies sat on the corner of the rustic bench beside the flickering firelight. Bud was reposing on his chopping block while the reverend sat on a log facing him.

"Any suggestions?" he asked. "I have nothing more that would be of value to you."

"Well, you know what I've been thinking for quite a while, don't you?" Bud answered.

"Which one do you want?" Bigalow asked.

"In the old days I might have traded you the team straight up for a night with both of 'em. But now I am an old rooster and I only have the capacity to handle one. Since you only own half a team I'll sell you the chestnut nag for a night in the sack with your dear lady, Minnibelle."

"Done," said the reverend. "Now, lets shake on the deal and have a drink to seal the bargain."

4

THEY CAME AT HIM FROM THREE DIRECTIONS. Bud was in the corral watering Suzy and two yearlings he was planning to show off in Bottineau in the fall. He noticed the horses were skittish, testing the air. Then he heard a whinny from far off and saw a rider coming up the trail about two hundred yards away.

When he left the corral, he spotted two other riders who had stopped west and east of him about one hundred and fifty yards out, with saddle guns resting on their mounts. He strode out, waving at the man who was coming relentlessly toward him with his head down, riding a huge, raw-boned nag. The men out on the sides were wearing dusters. Even from a distance they had a menacing look about them. The rider coming ahead was dressed in a bulky grey coat and had on a tall cap. When he rode closer, Bud could see he was wearing spectacles on his nose and had a sharp, grey beard sprouting from his chin. The man stopped his horse short of the cabin and made a rather awkward dismount.

"You Quigley?" he asked. "Am I at the right place?"

"Yeah, I'm Bud Quigley. What can I do for you?"

Bud was wearing only trousers held up by suspenders over his bare shoulders. He gestured toward the fire where the big coffee pot sat on the stone hearth. The stranger tied off his horses and waved at his outriders. They moved ahead until they were about fifty feet on either side and then dismounted and stood beside their nags. The man in the tall cap accepted the steaming cup of coffee that Bud held out to him.

"Your boys coming in for coffee, too, or are they just going to stand there after a long, hard day in the saddle? I know you must have arrived from somewhere. So if you want to water your horses and relax with a cuppa coffee, I have no objections."

The stranger in a great coat signaled for the outriders to ride in to the fire. Bud took a quick look into his face. His heart sank in his chest when he saw the man's eyes. He thought to himself, *If ever there was a human being with a shark's face this is him.* His cheeks were covered by a coarse, grey beard. One side looked as if it had been torn off and then left to grow back.

When the two outriders approached for their cups of coffee he took his time in giving them the once over. The rider from the west was a pimply-faced, overgrown youngster with the look of a pudgy killer. He'd seen his type before in the marauding gangs that haunted the countryside of his youth. The rider from the east had a swarthy look about him. He wore tight-fitting pants and fancy, pointed boots. A pearl-handled Colt on a leather thong was stuck nonchalantly into the waistband of his pants.

"Let me introduce myself," the stranger said. "My name is Jiggs Dubois. You may have heard of me. These are my guides, Charlie Parmer and Frenchie, who only goes by one name."

"Can't say that I have. How do you do? Now, what brings you gents all the way out here? I hope it's about horses, since about now I could sure use some business. Been a pretty quiet summer. I have a lot of good stock that I would like to move. Tell me, you work for the railway or a mining company? You have that look about you and I am raring to do business."

"Quigley, we didn't travel out here to beat around the bush. I just want to ask you a few questions. If I hear some satisfactory answers, why we'll be headed out of here in no time flat. Is that understood?"

"Well, my ma taught me that asking questions was a bit dicey when one was brought up to mind his own business."

"Let me give you my card. You can see plain as the nose on your face that I am the Jiggs Dubois who works for the Pinkerton National Detective Agency. These men are my guides and assistants in conducting my business."

When Dubois opened his jacket to pull out his calling card, Bud noticed the skull-crusher grip of a Merwin-Hulbert peering out from a shoulder holster. By the look of him, Dubois had twin Merwin-Hulberts in harness under his armpits. He also noticed that what he first took for a tall hat had a sharp brim on the front and was undoubtedly an officer's cap of foreign issue.

"Now, first question. Are you alone here or is there anybody else around?"

"I assure you, Dubois, I am the only one out here with my modest herd of horses, a dozen cows and flock of chickens. The nearest human being is probably about thirty-five miles away at Bottineau. There may be an odd cowboy around looking for a lost dogie or an Indian or two hunting moose or passing through the area, but I doubt it."

"Then you don't mind if we look around?"

"No, look around all you like. Maybe if you tell me what you're seeking, I can help you out. I can see you're not interested in my horses."

"On the contrary, Quigley, we're very interested in your horses. Where do you keep them?"

"Well, there's three in the corral. Another few that I'm training are currently hobbled in the brush down by the creek. The main bunch of them is about four miles west of here in a big, fenced meadow."

"Let me ask you this. At the end of spring or early in summer, did you meet with or encounter a lanky man wearing a duck-cloth coat and riding a chestnut gelding with three white stockings? The horse had a fresh wound on its right rump."

"No, I can't say that I did. I had a number of visitors about then who were looking for horses for one reason or another. A couple of riders passing through stopped long enough for coffee. A few camped out here for a night or two."

"Quigley, a man of your discernment would notice a horse marked like that, wouldn't you say?"

"No doubt about it," Bud answered, "I'd remember a horse like that just as I'll remember the Hanover you're riding."

"The fellow we're looking for robbed a bank in Bismarck on May 28th and killed a man. We're pretty sure he didn't ride into Minot or Bottineau, but we know he crossed the river forty-five miles south of here at Swedes' Ferry. The ferrymen remembered him."

Bud sat down on the chopping block and poured himself another tankard of java from the percolation machine.

"Dubois, because a rider gets off the ferry forty-five miles from my place doesn't mean he didn't travel in another direction and come out in a dozen different locations. Why should he bother coming this far up into Canada?"

"The man in question was riding a chestnut gelding with a severe wound on its backside. This horse was probably not travelling far without some attention. You're the only man with horses for sale on this side of the river. That's what the boys in the bar at Bottineau say. So what if you're thirty-five miles across the border? It makes sense that a desperate killer riding a stolen horse with a bad wound would venture your way in search of a better mount."

"I haven't seen anybody who fits his description and, thank God, nobody has bothered to steal any of my horses. I have a few chestnuts in my string up in the pasture. You are welcome to ride up there and have a look. I'm sure you'll find out to your own satisfaction that none of them match the description of the horse you're looking for. Now, you men are free to look around, but I have work to do and the day is not growing younger while we stand here gabbing about nothing."

Dubois stroked his chin whiskers and his shark eyes seemed to glow, staring into Bud's face as if he was trying to empty the old man's brain of its contents. Bud averted his eyes into his coffee cup and stood up.

"I have one final thing to say, Quigley, then I'll be on my way. I'm not here about murder. Nor do I give a damn about horse thievery. Those matters are up to the law. I'm here about the money. Our client's money was supposed to be safely stored in one of his banks. That's what I'm about. If you know the whereabouts of any of that money I would more than appreciate you speaking up. There's a reward for the apprehension of this desperado. You might be in line for it, and we quickly forget the sources of our information, if you understand my meaning. To know more than you're letting on and do otherwise would be folly. When Jiggs Dubois is on the case there is no rest for the wicked. Remember that, Quigley, the next time you think about lying to my face."

"Who authorized you to cross the border and throw your weight around acting like the law? I don't think you're recognized up here. You ought to go home before Manitoba's finest find out you're up here and send a recruit to kick your ass."

"I assure you, Quigley, that the Pinkerton National Detective Agency recognizes no borders. We cooperate with police forces in every jurisdiction we enter."

"Dubois, where did you find that swell hat?"

"It's a Prussian cavalry officer's hat I picked up along the way."

"You look like a music hall general."

"The boys will ride up to your meadow and examine your horses because I do not like your attitude. Good day, sir."

"Dubois, that Hanover you're riding is going lame on the left rear. If I was you, I'd walk him back to Bottineau before he gives out. You'll have to ride double with one of these two girlie boys you brought up here."

"You watch your smart mouth," answered the one named

Charlie Parmer. "For two cents I'd gladly straighten you out."

"Dubois, sorry I can't help you out. I'm not in the horse-selling business today or any other day you're around. I advise you to find better company than those two scum you have hanging off your posterior."

Dubois and his henchmen left straightaway. Dubois headed back on the return trip to Bottineau while the toughs veered off to check out Bud's horse herd.

Bud sucked in his bottom lip and thought, *Fish face didn't travel this far by accident. Now, he will be thorough in his investigation. He's used to intimidating and threatening people, that's plain. Imagine him asking me if I had ever heard of him as if he was some legendary figure. Jezuz, a pint-sized Pinkerton with a chip on his shoulder. He'll ride back to Bottineau and spend some time at the Bohunk's bunkhouse and bar. He'll sit around there and try and dig up some dirt to further his theory that I was lying to him. A dangerous adversary he is, to be sure.*

Bud went into the cabin, loaded his Parker and brought it outside and put it under his coat beside the coffee stand. He slipped on a fresh shirt, loaded the derringer and buttoned it in his breast pocket like an afterthought. In the future there was no way he was going to be caught unarmed by men who were no better than thugs.

He thought about saddling up and following them down the trail, but in the end he figured that for a waste of time. Bud decided he'd lie low for a day or two, watching the trails to see if the toughs were going to wait around before joining their boss. Maybe he'd sleep in a tent off the end of the corral in the aspen grove, where he could observe the approaches to the cabin, armed with his Parker, in case the two rat-heads riding with Dubois came back at night to surprise him. When they were in his yard he could smell the fear and anger they brought with them. Junior killers in training. Trash like them, buried six feet under, would be a blessing to humanity. The shark-faced pipsqueak looked like a puppet riding that big military plug. Rode a horse like a city boy. He was bluffing all the way.

There was no going back now. He looked at the grey sky. It was the middle of August and already snow was coming down. Soon, it filled in the dinner-plate-sized hoof prints left by the Hanover. Late in the afternoon the sun came out briefly. By evening again, it was raining black dogs.

I hope those bastards get soaked to the ass on the trail, he thought. *They should be wallowing in mud before they leave this country.*

His mind settled briefly on Tall Bob, wondering which direction he had taken. In the long run it didn't matter, better he didn't know. If Bob was smart he would have meandered a while and moved off as clear of the border as possible. Tall Bob was nobody to take lightly. He had a big head start and wouldn't be easy to find. Bud was sure the Pinkerton at least knew that much.

Dubois's flunkies were fools who knew more about guns than they did about men. That was a formula for disaster in this country. They'd be lucky to be alive within another year or two.

Dubois, the little puke, added up two and two and got four. *A dangerous man with simple arithmetic on his side,* he thought. *He wants the money, not the murderer or the horse thief. And he tries to make a deal to recover the money with no questions asked.* Bud focused on the grey horizon. *What bullshit! That bastard wants the money, also a hanging and a big newspaper story. He's dying to tell the tale of how he tracked down a bank robber and a killer and recovered the loot.* For one brief second he thought about the chestnut gelding with three white socks.

5

JIGGS DUBOIS AND HIS CONFEDERATES ARRIVED cold and soaking wet back in Bottineau the next afternoon. Sure enough, as Bud had predicted, the Hanover floundered, coming up lame on the muddy course. Dubois was forced to climb on up behind Charlie Parmer while the big Hanover followed along behind with the wind in its crazy eyes.

When big thunderstorms danced on the horizon, the Pinkertons were forced off their horses because of the danger of lightning strikes. They spent a miserable night camped out in the rain. They stretched a tarp between two saplings, but the rain pooled on it and they had to keep tipping the tarp with a long stick. None of them were able to sleep. They sat up around a smoky fire, burning wet wood, barely able to hear their own voices through the howling wind.

To make it worse, Parmer's skittish roan, spooked by a deafening blast of thunder, took off. Frenchie spent most of the next morning searching the area on his long-legged brown before he found the horse.

Late in the morning, after a lull, shortly after they set off for Bottineau, it rained torrentially again.

When they finally walked into the Bohunk's place and ordered whisky, nobody moved. Especially not the Bohunk, who stayed behind the bar peeling the onions he was about to add to the prairie chicken stew of the day. Jiggs, wrapped up, shivering in his soggy grey coat, reached into his pocket for his chewing tobacco.

"Just when I thought it couldn't possibly rain any harder, it up and started coming down in sheets that drummed like an army across the grass. Never saw anything like it," Dubois said, blowing his nose between his fingers.

"I'm not open for another hour," the Bohunk said as he worked his knife.

"Since when?" Charlie Parmer intoned as he stood barefoot ringing the water from his decrepit socks.

"Since now," the Bohunk answered, slamming his meat cleaver down on the bar in three powerful blows that completely dismembered the chicken.

"Don't you want our business?" Dubois asked.

"Come to think of it, no, I don't," the Bohunk replied. "In the long run I lose business when you hang around here with your brace of cheap thugs. Nobody with half a brain wants to enter here when you're hanging around."

"I want to talk to you about a man with a horse," Dubois said, dropping a few silver coins on the bar.

"What man with a horse? Didn't you already go and interview a man with enough horses to satisfy your curiosity?"

"My Warrior has ended up lame for the time being. I need to purchase another steed in order to complete my assignment."

"A man like you who runs gunmen around like checker pieces would have problems renting a Shetland pony in this town. Though you might have luck if you decide to turn that monstrosity you were formerly riding into a meat animal. There's a couple of Dutch prospectors out on the sand bars who relish the taste of horse flesh."

"You fellows are a sad sight, in fact you look half drowned," Gerry the Constable said when he came into the Bohunk's place for his afternoon shot of potato water, the ninety proof medi-

cine that the Bohunk ladled out from a barrel in a corner behind the bar.

"How can you drink that crap?" Charlie Parmer asked, as he
downed the double of cheap whisky he poured himself when the
Bohunk finally decided to put a bottle on the table in front of them.

"It's a lot smoother than the fiery rotgut you're drinking,"
Gerry answered.

In a surge of action, Parmer and Frenchie made short work of
the bottle and then started going quickly through a second.

"If I was you boys I would change out of those wet clothes
and into something dry before you all come down with pneumonia," Gerry said when Jiggs Dubois went on a coughing jag
and nearly chugged up his lungs onto the table. "You fellows take
life too seriously. Yip Hong down the end of the street does a
lovely boiled laundry. If you find MacGregor's duds too expen-
sive, Digby the undertaker has a selection of second-hand clothing. Somehow I didn't think you boys were planning on staying
around our fair town this long."

After wiping his nose on his damp woolen sleeve, Dubois
spoke up, pouring a little oil onto Gerry.

"Well sir, an experienced lawman like yourself certainly knows
about the trials and tribulations us devotees of law and order
must sometimes endure in bringing outlaws to justice."

"Jeez Dubois, I'm going to upchuck if you keep spewing that
crap. I assumed you were wasting your time when you went all
that way up to Bud Quigley's figuring your desperado went in
that direction. You certainly weren't well prepared for the elements. I hardly feel sympathy for your plight. If I was you I'd
move your horses down to old man Wilts' stable and tend to
them before they expire. I looked over that hulk you're riding
Dubois. I noticed his back left shoe is loose."

"I'll have to have that taken care of," Dubois answered.

"I told you the guy on the run would probably veer away after
the river and cross the grass on his way to another jurisdiction.

Seems to me if he travelled this far riding on one horse then it couldn't have been very seriously injured. I know one thing – he didn't pass through Bottineau and by now there's the possibility he has completely flown the coop and you're hooped. I'd say that's one tough hombre you're following. He ain't stopping for rest and relaxation until he reaches the Rocky Mountains. He's already more than likely high-stepped it out of this country. He ain't no fool to pull off what he's pulled off and make it this far. The fact he ventilated the bank manager means he knows he'll be dancing on a rope if he's caught. If you ever locate him you and your thugs might find out fast he has nothing to lose if he increases the body count."

Well," said Dubois, "the boys and I will be heading back to Minot in the morning. I'd say it's time for us to employ some modern techniques rather than brute force in helping us to close down on our criminal."

"You must have a swami with a crystal ball down there," Gerry answered, earning a big reaction from the Bohunk, who was browning his prairie chickens.

"You're a very funny man," Frenchie interjected, while his cheek twitched every twenty seconds as if to let him know he was still alive.

"Nobody asked your opinion so, if I was you, I'd shut the hell up before I run you in for impersonating a human being," Gerry said.

"I want you to keep an eye out for me, if you don't mind," said Dubois. "You can telegraph me at the Leland Hotel should any suspicious stranger fitting the description of that bank robber bird show up."

Gerry shook his head. "That desperado is long gone. He has a couple of weeks head start and I doubt he's going to stop running until he's at least half a continent away from this part of the world. Let me let you in on a little secret, Dubois. I am the law and order in Bottineau. I look after the town ordinances and,

38

every now and then, I have to rush over to the Bohunk's and bust the head of some over-zealous cowboy who can't find love or who imagines somebody insulted him."

"Just the same, sir, you have the same sworn duty to preserve the law as I do," Dubois answered from his glare.

"You ain't got the law on your side," Gerry answered. "If I see your man I'll contact the U.S. Marshal's office and call in Albert Price and his boys to do the job."

"Good luck," said Dubois. "He's busy trying to clean up Fargo."

"You're not much more than a bounty hunter who travels around under your Pinkerton disguise pretending you're an official legal beagle when you're really just a blowhard who hides behind a couple of greasy gunmen," Gerry said.

"I don't like the way you're talking about me and Frenchie," Charlie Parmer said, toothpick in his mouth, as he lurched forward on his chair, hand on his hip.

Frenchie was slowing uncoiling on his way to his feet. Before Charlie could utter another word Gerry grabbed the two of them and banged their heads together like a pair of odd-sized coconuts and they fell on the floor.

"That's it gents," the Bohunk said, smiling from behind the bar, demanding their attention with the sawed-off ten-gauge he was pointing in their general direction.

"Now stop it," Dubois hissed at his minions. "You knot-heads have been pounding down too much horse piss. While you two are under my employment you will do as you're told and keep your mouths shut."

Before they made it back to their feet, Gerry had their revolvers in his hands.

"I'm giving both of you a citation for being drunk and disorderly in the town of Bottineau. The circuit judge travels to town once a month, so unless you want to plead guilty and pay your fines, I'll have to escort you over to my jail. The judge was just here last week. You'll have to wait a long time until he comes back."

"That won't be necessary," Dubois answered in a cold, deliberate manner. "I'll be happy to pay their fines and vouch for their behaviour until we leave town in the morning. If that's all right with you."

"I'll release these men into your custody. I'll return their weapons in the morning when you turn up in my office and pay their fines before you leave town. That'll be five bucks apiece in fines and a buck each to cover the processing fees. In the meantime, you two road apples are no longer allowed in this establishment, so move your sorry asses out of here."

Looking over the bar at the Bohunk, Gerry asked him if he had anything to say about the situation.

"I'm sorry, but I have no room for you and your bullies in my bunkhouse. It seems a group of visitors have booked up all the beds."

"Oh come on," the Pinkerton said. "You're not going to pull that bull on me!"

"I worked very hard in the mines when I first came over from the old country. I signed a paper to immigrate over here and I worked three years like a slave and then I went to work on the railway. You probably don't remember how your Pinkertons behaved at the Railway Strike of '77, when we tried to gain better working conditions."

"I wasn't there," Dubois sniffed, and wiped his runny nose on his sleeve.

"There were 150 sorry-looking mutts just like you doing the dirty work for the railway bosses," the Bohunk answered.

"All in a day's work," Gerry said as he stood up to leave for the Widow Murphy's. "Being the law is a tough business, as you have pointed out Dubois. Never a dull day. Looks like the weather is still socked-in and this infernal rain is not going to let up. If I was you, Dubois, I'd pull your act together and find you and your employees a snug place to ride out this storm."

"You have a suggestion on that account?" Dubois asked, looking a bit nonplussed under the weight of his soggy hat.

"Frankly, no. I'm surprised you didn't travel prepared to live off the land."

"Who could predict this horrible, unseasonable weather was going to bog the country down in this infernal mud and damp?" Dubois said.

"I suppose there is that, but still you fellows are awfully helpless for professionals. Old Man Wilts, down at the stables, has been known to let men bunk in with their horses. If that doesn't work out, I would be willing to let you and your hirelings spend a night in my not-so-deluxe jail cells which, I warn you, are dank and musty. Of course, you'd have to be checked in by 8 p.m., when I go off duty. You'd have to surrender your weapon. I would have to lock you inside in accordance with the rules and regulations."

Turned out that Old Man Wilt didn't like the look of Charlie and Frenchie, even though they were disarmed and appeared quite sheepish. He didn't think his livestock would be safe with them prowling around the joint at night. When his mastiff curled its lip and started snarling before launching a full scale attack on Frenchie, he decided against the boys camping out with their equine friends.

"When all is said and done, you men are a lot of trouble," Gerry said as he opened the heavy grate to the subterranean cells. "Dubois, you're in the private room while you two blackbirds can bunk together in this other cell. I tell you, you make a lovely couple. Be aware that checkout time is 7:00 a.m. sharp. Dubois, by 7:05 I expect you will pay the fines they owe and your boys will be headed on their way out of town. I have no objections if you decide to hang around, Dubois since you have committed no infractions against the law. You beauties in the bridal suite are banned from returning to Bottineau for one month."

41

In the morning, Gerry opened the grate and ushered the boys out of the depths up to his office. Dubois, in a foul mood, quickly paid the fines. Gerry assured them that the sun had risen and it was a beautiful morning.

"I won't forget this," Dubois said out of the side of his mouth as his creepy shark eyes swam onto the far wall.

"Don't mention it," Gerry answered, just to goad him some more.

"I'm sure we'll pass by this way again," Dubois muttered.

"Do stop by for a chat," Gerry offered cheerfully. "Always happy to oblige whenever I have the chance."

When they came out onto the wooden sidewalk the sun was shining madly off the lightning rod on the general store roof.

6

BUD KNEW THEY WERE AROUND. He heard the birds stop singing as if waiting for something to move on before they'd start again. The silence was profound for one who had lived so long by himself in an isolated place. He could feel their eyes wandering over his body as they sized him up.

He ducked back to his cabin and loaded his Smith & Wesson Model 3. He tucked it into his waistband, leaving the handle sticking out in plain sight. Outside again, he dipped the big ladle into the rain barrel to fill up his coffee pot. He squatted down beside his hearth of loose stones and stirred the fire, adding a few lengths of dry wood.

In his mind, he could feel their breath on his neck. He imagined the trees had eyes and that the canopy of leaves covered their ears. Sometimes he felt the urge to pull out his pistol and fire into the heart of the silence in order to enable sound to start again. He lived in fear that one day somebody would sneak up behind him and tap him on the shoulder in the middle of nowhere, where no human being but he was supposed to be. At night he listened to the owl hooting at him from the trees, wondering if he should hoot back or shoot back.

While in bed, he left a candle flickering in the dark so he could catch the shape of the pack rat that had come out from hiding and was busy scurrying about in search of treasure. He practiced pointing the derringer. Pretty soon he didn't need the candle. He just pointed his arm, with the derringer in his hand, at the imaginary place where the pack rat stopped to sniff the air and squeezed the trigger – killing the rat every time. He wondered where the never-ending supply of pack rats was coming from.

When he looked up, he saw a lone rider standing about a hundred yards in front of him. About twenty-five yards to his right was another group of riders. At first, he counted three of them but, before long, he identified another horseman leading three ponies just a little behind them. He watched the wind tricking the feathers in their hair.

Bud stood up and walked down the path toward the lone rider sitting out in the open on a leopard appaloosa. When he was about twenty feet from him he stopped, took off his hat, bowed a little and said in a loud voice.

"How do you do. I'm Bud Quigley, and this is my horse rancheree. I'd be pleased if you and your friends would join me at my fire."

With that said, he turned his back and walked back to where his coffee pot was beginning to stir a little. When the rider followed, the rest joined him. They rode slowly up toward Bud and then suddenly all dismounted at once from their ponies. Bud's pulse quickened when he took a close look. He noticed that the ponies they were leading were three young snowflake appaloosas.

"Why don't you fellows help yourself to some water for your horses," Bud said as he cracked a few eggs into his frying pan.

"Hope you boys like plain country cooking," he quipped.

The man in front came forward, put his hand out and shook with Bud.

"Alphonse Pointed Stick," he said. "These men are my brothers."

"Glad to meet you," Bud said, shaking hands with each of them. "Will you rest a while here and join me for breakfast and a cup of coffee?"

When the coffee was ready Bud found a cup for all of them. After giving the cups a rinse, he poured and passed them around. He fried up a mess of eggs until each of them had a plateful, and he cooked bannock on sticks.

Alphonse quickly cleaned his plate and pronounced, "Why, you'd make a good wife for any man. This is the best coffee I've had since I was in New York City with Bill Cody. We put on Buffalo Bill's Wild West Show at Coney Island with some Sioux, Chief Bull Bear of the Cheyenne and cowboys from the Doggie Camp. We stayed at the Hotel de Clam and hung out on Brighton Beach. That's where I started drinking the good stuff."

"That's a mighty big compliment and I thank you for it," Bud answered.

He rose up and entered his cabin. In a while he came out with a package that he handed to Alphonse.

"I want you to have these beans so you can make some good coffee for yourself when you're out on the trail. Guess you boys don't have a coffee grinder in your gear, since you look to me like you're a hunting party, with them spare horses and all."

Alphonse chuckled and said something to his friends in his native lingo and they all laughed. One fellow with fur-trimmed braids started mimicking the motion of grinding.

"I told Big Swan what you said and he thinks you're very witty for a white man. I don't need a grinder," Alphonse said, "I use the same one the grizzly bear uses. A round stone pounding on a flat stone."

"I've never seen you around here before," Bud said.

"That's because we've never been here before." Alphonse answered. "The river-men gave me your message."

"Where you from?" Bud asked, beginning to think he might be getting a little too personal.

"From everywhere," Alphonse said.

"I take it, then, that you're from across the line or you're wanderers who don't have treaty?"

"That could be, but maybe not. Do you have treaty?"

"That's a good point," Bud answered. "I never thought about it that way before."

"Say is that a Boss of the Plains?" Alphonse asked, sweeping the long flow of wind-blown hair from his face."

"You have an eye for the finer things."

"I've always wanted one," Alphonse said.

"Then you must have it," Bud answered, brushing off the Stetson with his sleeve and presenting it. "My goodness it fits you perfectly, so that's that."

"You take a look at the three ponies we just put into your corral. You want them, you let me know. My brothers and I are full and now we want to rest before we ride back to where our people are camped near the ferry crossing."

"Why don't you just do that, while I take a ride? When I return we can talk about those horses."

Bud saddled up Suzy and rode to the meadow where both his cattle and horses were grazing. He roped a three-year-old steer and a dry cow. Soon after, he was on his way back down the trail to his yard.

The Indians were sitting in the shade, smoking. He sucked on his teeth as he looked over the prize stock the Indians had brought for him. An appaloosa stud in prime condition and two fillies. He climbed over the rails, walked over and sat next to Alphonse.

"Alphonse, your horses are blinding the sun. I want to make a trade with you."

"What do you suggest?" Alphonse asked, fanning himself with his new hat.

"You take these two beef back to your folks and let them feast. Then, on your way through Bottineau you stop and see Mac-Gregor at the store. Tell him I said you were to pick out the best rifle he has in the joint as well as five boxes of ammunition, three pounds of plug tobacco, ten pounds of sugar, a hundred pounds of flour and a new cast iron frying pan each for you and your brothers. Is that enough?"

"Shake," Alphonse said. "A deal."

"Meantime, you boys are welcome to bunk in here tonight and let me cook you a decent meal from the geese I ground-sluiced last night in the slough. I have 'em hanging in the meat shack. I was thinking of making goose jerky but now I think it's better I turn them into a stew with some potatoes and onions from my garden. I'll throw in a couple of old stewing chickens I have been saving for the occasion to give it a little variety."

"You're liable to go broke spoiling us," Alphonse said, inserting a hawk feather that he took from his hair into the band of his new hat.

"What are friends for?" Bud answered. "A man can't be alone all the time."

In the morning, over coffee, the sun was stuck in the clouds like a slice of lemon pie. Bud told Alphonse that if he brought him another stud and three or four fillies as good as the ones in the corral, he'd add plenty onto the deal.

"You come in the fall and put your tipis up in the sheltered coulee about two miles west of here. We'll go moose hunting. This country is crawling with those big black buggers. And if there ain't any around, I'll swap you beef for horses. It's up to you, if you don't have anything else to do. If you don't come, that's okay. Alphonse, do me a favour for my conscience. Before you and your people starve, if the winter is bad and the hunting is futile, travel here. I'll stake you to some good old-fashioned beef and potatoes."

In his racing mind, while he rode up to the cattle in the meadow, Bud had already figured it out. He'd refrain from selling any beef to the miners or the townsfolk in Bottineau. He'd leave that up to the ranchers who were usually too busy driving their cattle to the better markets at Bismarck or Devil's Lake. He'd forget about selling any spuds. He'd keep a good supply of food around in case he could talk these Indians into coming back later in the year with more deluxe appaloosa stock. Indians without treaty had a hell of a job making it through winter with enough grub in their bellies. Sometimes, late in the winter, they were forced to eat their moccasins. He'd trade them food for horses.

Bud was remembering the night six months earlier, in the Chandelier Room at the Leland House in Minot when Mr. James J. Hill, president of the Great Northern Railway, one of the great business moguls of the age, told Bud he'd pay handsomely for six appaloosa yearlings if they were perfect specimens.

Back then, Bud had driven a dozen of his best stock to Minot on spec and sold all but the animal he had ridden to a well-to-do local rancher who invited him to the hotel for dinner. There, they ran into a chum from the rancher's early days. Turned out to be the richest man in the west. Hill, a relentless promoter, was responsible for bringing in countless Scandinavian immigrants to the northwest. He had just delivered thirty prime Hereford bulls to local ranchers in an effort to improve local stock and sow the seeds of future cattle shipments for his railway. His private train with his luxury personal car, called Manitoba, was parked on a railway siding.

Hill was an avid lover of horses. He and Bud had a lot in common on that front. They spent an evening talking about the horse-breeding skills of the Nez Percé people of the Pacific Northwest and the beauty of the appaloosa horse breed.

"It was a sad day in 1877 when Chief Joseph and his people surrendered to the U.S. Army in the Bear Paw Mountains," Hill said, blowing a huge cloud of smoke from his Cuban cigar.

"Only forty miles from the Canadian border, after travelling so far, enduring so much hardship and surviving so many skirmishes," Bud said.

"Skirmishes! What do you mean skirmishes? Those were full-scale battles." Hill was filling the room with smoke from his Double Corona like an engine on one of his trains.

"I have no respect for that cretin, General Miles. I have made my opinion well-known at the highest levels of government. That bastard should have been horsewhipped and run out of the service. Do you know, after they surrendered he stole hundreds of their horses? Disposed of them for tawdry purposes to shysters and had his troopers shoot hundreds more? Then he refused to allow them to breed appaloosas anymore. The most beautiful horse in the history of the world! And, perhaps, the greatest nation of horse breeders on the continent. Damnation! We are an ignorant country in so many ways! Have a Havana, my friend, and let's have a drink in honour of Chief Joseph. Corrupt government flunkies are holding him prisoner in Oklahoma."

"I hear tell there's still some of those horses around from the pure Nez Percé stock," Bud answered, puffing away. "The Crows have some and I have seen the Assiniboines riding appaloosas as well."

"You don't say," said Hill, pausing to pour another shot into his glass. "The stock Miles scattered to the winds have been bred by every scabby stallion in the country. Miles is a pompous horse's ass. Have you met him? I tell you, I have never encountered such a pedantic dullard and I have met some stuffed specimens in my time."

Bud was having a little trouble following Hill's colourful prose but he understood the gist and spirit of it. It was obvious that Hill was an expert on many facets of the horse business. A passion which he had heavily invested in, as he liked to point out. His passionate side dominated and Hill became more vitriolic toward Miles, and General Howard for that matter, as the whisky went down.

"Now they're each trying to one-up the other to take credit for the disgraceful treatment of the Nez Percé. Mark my words, Mr. Figley, history will not be kind."

Giving his tongue a good work out, Bud thought as he marveled at Hill's staying power.

"I'd pay a pretty price for six good, young animals. The real thing in prime condition – not some amateur breeder's interpretation."

"Is it that bad?" Bud asked.

"Yes. I have seen some abominations in the east. Generations of breeding have been besmirched."

"How much?" Bud asked out of curiosity.

"I don't know," answered Hill. "Let me think about it."

"Be a tough thing to pull off," Bud went on. "A man would have to invest a lot of time and effort and, hell, who knows if anybody'd be capable of finding real good, young stock."

"By God! I'd pay five hundred bucks apiece for them if I was to acquire, say, a stud and five good young fillies. I recognize it would be a feat to pull this off nowadays. Hell, it's only money and money is one substance I have more of than I'll ever need. Not that I'm about to throw it away or let any son-of-a-bitch take it from me."

"If you could put your hands on those horses what would you do with them?" Bud asked.

"Never mind what I'm going to do with them," Hill said. "You're a wrangler, I don't tell you how to do your business, you don't tell me how to run my railway or ask me any questions about what, or where. Just send my secretary a telegram about the 'when' and I'll have the details taken care of. God bless your yellow eyes! What the hell's the matter with them anyway?"

Mr. Hill was a man surrounded by beautiful women. He sponsored opera houses and encouraged the development of cultural institutions in the towns his railway serviced. Hill liked to pontificate on how the spread of so-called civilization could only benefit his business aspirations. Several times a year he came west in his private railway car, with a number of his business pals who took to the whorehouses in rustic prairie towns like fleas in a circus.

He was currently travelling with the diva Emma Calve, the buxom canary from Europe who sang the popular songs of the day by request, as well as performing classic operas in opera houses and theatres across the land. Hill made it well-known to the boys in the bar that he was putting it to Miss Calve. It was rumoured that he ordered a hole drilled into the boudoir of his railway car and had a magnifying lens inserted into the wall so that his lecherous friends could take turns watching him banging on Emma, whose screams in eight octaves threatened to shatter the windows in the car.

Hill's last words to Bud, as he snacked on caviar and blue cheese on dry toast, were something as follows: "Remember, Quiggles, or Figgles, or whatever your name is. Money talks and bullshit walks!"

Bud had nodded in agreement like a puppet. He was already thinking about the three thousand bucks. He'd dance on the head of a pin for that kind of money. Hill was charmed by Bud's picturesque way of talking and by his stories. He offered Bud a couple of nights lodging in the hotel. After all, Hill was a silent partner who owned a piece of it.

Miss Florence Mouton, Hill's private road secretary, was instructed to advise Bud on the details of how to go about contacting Hill if he was to personally deliver said ponies to Hill's railway supervisor in Minot. She was not willing to fill him in on the plans he had for the appaloosas except to state that Hill was intending to impress and influence a foreign dignitary. Later, in a drunken conversation at the Leland Hotel, one of Hill's associates confided to Bud that the hypothetical horses were intended as a present for the Prince of Wales.

"A man," he said, in a jumble of slurred words, "who has nearly everything."

Miss Florence was the pinnacle of Bud's taste in the female form. She was an Amazonian woman with a massive bosom. She had an unconventionally attractive round face. She moved easily among Hill's gentlemen followers, giving them details about the train schedule and the various events that Hill had planned for them in the sundry towns they stopped in on their sojourn across the country. She took notes in a stout, leather-bound notebook and bossed around the staff as if she were the president of the Great Northern Railway, herself. Whenever she appeared, Hill tuned out whoever he was talking with and gave her his undivided attention. When she wasn't on duty as Hill's surrogate, she spent her time socializing with the other female members of the travelling party. She towered over Emma and the other singers and most of the musicians. She led them about as if she were the leader of the flock. The parrot feathers in her hat bounced above the throng. When her silk dress rustled during one of her walkabouts, the material seemed to come alive as it announced her presence to the room.

Bud, charming Miss Mouton with his gentle manners and rustic humour, had soon had her blushing in an animated private conversation.

"Miz Flory, you're the woman of my dreams, I'd love to see the sun come up in your eyes," Bud had crooned in her ear after a few too many shots of whisky.

"You're a tolerable good-looking figure of a man, but you're not a man of enough substance for a woman like me," she'd said, patting him on the cheek.

"Don't you dare trifle with me, Mr. Quigley. If you are ever able to fulfill Mr. Hill's request for a half dozen of the finest appaloosas in the land, then send a telegram to me at this address, marked 'urgent request,'" she said, handing him her card. "I will see to your needs. If not, I don't wish to hear from you under any circumstances, and neither does Mr. Hill. I have had my fill of you western types who are all guff and bravado and seldom perform when necessary."

For an instant, Bud felt inclined to invite Mouton up to his hotel room to see if he might be able to perform on her behalf, but his libido would not allow it. He found himself strangely attracted by her assertive personality as well as by her considerable physicality, although he would have never been able to put it in words. In truth, few men dared to make advances on Miss Florence. Flo Mouton kept a low profile at the Great Northern headquarters in Saint Paul, Minnesota. A dutiful James Hill, and his wife Mary, parents of ten children, were the centre of an enormous social circle as befit a man of Hill's status as railway magnate.

On the rails it was another story. Miss Mouton put on her dominatrix leathers and used a cat o' nine tails on Hill's posterior to keep him in tune. The result was a strong relationship between the pair that manifested itself with Mouton gradually taking more responsibility in translating Hill's orders to his employees and staff on his many rail trips around the country to consolidate his empire.

Hill could relax, out of sight of home, travelling with his pals, knowing that Florence Mouton was on the job. She had a sense of propriety and was more loyal than some of his male employees, who were prone to embezzling funds or promoting indiscreet behaviour that reflected badly on the Great Northern image.

"One last thing, then. These horses have to be fit for a king. If they aren't you'll be wasting our time, as well as your own."

Recollections of his two days spent in the company of the Great Northern Railway entourage flooded back into Bud's mind long after Alphonse Pointed Stick and his brothers had left his yard to rejoin their people camped at the river. It seemed a long shot when he had asked the Swedes at the ferry crossing to tell the Assiniboines that he was interested in purchasing horses from them. Now the future seemed clearer as he looked over his new acquisitions prancing in the corral.

Bud Quigley figured that if everything worked out according to plan, it wouldn't be long before he would be increasing the already considerable pile of cash he had stashed near his home. He thought about how the odds in a man's life even out when one considers that opportunities and luck are often self-generated. He briefly considered the arrival of Jiggs Dubois on the scene with his hired lackeys. The only cloud on the horizon in his scenario was the prospect that he might see them again. Dubois was not the kind of a man who let go of a notion once he fixated on it. Bud knew that Dubois did not believe his story. However, without evidence or witnesses, Dubois had nothing to link him with Tall Bob. He figured the two henchmen for unpredictable hotheads. There was the slim chance they might return on their own if they considered there was any advantage in it. He would trust his instincts and his friend Mr. Parker to deal with Charlie Parmer and Frenchie "Who-Only-Goes-by-One-Name" should they show up on his doorstep. They were miserable vermin, of a type he had learned to deal with when he moved out into the wild country. Dubois was another matter.

Now his path to further riches was written in the deal for horses that he was beginning to pull together. Bud resolved he was not about to let anybody stand in his way. Often, during the long, winter nights in his snug little cabin, he dreamed of sailing across the oceans of the world on a sleek clipper ship to magical lands. Sometimes, when he travelled the wide expanse of grass, he conjured up a vision of watching the wind blowing waves across the sea. He imagined he was on the deck of a ship bound for adventure under the tumultuous piles of clouds that were gathering.

7

May, 1894
State of North Dakota, United States

WHEN TALL BOB SET OFF from Bud Quigley's homestead on Foxy in early spring, he had a fixed plan in his mind. The vigorous economic activity in North Dakota, illustrated by the two railways that were aggressively pushing across the region, led him to suspect there could be a large amount of cash in the First National Bank in Bismarck, the state capital. He reasoned that just before the first of the month would be the perfect time to act on his hunch.

However, the events at the bank had not unfolded in any pattern that he understood. When his revolver had gone off, the last thing he saw was the bank manager falling in the doorway. He knew by the way the whole scenario unfolded that the slug had caught the unfortunate fellow in the head. He saw a bright puff in mid-air, where the man had stood, like a fine red mist.

He could hardly believe his luck when he walked into the bank on Fourth Street and Main Avenue, in Bismarck, on a bluebird day. The streets were empty and, miraculously, only one man was on duty in the bank. It was the manager, busy returning some ledgers back to the vault. Tall Bob hauled out his weapon and addressed the florid executive, who readily agreed to give him the money in his already-open safe. It was as if the man had been caught with his pants down. The drawn gun was a real attention-getter. What could he do but fill Tall Bob's sacks with money without a second thought? It was a civilized encounter between two men with very different intentions. As he calmly left the bank, he stopped briefly to gaze up and down the deserted street. There was nothing to see but whitewashed walls and storefront signs. Tall Bob recollected the last words that came from his lips before he left the building –

"Don't do anything crazy. Sit down and have a smoke before you sound the alarm. I wouldn't want to see you get hurt by dis-playing rash behaviour. It's only money and probably not yours, so don't try and be heroic."

The middle-aged man nodded as if he clearly understood the need to stay inside. Tall Bob had left the chestnut out front, snugged up on a hitching rail. He slung the two potato sacks stuffed with money over the horse's withers. After he was aboard he pulled his revolver again. Suddenly all hell broke loose. The chestnut, startled by a small yapping dog that had appeared from between buildings, reared in the air and came down hard. By now, the hysterical bank manager had arrived in the doorway, scream-ing for help at the top of his lungs. When the horse landed, the gun in Tall Bob's hand bounced against the saddle horn and dis-charged. He took off on a runaway horse headed in the wrong di-rection down Main Street. People looked out from their windows to see what the commotion was about, but nobody dared go out into the street and there were no additional shots fired.

Tall Bob was back in control of the horse by the time he hit the dead end. He decided he had no choice but to navigate his horse over the fence enclosing the graveyard. He passed a half-grown boy in the street taking a bead on him with a long-barreled rifle. The boy fired the weapon just as the chestnut stretched over the boards. Tall Bob felt the shudder from the horse as it veered sideways when the shot grazed its rump. They continued running through the graveyard, dodging headstones, until they reached the far side. One more time he asked the horse to jump the fence and the chestnut answered in style.

As Tall Bob rode away, he could not stop the twenty-second memory that kept going around in his brain. The rearing horse, the gun going off, the manager taking the slug, the rush down the street, the boy staggering under the weight of the ancient rifle, the flight over the fence into the graveyard. It played over and over again while he vamoosed from Bismarck. After an hour, he steered the chestnut down the shallows of a creek for a mile before vanishing into a thicket. When he came out the other side he cut through the fields for some time before he arrived back onto the road. After another few miles he left the road and headed for higher ground on a ridge. When it became too steep, he dismounted and led the horse up the side hill into some trees, where he stopped to rest. It was a place that afforded a clear view of his back trail in case he was being followed. He reached into his saddle bag for some jerky. He was so excited he could hardly chew. His dry lips could do little more than sip at the water from his canteen.

Tall Bob reflected on the balding man with the ruddy complexion taking a bullet in the head. He was sick at the thought of it. How could an isolated act on a perfectly calm day turn into such a hash?

Luckily, the gun had been too heavy for the lad to hold for long in the air. Considering the range, it was fortunate the horse had only been grazed instead of being gut-shot. Now he was in a dilemma. He had no idea how long the wounded horse would travel before it lost hope and played out.

He decided that, after a rest, he would set off for the secluded location he had left the packhorse and supplies, a journey of about two hours. He walked the horse down the other side of the ridge and mounted up. The horse, champing at the bit, seemingly oblivious to its injury, had found a second wind and they moved along at good pace. He did not encounter another soul on the road.

Tall Bob figured that, if he could reach the packhorse and his extra gear before the chestnut broke down, at least he would have a fresh horse to ride. He would give the chestnut a chance to rest and time to feed and water. If the chestnut couldn't continue he would put it out of its misery and ride the knobbly packhorse until he had a chance to steal a better mount. By the time he reached the packhorse, staked out in a small, wild meadow beside a creek, he realized the chestnut was in it for the long haul. He took off the saddle and allowed the horse the freedom to graze and take on water. He decided he would camp there for the night and risk a fire before pitch-black darkness set in. He would boil some water for tea in his pail and eat the hard-boiled eggs and jerky that Bud had given him.

After he finished eating, drinking three or four cups of tea and rolling some smokes, he continued reliving the awful twenty seconds of the shooting that had been turning over in his brain. Tall Bob grabbed the potato sacks and untied the knots that secured them. He dumped the money out on his bedroll. He counted out forty-four thousand dollars. *My gawd*, he thought, *for once in my life I guessed right.* His hunch that there might be a big payroll in the bank at the first of the month had been correct. He'd hit the motherlode. He had a sudden flash of insight as to why the bank manager had taken the unfortunate chance of yelling wolf.

It was then that he began thinking. This was enough money to set him up as a wealthy man in a style he could never have imagined a few short hours before. He knew that killing the bank manager was an act that would haunt him for life. There was no giving-up by the law when somebody was shot dead.

The bosses Tall Bob had just robbed were usually more relentless when it came to recovering money than they were about catching a killer. Their ideal solution was to get the money back as quickly as possible. If the robber was also brought in, dead or alive, then so much the better. When dealing with robberies, most banks, stage lines or railways brought in the Pinkerton National Detective Agency to recover their funds and eliminate the threat of hold-up men who had a habit of repeating once they had a taste for the outlaw life.

Pinkerton billed itself as a "private law enforcement agency." The agency motto, "We Never Sleep," was illustrated by a logo of the all-seeing eye which, in turn, gave rise to the term "private eye." The company operated in the United States, Canada and Mexico. Unpunished robberies and unrecovered stolen goods were bad for business. Bankers and other employees who tried to stand in the way were easily replaced. Lawmen were constrained by their need to keep law and order in their jurisdiction while they hunted down criminals. Pinkerton agents pursued outlaw vermin with all the enthusiasm of a terrier stalking a rat and they were free to range widely. They were limited only by the resources of their patrons, who usually had deep pockets. The law meant little to them when a client's assets were on the line.

Tall Bob's mind was working overtime. He was certain there was a posse following him. By the time the sun had burned off the morning haze, he was already back on the trail. He travelled overland, leading the packhorse for the better part of day, until he came to a place where he had camped on his journey to Bismarck. He had a fishing line and knew he would have no trouble catching fish in the good-sized creek there. He used a hook with red wool wound round its shank and soon enough he had three pike gutted and split on sticks over his fire. He would eat what he needed and take the rest along with him.

Travelling north, he stayed off the official roads as much as he could and journeyed overland whenever he had the opportunity. Sometimes, he was forced to take to the more well-travelled routes. Twice he encountered travellers on the road. He passed with a wave of his arm while he kept his hat tilted down over his face. Once, he stepped off the road into the brush for a rest and watched as a wagon and three riders clattered by. They appeared to be in no hurry as they leisurely plodded along. Still, he surmised that the authorities in Minot would have already been apprised of the events that transpired in Bismarck and that the law would be watching the roads.

Finally, he came to the outskirts of Minot. Tall Bob rested in the late afternoon in some brush, waiting for the light to leave so he could chance the trip into town. He would try to cross the Mouse River and head northeast, bound for Quigley's place. He knew that his best chance at survival was to reach Bud's as fast as he could, so he could stop and rest for a day or two. He'd let Bud watch his back trail while he caught up on his sleep, then he'd pay Bud off and plan his getaway in earnest.

That night, under a full moon, Tall Bob sucked in his breath and started the torturous journey through Minot and onto the bridge across the Mouse River. He was fearful it would be guarded by law enforcement officers. Dogs barked but no shots rang out as he passed. He encountered only one drunken man waving an empty bottle, screaming profanities at the moon. The drunk paid no attention as Tall Bob and his animals slowly plodded by.

A couple of hours out of Minot he noticed that the packhorse had come up lame. He had no option but to slow down and figure out how he was going to proceed. Tall Bob then made a decision that would have great impact on future events in his life.

It dawned on Bob that maybe the best thing to do was to bury most of the money until he could return at some future date and recover the cash. He decided he would stuff his boots with money and wrap up a good wad of it in the oilcloth he kept in his saddle bag. He'd slip that down the front of his jacket, under his underwear top and baggy shirt. That would give him enough money to take care of his debt to Quigley and look after his obligations. He'd use it to tide him over in a carefully-arranged, low-profile lifestyle until he could find the opportunity to travel back for the rest.

On his run for the border he'd cut down on his baggage, eventually ditch the packhorse and reduce the chestnut's load to the bare essentials.

Tall Bob stopped in a small marshy area that had a fringe of bur oak and American elm trees, as well as a few scrubby evergreens. He took the small shovel from the packhorse and the bulky potato sacks he had tied down on the back of the chestnut. Locating the tallest evergreen, he marched off twenty strides to a pile of rocks. There, he shifted the rocks then quickly dug a two-foot-deep hole. Consolidating the money into one bulging potato sack, he wrapped the whole issue in his slicker. Depositing the package in the hole, he shoveled the dirt back in place and restored the rocks so that it appeared they had never moved. Taking good notice of the tall elms, he memorized the features of the landscape from every angle. Tall Bob knew he would never forget this place. He would return in the future when the heat was off to recover his hard-won fortune.

He rode for another hour with his lame packhorse following behind. When he came to a coulee, he unloaded the gear and scattered it in the brush on the bottom land. Later in the afternoon, when he chanced on a herd of horses, he took the halter off and let the old fellow loose. He mounted the chestnut and watched the packhorse wander down the field in search of new companions.

Deserved it, he thought.

By the time whoever owned the horses discovered another nag had been added to his eaters, Tall Bob planned to be well free of this territory.

The Mouse River, called the Souris in Canada, meanders across the prairie like a slowly uncoiling snake. Tall Bob speculated on swimming the horse to cross it, but the river was high from all the rain that had fallen in the spring and summer. He reckoned it was too dangerous for an exhausted horse and man. He had no choice but to pay his fare and ride the ferry. Tall Bob concluded that the Swedish ferrymen were mind-your-own-business types. Even if the law arrived at their ferry they might be vague in their descriptions of man and horse. He was sure they'd fail to notice the wound on the horse's rump because of the tarp. The three white socks and the description of the man were more problematic.

"How do, that'll 'a be one dollar," said the ferryman who came out of the hut beside the river.

The Swede was not interested in making small talk. His brother cracked his black bullwhip in the bright sunshine, the mules moved in a circle and the ferry lurched into the current. When Tall Bob reached the other side, he mounted the gelding again and headed along the riverbank into the lush grasslands.

When he finally reached the outskirts of Bottineau he took the scenic route around the town to avoid being seen. Now he had thirty-five miles to go and would sometime soon be crossing the U.S. border into Canada.

After the robbery it had been two hours before anybody in Bismarck even thought about arranging a party to go after him. The local lawman, John Humphrey, was too old and bothered by his aching back to commit to a serious chase on horseback. His underpaid deputies had no gumption to pull it together, either. When they entered the Bismarck bar to raise up a posse, they started drinking instead. Pretty soon they were all too well-lubricated to sit on a horse.

When they were sober enough to set off, they rode for only a short distance before being befuddled by the trail petering out at the creek that Bob had ridden down. Darkness was setting in so they went back to town and resumed their deliberations in the bar. The next morning they were back at it again, riding up and down the road leading into town until they concluded the desperado had turned into the will o' the wisp, having vanished without a trace. They sent out telegrams to Minot and a few other places but, unfortunately, at this stage in the investigation, nobody had a handle on a decent description of the robber or the horse he was riding. Truth was, once Tall Bob had navigated his way through Minot, he could have stopped and camped for a week. His fear that a posse of angry riders, bent on revenge for the robbery and murder committed in their town, was on his trail was totally unfounded. Just the opposite. There were no heroes in Bismarck, only talkers who were bullshitting while getting liquored up in the hotel bar.

When Tall Bob rode that worn-out chestnut nag with a heart as big as they come into Bud's yard, he already had decided on an approach to paying off Bud. He'd show him the money he was carrying on his body to give Bud the impression that it was the total take from the robbery. Tall Bob planned on rewarding old Bud with a substantial cut to keep him onside. He was starting to feel optimistic now. If he could replace the chestnut with a fresher pair of legs, his chances of escaping were increasing by the mile. When the trail changed from prairie into rocky bush, the horse began to tire, so he stopped to rest for the night. The next day, on the final ten-mile stretch, he felt its strength wane even more, as if his knees were pushing the animal down into the trail, but the faithful chestnut kept plunging forward. When they arrived in the old man's yard, the horse was glistening and foaming at the bit under the beating sun.

8

September, 1894
State of Minnesota, United States

ON SEPTEMBER 16TH, 1894, ON HIS BIRTHDAY, the Canadian-born railway magnate James J. Hill, known widely as "the Empire Builder," was in residence at his new thirty-six thousand square foot, palatial home at 240 Summit Avenue in Saint Paul, Minnesota. Early in the morning, Hill had travelled the ten miles into town from his six thousand acre farm for an important meeting.

Hill, a self-made man, was a major player in the gilded age of railroading, associating with many of the movers and shakers of the times, including Donald Smith, Sir William Van Horne, J.P. Morgan and future president of the United States, Theodore Roosevelt, who named him to his blue ribbon conservation group. Hill's empire-building vision was from a far different perspective than his competitors. He built his seventeen hundred mile railway from Saint Paul, Minnesota to Seattle, Washington in two-hundred-mile bites. All along his Great Northern railway line, he sold homesteads to the immigrants he helped recruit, then sold them the wood and other commodities they needed. At the same time, he enriched these new farmers by presenting them with pedigreed cattle free of charge and providing herds of Clydesdale horses.

Hill employed agents to attract immigrants primarily from England, Scotland, Norway, Sweden and Russia. Hill was quoted as saying: "Give me snuff, whisky and Swedes, and I will build a railroad to Hell."

He invested heavily in the communities that came to life with the arrival of his slowly-but-steadily advancing, railroad. He was a visionary, driven to succeed in his railway ventures while he furthered his long-term ambitions of doing shipping business in the Orient.

Hill was an avid art collector and patron of the arts. He thought nothing of purchasing a painting for one hundred thousand dollars. He built a big house lavish enough to display his collection of European masters.

Hill, a notorious hands-on operator, obsessed over the details in his ever-expanding business enterprises, which included banking and finance. It was in his role as President of The First National Bank that he summoned William Pinkerton, of the Pinkerton National Detective Agency, to travel to Saint Paul from Chicago to meet with him on such an auspicious day.

Late in the morning Pierce, the butler, admitted Pinkerton into the drawing room where he waited for Hill to finish dictating letters to his private secretarial staff. The Pinkerton National Detective Agency, founded by William's now deceased father, Allan, was firmly under the direction of William and his brother Robert. William was in charge of the Pinkerton head office in Chicago, while Robert ran the company's new office in New York City. The Pinkertons enjoyed a long, prosperous relationship with most of the railways, including Great Northern. The times were changing and workers' associations and labour unrest were beginning to become troublesome for the industrialists, who were reluctant to share the wealth. The Pinkerton Agency provided heavies as well as spies and infiltrators to provoke the workers. They often committed acts of violence, as the company did the bidding of the bosses.

Pinkerton was sure he had been summoned by Hill to receive instructions on how to proceed against Hill's railway workers. He was wrong. James J. Hill took no man's counsel when it came to making policy concerning his businesses. He had already decided on his course of action in dealing with his labour problems and the declining economy. He would ruthlessly sack a third of his work force to avenge their wildcat strike earlier that summer. In addition, he would reduce the freight rates on his shipping and railway lines in order to increase business. It was a clever ploy. While reducing the work force he would target unionists and troublemakers, thereby weakening the will of his surviving employees. By lowering freight rates he would increase the volume of freight handled and keep his thriving business on an even keel. Hill was just a few months short of celebrating the one-year anniversary of his railway linking the east with the west coast. Now, his business vision was widening and he was turning his attention to expanding his empire into the Orient.

However, for this particular meeting, Hill, in his role as president of the First National Bank, had something else in his mind. He had summoned Pinkerton to discuss the robbery of the Bismarck branch of the First National Bank earlier in the spring of the year. Hill was eager to have a progress report on the state of the Pinkerton investigation into the robbery and the subsequent murder.

"I assure you, sir, I put the bloodhounds out on this case. I have scattered them widely over the area. I believe it is only a matter of weeks, months at the most, until we apprehend the man responsible."

"You must see my position clearly, William. I cannot tolerate my banks being robbed and my employees being murdered by crude morons who live by the gun. I have grown impatient with the lawmen coming up empty. I am distressed that you have made little progress in this matter."

"It's a big country out there, sir, but we have made progress. We believe the man who committed this robbery and murder is not the usual criminal type who commits this kind of act. He does not hang out with lowlifes or frequent the saloon scene. He is not associating with the known criminal element who always seem to have buzz on events such as this awful Bismarck robbery. At this point, four months since the robbery, we have heard no speculation from the public."

"Then why are you telling me you're making progress?"

"You see, sir, my network of informants and investigators have determined that our man is not going to be located in the usual haunts, blowing the money he took from the robbery on wine, woman and song."

"That doesn't make me feel very confident you're going to find him."

"Well, sir, it will take time, but I assure you we will apprehend him."

"I admire your conviction, William, but this lack of resolution doesn't exactly inspire the confidence of my bank employees. Never mind the depositors who might be worried about being shot by some deranged robber in one of my branches."

"Yes, Mr. Hill, I'll take that last point under advisement and do what I can to accelerate our pace of investigation."

"Yes, why don't you? Further more, William, I don't find it humorous that our bank robber not only robbed one of my banks and killed the manager, but that he also made off with the payroll for my railway workers. So I have been doubly injured. I do not intend to tolerate this kind of activity perpetuated against my interests. I can always hire a new bank manager, but forty-four thousand dollars does not grow on trees. It is a substantial amount of money. I want you to nab this villain so we can recover the damn payroll. If this man gets away then I will be a target for every warped saddle tramp and itinerant fool who can afford the price of a revolver. Up the odds, shake a few more bushes, bring him in fast, dead or alive. Makes no difference to me, providing he's the right one."

"Yes sir, I will do my best."

"Listen carefully, William. I am willing to increase your fees and expenses and I am up for providing more reward money if necessary, but you must show me some enthusiasm and vigour in attending to this matter. I want you to double the bloodhounds and turn over every rock within five hundred miles of Bismarck. I will be furious if he's just some local schemer who was out for an afternoon lark, knocked over my bank, and is now secluded right near the scene. Don't suppose you figure the robber went over the border and is hiding somewhere up in Canada?"

"A possibility, but not one that daunts us, sir, since we operate equally well on both sides of the border. In fact we don't recognize the border. By that I mean we are a private police force that co-operates with the legal authorities in every region in our pursuit of criminals."

"Spare me the bloody speeches, William. It's damn slack north of the border on the prairies. There are just those few redcoats wandering around, mostly herding Indians from point A to B. I doubt whether those birds could catch a cold. Bunch of pointy-headed rubes who'd rather be in the cavalry. You put some agents north of the border and start looking for a spendthrift."

"We're already there, sir, and I have received an encouraging report from one of our most tenacious investigators in North Dakota. This detective is pursuing a particular line in his efforts to run down some leads that we turned up in the original investigation."

At this point in their encounter Pinkerton was grasping at straws. The only possible lead he had, apart from a description of horse and rider, was based on the theories expounded on by detective Jiggs Dubois, a man who achieved results at times but was far better at initiating violence than he was at solving cases. Dubois was sure the fleeing suspect had crossed the Mouse River on a ferry run by Swedish brothers. He was also suspicious of a horse rancher across the border who was far too old to have been the perpetrator. Dubois thought perhaps the man in question knew more than he was letting on but had no evidence to support his gut feeling. Under William Pinkerton's administration, gut feeling was something that was attributed to lunch, not to cases.

"I must say, William, it sounds like piffle. I'd rather drink a glass of warm spit. Let's start moving on this matter. I want my damned money back! Damn it, I don't care how much money I have to spend to get it back. I want the same damn bills, the very same pieces of legal tender that were taken from my bank. If you have to shoot the bastard to bring him in, then shoot the smart bastard right in the forehead, just like he shot that poor soul who worked for me. Everybody concerned will be served notice that robbing me doesn't pay and I'll be a happy man again."

"Yes sir, Mr. Hill. I'll prime the pump and light the fuses. We'll double our effort and turn the country inside out until we find him."

"Jesus, William, you sound like a salesman. Take it easy or I'll have you selling debentures and bonds. William, I want you to follow my lead. Meet with your agents in order to exhaust every lead in this case no matter how trivial it might be. Do you understand me? I want action, not rhetoric!"

"Perfectly, sir, I understand every word and I will take appropriate action."

"Very good, now that you've heard my spiel, how about we adjourn this meeting and have lunch."

Pinkerton helped James J. Hill celebrate his birthday by sitting down with him and demolishing three dozen of the native Matin oysters from Puget Sound on the Pacific coast as well as a brace of two pound lobsters each, brought alive overland from Maine and the Atlantic Ocean for the occasion. They washed that down with several bottles of Lafite Rothschild Medoc 1870. The power of the railway did not go unnoticed by Pinkerton as he dined splendidly on live seafood from opposite coasts in one of the inland power corridors of the times. After the lengthy, sumptuous lunch they toured Hill's art gallery and viewed his collection which included works by Courbet, Millet and Delacroix. Proud of his opulent new digs, Hill followed this up by giving Pinkerton a look at some of the state-of-the-art features that were incorporated in the construction of his mansion. These included plumbing, central heating, and electric lighting as well as a security system to ensure his privacy.

"One more thing, William. I want you to undertake an immediate, first-hand investigation of the case yourself. It will entail you leaving immediately on a trip to North Dakota to personally go over the ground and interview your agents in the field. To that end, a private car will be attached to a train heading west in the morning. You and your luggage will be on it. Is that clear?"

"Yes sir!"

Pinkerton was no fool. James J. Hill was not a man one refused. Great Northern Railway was one of the Pinkerton Detective Agency's biggest accounts. James J. Hill had his fingers in too many pies right up to his elbow to be ignored. James J. Hill usually got what he wanted, when he wanted it, from whomever he wanted it from. Pinkerton was in no position to turn down the request. William hurried to the telegraph station to send his brother Robert the message that he would be taking a sudden train trip to Minot, North Dakota.

The Pinkerton brothers were under a huge amount of stress. On July 6th, 1892, all hell had broken loose when industrialist Henry Clay Frick, working for Andrew Carnegie, authorized the Pinkertons to send a force of three hundred and fifty men, armed with Winchester rifles, to subdue the workers at Carnegie's steel mill in Homestead, Pennsylvania. A gun battle broke out. Nine strikers and seven Pinkertons were killed and the ground was littered with scores of wounded.

This was the beginning of a disastrous series of events with tragic consequences for both sides. In May, 1894, the Pullman strike in Chicago turned from an isolated union grievance into a full-fledged national railway strike with railway workers under the leadership of the American Railway Union head, Eugene V. Debbs, refusing to work on trains that included Pullman cars. Once again, the Pinkertons were front and centre, spying, agitating, and disrupting while on the payroll of the bosses. President Grover Cleveland ordered General Nelson Miles and twelve thousand United States army troops, along with United States Marshals, to move against the workers. Subsequently, thirteen strikers were killed and fifty-seven were wounded.

By fall of 1894, Pinkerton was still putting out brush fires that were left over from the conflict that took place earlier in the summer. James J. Hill was a tough opponent and he expected nothing less than total diligence from Pinkerton as he set about continuing his vicious campaign against the workers. Hill vowed that never again would one of his trains sit on a siding because of labour problems. The workers and the newly-established union would be made to pay a terrible price for their impudence.

Reluctantly, early on the morning of September 17th, 1894, Pinkerton climbed aboard a private car that was added to a Great Northern train heading west, and found himself on his way to Minot. The night before he had sent another telegram, this time to North Dakota, to his top agent in the field there, asking him to make sure his detectives, including Jiggs Dubois, would be available for interviews when the train pulled into Minot.

Pinkerton was not happy. This problem of a robbery and a murder was low on his list of priorities. He had been content to let his men work this case at their own pace. Now Hill was escalating the situation by demanding immediate action. Pinkerton saw a strange trait in James Hill that worried him. Hill seemed more focused on solving this bank robbery and killing than he was in the much larger picture. Workers were becoming organized under dynamic leaders and the times were changing. How long could men like Hill and his ilk continue to suppress worker's rights and bring down wholesale bloodshed on their labourers? The things that Hill and his contemporaries asked of the Pinkertons were becoming unpalatable for William and his brother. He resented that he was forced to waste his valuable time on a Hill whim.

When the train arrived in Minot, Pinkerton's private car was parked on a siding. Soon after, he began the laborious task of interviewing the detectives and agents who had been out in the field running down leads on the Bismarck robbery.

Detective Balfour Smith, a hard nut with an enviable record of success in his investigations, had ridden the stage line from Bismarck to the notorious town of Deadwood to pursue inquiries. Travelling under the guise of mining promoter, Smith was a friend of the long time Deadwood hardware merchant and sheriff, Seth Bullock. They had known one another from the days when they were both involved in politics in Helena, Montana. Bullock, a man of impeccable reputation had formed a lifelong relationship with future president Theodore Roosevelt, beginning in 1884 when Roosevelt served as a deputy sheriff in Medora, North Dakota.

Bullock's wife, Martha, was the leading social figure in Deadwood society, which had been much cleaned up by her husband's diligent attention to enforcing the law. Bullock, who by 1894 was running a very tight little town, assured Balfour Smith that no rider fitting the robber's profile had recently passed through Deadwood. He promised that he and his deputies would keep a look out for anybody who fit the description of horse and rider. Smith spent a week in Deadwood sizing up the characters he saw in the streets and saloons before he made the return trip to Bismarck. His partner in investigations, Harold Moss, had spent his time travelling around the environs of Bismarck, talking to local ranchers and settlers in the hopes of turning up a suspect.

Both Smith and Moss were of the opinion that, since the robber had only hit one bank and made a big score, it seemed more likely he was not a professional but a one-time amateur with good luck. Therefore, they could not overlook what might be right under their noses. Pinkerton agreed with them. It was unusual for banks to be held up by a single gunman. The murder had been an afterthought that occurred in the panic that ensued before the getaway. He concurred with Smith and Moss that the robber/murderer was undoubtedly an amateur who scored more money than he had ever imagined. It was possible that by now he was at home hoping to live a near-invisible life without ostentatious spending that would attract attention. The fact that there were no subsequent criminal activities gave credence to the above premises.

Jiggs Dubois, uncomfortable in the louse-infested underwear under his heavy wool suit, turned up five days after Pinkerton's train arrived in Minot. Dubois had left his two boys, Charlie and Frenchie, in a cathouse in Bismarck, where they had gone in search of leads. They were not the quality of men that Pinkerton would waste his time on. Dubois expounded on his theories. He believed the Swedish ferrymen at their tiny station on the Mouse River had given passage to the robber on their short-run ferry that crossed the river.

"Them Swedes don't say much. In fact, every time I interview them they talk less than the time before. The damn foreigners barely speak American, so it's damn hard to understand what they're going on about half the time," Dubois said, looking for the spittoon.

"If you don't mind, I'd rather you not chew in here," Pinkerton remarked with an exasperated look on his face.

"I can't swallow it!"

"Well, spit the damn stuff out the door. It's a filthy habit." Pinkerton answered, plucking a loose thread from his jacket sleeve.

"Fact is, first time I talked to them they remembered a tall stranger in a white hat and a duck coat riding a chestnut gelding with three white socks. They had no opinion on the ass end since the back of the horse was covered with a folded tarp. It seems to me anybody riding a getaway horse with a groove in its right rump from a bullet would do their best to cover up the injury if they were boarding a ferry. They also have no recollection of the rider having a bag on board. Forty-four thousand dollars in small bills is a considerable pile of cash and would need to be carried in a pretty large container."

"This is a firm lead that is more than we've come up with so far. Tell me how you think this horse rancher north of the border fits in?" Pinkerton inquired.

"After the boys and me left the ferry we travelled into Bottineau, the next town, about ten miles north of the crossing. Let me tell you, the constable there is a real prick! The barkeep, some kind of hunky devil, hates our company. We made some inquiries and found out that the only man on the north side of the river who has decent horses for sale is this man Quigley. He lives about a day's ride over the border on the Canadian side. So, we travelled up to see him. Parmer and Frenchie went out and checked on his horses, but nothing matched what we were looking for.

"Now, this Quigley fellow's also a smart ass. In my opinion, he was lying through his teeth when I questioned him. I base that on my years of experience in interviewing people. Not only that, but he was rude and uncooperative."

"Maybe he didn't like the appearance of you and your companions, Dubois. You don't look like you sing in a choir and I doubt your interviewing manner is very subtle."

"What the hell does that mean?" Dubois asked. "The boys and I did our best to talk this Quigley into leveling with us, but he evaded our questions. We think the suspect took a chance on the ferry crossing because he had a tired, damaged mount that he had to replace before long. It seemed to us he was making a beeline for a place that had good stock. If you look at the map, you'll see there aren't many choices when you arrive up in that country. Not only had his wounded horse travelled a lot of miles under stress, but it was a chestnut with three white socks. Even a dumbbell would know he would eventually have to ditch that nag for a healthier, less-noticeable ride!"

"Now you're cooking, by God!" Pinkerton answered.

"Yes sir, I know," said Jiggs Dubois, admiring his own image and his new going-to-town bowler hat in the train window.

"In your preliminary report to me in the summer you pointed out that this horse wrangler –"

"Bud Quigley's his name, sir."

"You reported this Quigley fellow is too old to be the suspect."

"Yes sir, I believe Quigley is just what he appears to be – a horse wrangler who lives alone in an out-of-the-way place and prefers it that way."

"You figure, then, that our suspect rode up to Mr. Quigley's ranch to ditch his horse and find a new mount."

"Possibly," Dubois answered.

"Dubois, you have any ideas on how this investigation should proceed?"

"Well, sir, the boys and I could go up and put the screws to Quigley and see if we can beat some information out of him."

William Pinkerton blanched at Dubois's final statement.

"You're advocating crossing the border into a foreign country and beating the snot out of somebody in the hopes of gaining information?"

Dubois, with a sheepish look, answered that it was his understanding that Pinkertons didn't recognize international borders when it came to conducting investigations.

Pinkerton looked intently at him then explained to Dubois that, while the Pinkerton National Detective Agency crossed borders in the pursuit of criminals, it did so in a more subtle manner than arriving abruptly somewhere in another country and bludgeoning information out of a possibly-innocent citizen. Pinkerton explained that Pinkertons had agents on the other side of the border. If a strong case could be made that the suspect fled into Canada, these agents would be called into play.

"Dubois, cheer up, you've done a good job. Your theories are the only ones we have at the moment," Pinkerton stated, giving him a pat on his shoulder.

"Thank you, sir, I appreciate your confidence in me."

"Dubois, times have changed and the Pinkerton National Detective Agency has had to move with them. We are living in a new era of transcontinental train travel, with rapid modern communication tools and a new world of investigative techniques that we haven't even scratched the surface employing. Here's what we are going to do – we will send out circulars to every government office, post office, train station, stage coach terminal, sheriff's office, military establishment and hotel within five hundred miles of Bismarck. Add to that any other establishments we can think of that might post a notice. As well, we'll be taking out ads in all the newspapers within the region. Our Bismarck office will orchestrate the campaign with the First National Bank staff. There will be three key words, Dubois: circulars, telegram, reward. Let me put it down on paper for you to view."

William Pinkerton penned the message in a bold hand.

REWARD FOR INFORMATION
**Anybody who has come into contact with a chestnut gelding
with three white socks and a gunshot wound on
the right rump contact Jiggs Dubois by telegram
at the First National Bank, Bismarck, N.D.**

"There's one last clue, sir, that may shed light on the identity of our shooter.

When I heard you were coming out here by rail, I decided to take a quick trip to Bismarck to go over the details of the robbery one more time with the Bismarck sheriff. That is why I stood you up so long."

"Well Dubois, what is it?"

"This, sir," Dubois answered, unwrapping his handkerchief

and revealing a cartridge casing.

"During my original trip to Bismarck to investigate the robbery and subsequent murder there was one piece of evidence that was overlooked. It seems the posse that followed the shooter's trail found a location where the robber stopped briefly before he took to the countryside. I believe the suspect discarded this cartridge casing when he reloaded his weapon. Remember, he only fired one shot outside the bank. So he only had one cartridge casing to discard when he reloaded. One of the sheriff's deputies put the casing in his jacket pocket. He only remembered it later, some time after my first visit to the sheriff."

"Good work, Jiggs," Pinkerton said, referring to Dubois by his Christian name for the first time in their relationship.

"It's from a .476 Enfield cartridge. One that is normally fired from a Enfield Mark II revolver, which is a weapon commonly in use by both the British military and the North-West Mounted Police."

"What a dandy surprise and a bit of bonus! Don't you agree, Jiggs?"

"Yes sir, it gives us a whole new angle to investigate."

"Now, Jiggs, here are your instructions. Firstly, I am giving you a substantial raise in pay and increasing your expenses. I am putting Roger Filbert in charge of this investigation because the northwest is his area of operations. You will handle the field work but you will answer directly to Roger. He is an experienced man with numerous invaluable contacts. In addition, you will report to me as well, by telegrams and biweekly letters sent to my office in Chicago. Keep your messages brief, current and to the point. I will return east in the morning. Harold Moss will travel to Bismarck and reside there for the next month, keeping in close contact with the people at the bank to monitor the results of our advertising campaign. If this killer is smart he will have disposed of that horse in a manner that would defy investigation. On the other hand, if he's foolish he might have sold, traded or dumped the animal in a place that could betray him. In the meantime, you will sack those two reprobates you hang with. Then you and Balfour Smith will cross the border to Assiniboia and make contact with the North-West Mounted Police authorities at their headquarters in Regina. You will apprise them of our investigation and ask for their assistance and cooperation. You will inform our clandestine operatives in Canada about the manhunt we are undertaking in earnest to catch this rascal. Roger Filbert has checked into the Leland Hotel. He will fill you in on the details of how to make contact with our agents in Regina."

"Thank you for your confidence in me." Dubois said while he digested William Pinkerton's bold initiative.

"Dubois, one last thing. I want this investigation conducted in a thorough manner. I am pleased with your diligent work. This is an impressive new leaf you seem to be turning over now that you're using your brain as well as your brawn. This is a recent development for you, Dubois. It bodes well for your possible advancement further in the company."

9

July, 1894
Province of Manitoba, Canada

WHEN TALL BOB LEFT BUD QUIGLEY'S modest little spread in
Manitoba, he had already decided he would go north for a day
and then head east on his way home. Cleaned up, riding a fresh
mount and with thirty-six hundred dollars wrapped up in packages in the lining of his coat and in his saddle bags, he felt re-
newed. Tall Bob, as Quigley named him, was trying to revert
back to his true identity – Leslie Simpson, a constable in the
North-West Mounted Police on leave, headed home to visit his
family.

On July 1st, well into his two-month leave, he felt like he had
been in the saddle for a year. So much had happened in the pre-
ceding few weeks that it made his time in the service of the
North-West Mounted Police seem slightly distorted, like memories from the deep past.

When Les had been in the Mounted Police service for two years,
he applied for a leave to go home but had been turned down. His
superiors told him that it was unlikely they would grant him that
privilege unless, toward the end of his five-year contract, he would
commit to another term. Les bided his time, waiting until the
fourth year before applying again. He maintained that he was

happy in the service and was likely to sign on for an additional three-year term. Under the circumstances, his betters were happy to grant him two months leave with the understanding that he would be continuing in the force.

Les had taken the bold step of becoming a criminal while on his leave. His side trip to Bismarck and hundreds of miles of travel were testimony to his change in character. Leslie Simpson the Mountie was also "Tall Bob," a murdering bank robber. In a matter of a few weeks, Les had abandoned his law-abiding up-bringing and disavowed his sworn duty. Arguing in his own head, he was having trouble rationalizing his actions. A little voice in the silence of his mind was compelling Les to wake up and realize he was living by his gun now.

Eventually, he came upon a rutted road – really a glorified trail – that led him in a northeasterly direction, further into Manitoba. It was a Métis route made by the Red River carts of hunters who had come every year for decades out on the Assiniboia plains to hunt buffalo. That is, until recent times. By the 1890s, there were no buffalo left to hunt. On his way east, on this once well-travelled route, Les began the process of trying to turn back into the person he was before he had taken a man's life in a robbery. If that could ever be possible.

On the trail to his destination, the community of Brandon, he spent the miles on horseback thinking about his future. In the Blue Hills south of town he pondered how he would go about giving some of his ill-gotten wealth to his family without arousing suspicion.

Arriving in Brandon, he was shocked by the dramatic changes that had taken place in the five years he had been away. The city had nearly doubled in size. There was an atmosphere of a boom town as he plodded down the bustling streets on Red Ned. Les was returning home with money in his pocket and the death of the bank manager weighing on his conscience.

When he pulled up at his family's home on the far outskirts of town, he saw two youngsters playing a game with a puppy in front of the shack. He dismounted from the sorrel and walked toward them leading Ned. They stopped what they were doing and stood transfixed.

"Well," he said, "don't you have a hug for your big brother?"

The girl, Agnes, buried her face in Les's shirt and started to cry. The boy, Arthur, ran toward the back of the property, shouting at the top of his lungs for his mother, who was working in the garden. Before long, Les's mother and his sister Mabel came quickly from the back of the property. Both were in tears as they hugged Les and stood leaning against him for several minutes.

When he set eyes on his mother, Les immediately reflected on the letters his sister Ida Mae had sent him, warning him of their mother's deterioration in both physical and spiritual health. He remembered how mature he felt Ida Mae's letters were in advising him about the danger of their mother wearing out before her time. Now that he saw her, he was shocked by the difference in his mother's appearance since he left home. Her beautiful auburn hair had turned a ghastly shade of yellowing grey. Rounded shoulders and stooped posture told the story. She was only in her early forties. Her looks had faded, it seemed, in much too short a time.

My God, he thought to himself, *Father Time is on a runaway horse.*

Seven years earlier, John Simpson, Les's father, caught a cold and, before he knew it, his illness had turned for the worst. Within the week he died from pneumonia, leaving his widow poorly-off with six children – Les, sixteen; Ida Mae, fourteen; Mabel ten; Robert, seven; Agnes, five and Arthur, four.

Les was eager to contribute to supporting his family. To help make ends meet, he found a job as an assistant horse wrangler on a railroad crew. The paltry wage he made helping to sort out draft horses didn't go very far in sustaining his siblings. He and his mother struggled for a few years to put food on the table. Then Les joined the police force because it seemed the best opportunity for him and his family.

While he was away, the letters he received from Ida Mae outlined the hardships they endured despite the money he sent them every month. Combined with the reports about his mother's poor health, this had started Les thinking about finding a way to rescue his family from their poverty. He began to muse on schemes for making money. None of them were legal. Gradually he seized upon the idea of becoming an adventurer. He'd take a big chance to gain a stake that he would use to become even richer. Now he was the living embodiment of his own invention, trying to figure how to share his lucre with his family without revealing his sordid deeds.

While he was drinking tea beside the summer kitchen behind the shack, Les's fourteen-year-old brother Robert showed up with a string full of pickerel that he had caught that afternoon in the river. After they cleaned the fish, Les and Robert fetched Ned, who was tethered to a fence post.

"Good to see you're a good provider, little brother," Les said as he lifted Robert off his feet and sat him up in the saddle on Red Ned. "When I leave here this old horse is going to belong to you."

Les led Ned toward the corral where he and Robert took off the saddle and pumped some water into the trough

"We'll have to buy some feed to keep Red Ned eating all winter," Les said as he slipped off the halter. When they had finished brushing and grooming the horse, Les carried the saddle with its gear to the shack and put it inside the porch.

It was after 6 p.m. when Ida Mae returned home from her job working for the town doctor. "Why didn't you tell us you were on your way, so we could have done something special to celebrate your homecoming?"

"Don't worry about it," Les answered, hugging his sister. "In the Force you never know quite which way the wind is blowing. I thought it best to keep it a surprise in case I had to change my plans and disappoint you."

"Now that you're home, we'll have a chance to catch up," Ida Mae said.

"So what do you do for this doctor?" Les asked.

"It's Doctor Fleming, remember? He tended to Dad just before he died. His wife is a lady and a bit of a princess so I clean their house and the infirmary and help the doctor when some of his patients need tending to."

"We're having Robert's fresh-caught pickerel and some vegetables from our garden for supper," Les's mother said as she fired up the stove in the summer kitchen.

After eating, they sat on the porch watching the children play with the new pup.

"Les, if it wasn't for your money coming every month we'd have been in sorry straits around here," his mother confessed. "Now, with Ida Mae and Mabel helping me with the chickens and the garden in the summer, we are doing much better than before. And there's more money in town now, with more houses and buildings to clean. Mr. Waldo, who manages the Prince Edward Hotel, has indicated that he will take Mabel and me on as chambermaids this winter when he completes the finishings on his new wing."

"Do you still do business with Meredith?" Les asked.

"Henry has been wonderful to us since your father passed. He gives me credit and I pay when I can."

"Let's leave it till tomorrow," Les said. "I'm exhausted and need to sleep, otherwise it's all too much of a rush. I want to do something positive for you all during the next few weeks before my leave is up. Now, if you will excuse me, I'm going to bed down on the porch. All those miles on Red Ned have left me feeling somewhat fatigued."

In the morning, as was his habit, Les was up at dawn and saddling Ned. He headed into the centre of town where he stopped at the feed store. Mr. Grover was just opening up for business.

"Remember me?"

"Can't say that I do."

"I'm Les Simpson, Mary Simpson's boy, and I'm home on leave from my job. My mother's going to be feeding a horse this winter so I want you to supply enough oats and hay to carry the old fellow through. You deliver it to my mother's acreage on the edge of town and unload it in the barn. I'll be in to settle with you a day or two after that. In the meantime, here's three bucks on account."

"No problem, I'll have it hauled out to you tomorrow afternoon."

"By the way, does Archie Fisher still own the lumber yard?"

"Yes he does. That Archie's a real card."

"I remember him well," Les answered. "I was in the same class at school as his son."

From the feed store, he went to the livery stable to fork Ned some hay, then down the street to Henry Meredith's general store. Henry was up on a ladder hanging bunting around a display of women's fashions.

"You have to do it all to stay in business these days," said Henry as he was coming down the ladder. It didn't take more than a few seconds for him to recognize Les.

"The Simpson boy," he said offering his hand. "Heard you made good in the Mounted. Your mother talks about you on occasion. Welcome home."

"Thanks," Les answered. "Haven't been home for nearly five years. Stationed mostly in the wilderness. No place to spend my pay. I'm happy to be able to use what I have to help my mother bring up the kids. Henry, can you tell me how much my mother owes you right now?"

"Just give me a second to look at my records," Henry answered.

"Your mother currently owes nineteen dollars and forty-seven cents."

"I'll be paying that off immediately."

"Thank you Les, I'm glad to give your mother credit. She's a tough survivor."

"All the credit's to you, Henry," Les said. "Let me shake your hand. You're a good man and you'll have your reward in time for all the good you've done."

Henry stayed silent, looking out the window. He didn't know how to react.

"One more thing," Les remembered. "Do you sell rolls of paper? And I wonder if you have anything to draw with?"

"In luck on both accounts. I do carry some small rolls of paper and I have a box of fancy pencils, the latest craze from Paris, France. I brought them in for the teacher at the school. She has the notion she can teach the kids to draw. I can sell you one."

Les left Meredith's feeling he was well on his way to accomplishing his objective. He would pay off his mother's debts and spend about what a thrifty constable could have saved in five years of duty in the Mounted Police. His next step was to ride down Rosser Street and head out to the east end of town to visit the Darrach's.

Their son, Tom, was one of two locals who had travelled with Les to Winnipeg to join the Force. They were both eighteen years old and in good physical condition. The North-West Mounted Police was desperate for new recruits, but leery of signing men of the minimum age of entry. Years of recruitment had proven that older candidates, especially with military backgrounds, performed Mounted Police duties better than inexperienced youths. Les was accepted into the Force because of his father's previous record in the British military and because he had worked with horses on the railway. His fellow applicants from Brandon were rejected because both were bull workers without experience handling horses and neither had a military background in their respective families. It didn't matter that Les was wrangling draft horses in large teams that were leveling grades, rather than handling riding stock.

"A horse is a horse," the recruiting officer stated.

Only Tom's mother was at home, his father worked at the brick yard. She told Les that both Tom and the other North-West Mounted Police hopeful, Roger Horne, had quit the railway and were busy working on job sites in Brandon. She said they were currently putting up siding on a new store downtown. Mrs. Darrach was happy to see Les and told him she would tell her son that he was home.

Les had decided that he ought to teach his brothers how to take care of Ned. He'd work with the boys and the horse to get them working together before he had to leave. They'd have to rise early to feed and water Ned before they went to school. Les would instruct them in riding and handling a horse, as well as how to take further care of it. He told them he would give them the horse, saddle and other tack. In return, they would promise to look after the horse without fail.

"I know times have been tough for you guys and you don't have a lot. But guess what? Now you have a horse. That's a lot more than you had yesterday. I'm giving you guys five bucks apiece and I'm leaving Ma money to give you fifty cents a month that goes for taking care of Ned. You be good to Ned and, in return, he'll be good to you."

Les had grown fond of Ned as he rode him up from Quigley's place. Ned didn't kick or bite but he wasn't a pushover either.

One evening, before it became dark, Les sat on the porch talking with Ida Mae, telling her of his plan to add rooms onto the shack to turn it into a better home. Ida Mae had drawing ability. Les gave her the roll of paper and the pencil to sketch the shack with two large rooms added on, complete with measurements. She also came up with the idea of enclosing the porch, creating an additional room on the back side. When she finished they showed the plan to the rest of the family.

"How can we afford it?" his mother asked.

"I have some savings," Les answered. "There was nowhere to spend money where I was posted."

Les rolled up Ida Mae's drawing and rode Ned downtown to Archie Fisher's lumberyard.

"I'll tell you what, I'll sell you all the lumber you need plus shingles, delivered and stacked at your place, for eighty-five dollars."

"How soon can you do it?" Les asked.

"Give us a week and we'll have it there," Archie replied. "So what it's like being in the Force?"

"It's fine," Les answered. "Good food, benefits, decent pay, good companions, mostly, and you sure manage to see the country. I feel kind of homesick sometimes and I worry about Ma and the kids. Saved some dough and I'm spending it on improving the shack rather than blowing it on foolish things."

"That's a damn good idea," Archie answered. "I just looked at this latest bill for lumber that came in here and damn if I didn't make a miscalculation. I'll sell you the whole works for sixty-five dollars."

Les paid Archie the money up front before he left to find Tom Darrach and Roger Horne, whose hammers he could hear banging away down the opposite side of the street. When they saw him they put down their tools.

"Wondered when we'd see you again," Tom said.

"Yeah, Tom and I were disappointed when we failed to make the grade, but somehow things worked out for us."

"They made a mistake passing on you guys," Les answered. "It was hard at first, but the training was good. Now I have a steady, better paying job. I like seeing the country. I've had some memorable adventures."

"Shoot anybody lately?" Roger quipped.

The comment hit Les like slug. He stood tongue-tied unable to deal with the question as his mind flipped back to the longest moment in his life, when his bullet had tumbled into the bank manager's forehead.

Tom was grinning at Roger's forward question.

"Can't say I've had occasion to pull out my revolver in the service yet," Les answered, truthfully.

Tom and Roger told Les they quit the railroad when they discovered they could make more money as carpenters due to the boom in Brandon. Initially they worked for one dollar a day for contractors before they decided to form their own business. Les unrolled his plan and showed them what he was hoping to do with his mother's shack. He told them he had already made a deal with Archie Fisher to have the lumber delivered, then asked for a quote on the additions, as well as framing in the porch and doing some finishing work.

"For you, Les, and your ma, we'll do the job for sixty dollars," Tom answered, after conferring with Roger.

"How long you figure it will take?" asked Les

"Oh, at least a month to do a real good job and build in some comfort for your family," Tom replied.

"I'm not hiring you and Rog by the hour," Les replied. "I'm paying you eighty dollars. I'll be gone before you get started. You'll have to get nails and hardware. Ma has an account at Meredith's. When can you start?"

"We're nearly finished here. Then we're committed to finishing a storefront. I'd say we could be onto your job in about two weeks."

"That's good, I'm counting on you. This will be big for Ma and the kids and will give me some peace in my mind," Les answered. "Here's the money. You might as well have it now because I won't be around to pay you."

Silent until then, Roger said, "We have nails and hardware left over from other jobs. We'll add on those rooms and enclose the porch, put in a chimney and pick you up another stove. We'll talk to your ma and see what she wants in the way of finishing.

It won't be fancy but it'll be solid."

After he had finalized his construction details, Les occupied most of his time hanging out at home. He had spent the bulk of his Mounted Police savings on buying things that would improve his family's living conditions. He had done it in such a way, with people of good reputations, in order to minimize screw-ups that might have ensued otherwise. In the future, his family would be living in something closer to a house than a shack. He spent his money wisely and attracted no attention flashing it anywhere else in town.

But now he had a shocking confession to make to one member of his family. It was the only way his plan could work. He knew that he was a wanted man, even if unidentified, and every mistake he made would be magnified. He was sitting out with Ida Mae on the back porch, looking for shooting stars.

"Ida Mae, I know you keep this place going. You're wise long before your time. I knew I had a smart sister, but not one with the backbone that you possess. Ma doesn't look great. I wonder what we can do for her?"

"What do you mean?" she asked.

"Well, it seems to me life around here would be better if Ma stayed home and looked after the place, especially in the winter. She could continue on with the garden and chickens in the summer with Mabel and the other kids helping out. You, being the oldest and a sensible young woman, could take care of Ma and look after the family interests. Eventually, when I am out of the service, I'll no longer be able to supply income on a monthly basis. So I'm giving my contribution in advance."

"How are you going to do that?"

"Like this," he said. "Take a look in this package."

After she unwrapped the parcel, Ida Mae said, "Les, there's a lot of money here."

"Yes, over three thousand dollars U.S. in mostly tens and twenties."

"Where did you get it?"

"That's my business."

"What do you want me to do with it?"

"I'm giving it to the family. You and I are going to hide most of this money. American money is common currency around here so you can spend a little of it now and then. But only to pay bills and not in big amounts. Try to keep the bills manageable so you don't have to hit the stash too hard. It's enough money to keep everybody going for a long time if you all keep contributing as well. Gradually, as the kids grow up, you can give each a stake when they leave home. Mabel's getting there fast and so is Robert. Sad to say, Ma's coughing and rattling in the mornings is enough to scare a man to death. I want you to take her over to see that doctor of yours."

"She won't go. She says she doesn't want to know."

"Well that's fine for her, but it's not great for the kids."

"Where did you get the money?"

"You already asked me that question. It's none of your business."

"Of course it's my business, if you want me to take care of it."

"Look, I have the money, *how* is a long story that is not in your benefit to know. It's the ticket to save Ma from dying on a mop. I want you to take the money and hide it. Then I want you to continue on being the practical, stoic, big sister who can handle Ma and the kids and who will take care of our money and the family business.

"Just like that. You're putting that responsibility on me," Ida Mae said.

"Yes, I am. There's no other option. Ma is not up to pulling this off and the others are too young, so you're the one. Ida Mae, what's done is done, there's no going back. I want you to put this money to good use in helping the family. Ma's sick, she and the kids need looking after. You and I are going to do it. That's all there is to say on the subject."

Ida Mae's face puckered up like a sour apple. She sat helplessly, listening to Les, confused about who the person she called her brother really was. She knew that he must have done something drastic to put his hands on that much money. He was rationalizing his reason for going off the rails, saying he did it for the good of the family and cutting her in on the deal whether she liked it or not. Suddenly the loving brother she was so proud of was a mysterious brother who had secrets and who possessed a darker side. Ida Mae thought about the dilemma before she responded.

"Damn you, Les. This is no way to act. We weren't brought up to rob people or take advantage of them. You're asking me to hoard stolen money and dole it out to the family. That's a novel thing to say to your sister. 'Here's a stack of dirty money from God knows where. Put it away and enjoy it with the family!' Are you really giving me a choice? Have you ever thought of the consequences for all of us if you're caught?"

"An hour never goes by when I haven't wondered about it, gone over it in detail. It's too late for second thoughts. The horse is out of the barn and he's running hard, right into oblivion, maybe. Ida Mae, take the money. If you're half the shrewd personality I think you are, you can handle this bad but necessary business."

"Les, I thought you were supposed to catch people committing crimes, not joining them."

Her rebuke caught Les right in the chops. He felt like he had been hit by a runaway train. "There's no point in trying to deceive you. I've hit bottom by taking a big risk and screwing it up. Ida Mae, hide the money and forget about it, if you must. If somebody finds it, then deny knowing anything about it. If a bulldog comes sniffing around tell him you're not your brother's keeper or his confessor. Bury the damn money and ignore it. I can't take it back. At least you'll have it available if Ma needs treatment. Promise me you'll do that much."

"I'll try," she said. "I can't guarantee anything. But I can't throw my own brother to the wolves."

"That's all I can ask," he answered.

They sat up talking long into the night, reminiscing about the things they both could remember about their childhood.

"Do you remember when Dad was transferred to work at the railway station in Brandon and we all arrived from Winnipeg on the train? And we moved into the hotel before he found us a place to live?" Les asked.

"Funny thing," she said, "I was probably too young but I do have memories of it. Just vague ones that pop up in my head like a picture, without many familiar details but still important."

"Remember Bill, the funny-looking horse that Dad bought from the preacher?"

"Yeah, he pulled the buggy in good weather and the sleigh in winter," she said. "I remember the bells and his breath like a cloud above his head."

"He had a sway back and he was prone to biting. He bit old man Jones on the neck when he was leaning on the corral," Les said. "Old Jones was madder than a hornet. Dad had to step in to keep him from shooting Bill."

"He only bit crabby old guys like Jones and that preacher who owned him. He never bit one of us kids," she said.

"Those were better times," Les said.

"When Dad took sick and died so sudden, it was like a bad dream. It's been downhill ever since. If it wasn't for Ma being stubborn, all us kids would have ended up in the orphanage. She kept us together. Works night and day. I don't know how she does it," Ida Mae said.

"She won't be doing it much longer if we don't help her ease up," Les answered. "Believe it or not, I did it for her."

"I believe you, Les, but I'm scared."

"We'll make it through this," he said. "In the future, I'll have to take some chances, but we're the same blood and I can't forget it. I never give up and I don't think you will either. I brought you this proposition. I know you didn't ask for it. In a few months, if I'm lucky, I'll have disappeared. You'll hear about it, if I come to the end of the line. If I get away with it you might not hear anything. Don't make me tell you too much, Ida Mae."

"Les, you've already told me enough."

"One last thing – I'll communicate with you by occasionally sending you a letter or package in the mail, or maybe something by freight. It may have a strange sender's name and return address. Don't accept the goods at face value. Look further into the objects inside, in case I'm sending you something valuable. It'll just be me letting you know I'm still out there. A letter from a stranger that makes no sense is a letter from me letting you know I'm in a safe place. If anybody official notices you have more money than normal, say it was a small windfall inheritance from Uncle Ebenezer who died last winter in Ottawa."

"But he didn't have any money. The executor sent us just that trunk full of the silver tea service and those clunky candle sticks," she answered.

"Aren't you forgetting the cash in U.S. funds that was under the knick-knacks?"

"I see what you're suggesting."

"Solid dependable Ida Mae, you're the one who can pull it off. You dole it out. You help the other kids move ahead. When they get jobs, everybody contributes to Ma. You continue to nag her about going to the doctor, maybe ask him for a favour and talk him into coming here to look her over."

"I dunno about this."

"It's too late to go back now."

"It was money from Uncle Ebenezer's trunk," she said.

"You stick to that line no matter what happens," he added

"What are you going to do when your time is up?"

"I'm not certain."

"You sound certain to me."

"Maybe I'll ship out to South America."

"Then we won't see you again for a while."

"I think about five years or more."

"It'll be okay," she said.

"I'm not so sure about me," he answered, truthfully.

Time went by quickly. Les's leave was close to running out. He gave his mother one hundred dollars in twenties and convinced her to put eighty of it into the bank.

"How about you take the winter off this year, Ma. Stay around the house, keep the home fires burning. Make sure Robert and Arthur are taking care of Ned. You need to go and see the doctor. He'll perk you up. It's time we let Ida Mae look after dealing with the merchants and doing the family business downtown. She can do your banking. She has the gift of the gab and a level head. She can be your legs and get things done."

"Maybe you're right," his mother said. "It was a bad winter last year and I had to go out to work every day and take care of the home front as well. Les, you're a blessing to your family."

His mother's comment hit him right between the eyes. He fixated on the image of the awkward bank manager, iced in the doorway from his careless bullet. He was thinking to himself that he could turn out to be anything but a blessing to his family, depending on which way the chips would fall.

"I'm going to Regina on the train the day after tomorrow," Les announced at supper on a Saturday night. "I already have my ticket. My leave is nearly up. I must return to the barracks. On Monday morning, Robert can double-ride Ned with me down to the train station. Then he can ride his and Arthur's new horse home and give Ned some hay and oats and a good watering. Ida Mae's the gabby one, so she's going to be writing me. I'll be sending her mail back whenever I have the chance. I hate goodbyes so let's spend the day together tomorrow and I'll slip out with Robert and Ned early on Monday morning."

Later that evening, Les told Ida Mae that, in the event of his death, she needed to stay focused and resist going to the money unless it was an emergency. She should try and wait a year before she spent any of the money.

"No matter what happens, stay calm and forget the details of this visit in a hurry. I came home, helped the family out with my savings and went back to the job. That's all you know. If any investigators nose around, tell them you're too busy working to spend time speculating about a brother who hasn't been keeping in touch with his family."

At dawn, Les packed his possessions into a new rucksack that he purchased at the general store along with a pair of pants, a shirt and a winter coat. He had two hundred dollars left in his money belt. Robert was wearing the worn grey hat that Quigley had given to Les. Robert and Les rode Ned to the train station. Before he entered the building, he watched his young brother ride Red Ned down the road beside the tracks before he turned at the corner and headed for the outskirts.

10

September, 1894
State of North Dakota, United States

WILLIAM FLUMERFELT, MINOT POLICE CHIEF and already a legend for the unique law enforcement tactics he invented, invited Jiggs Dubois, Balfour Smith and Robert Filbert to meet with him in his office – a lounge behind his saloon in downtown Minot.

"You boys can have a quiet conversation in here without being bothered by the rabble drinking cheap liquor out front. I'll send Slappy, the barman, to take care of your needs. You'll have to excuse me, gents, I have some urgent business to attend to in another establishment down the street, but I will be back soon to join you."

The barkeeper put a bottle of the best Kentucky bourbon on the table with four glasses and a silver bucket of ice, as well as a heaping plate of mountain oysters, some smoked salmon and a large jar of pickled herring.

Robert Filbert was giving the boys the low-down on how best to proceed with the police authorities in Assiniboia and Manitoba. Filbert was a small wiry man and a bit of a dandy, with his slick hair parted down the middle. He was dressed in a three-piece blue suit with a gold nugget fob on the end of his fancy watch. He had finely-manicured hands and he kept a nickel-plated Tranter in a shoulder holster under his right arm. All three men agreed that whoever pulled the bank robbery and committed the murder in Bismarck had likely passed by Bottineau on his way across the border. There he had likely ditched the chestnut, hooked up with a new mount at Quigley's ranch, then disappeared somewhere further north. Finding a cartridge casing fired by an Enfield Mark II revolver only increased their suspicions.

Balfour Smith assured the other two that whoever committed the crime had made sure that the chestnut gelding with three white socks and a groove in its ass was by now a bleached-out pile in some unknown gully. He was certain William Pinkerton's reward would go uncollected. Smith, a wise operator in his mid-forties, was a large, shambling man with a curly head of steel grey hair, who gave the impression of being a jolly, teddy bear of a man. His exterior was designed to fool whoever dared take him for granted. He was armed with a snub-nosed Webley Bulldog. He had a special pocket sewn into the lining of his coat to hold a blackjack that could crush a human skull with one blow.

Filbert was of the opinion that if the killer had fled northeast into Manitoba he would be virtually impossible to catch, unless he happened to be some kind of braggart who started throwing the money around. Filbert claimed it was almost impossible to attract the attention of the Manitoba Provincial Police. They had few officers on patrol. The bulk of their force was concentrated in the eastern region of the province, dealing with the epidemic of gunmen who spilled over the border from Fargo.

"Haven't had a lot of success trying to hook up with them," he offered.

Dubois was of the opinion that the killer had picked up a horse from Quigley and probably turned and headed north-west into Assiniboia, putting some distance between himself and the border.

"Look, the brazen bugger's killed a man with the same make of revolver that's issued to the North-West Mounted Police.

Who's to say he's not a deserter from their service, or somebody who was mustered out and left with his weapon? We know one thing. The SOB can ride a horse like a madman. He covered the distance from Bismarck to where he was spotted by those Swedish ferrymen in record time. That makes me think he's had some expert training."

Filbert confided that William Pinkerton had told him James J. Hill was putting enormous pressure on the Pinkertons to have this case solved. "Pinkerton still has his ass in a beehive over Homestead and the Pullman strike. With all that on his plate, Hill calls him in and craps all over him about this robbery. Pinkerton couldn't give a damn about it because he's frying far bigger fish. But, alas, Hill is such a gold-plated client the Boss has no choice but to drop everything and take a week-long ex-cursion by train, to a place he considers godforsaken, to deal with this, by his standards, puny issue. We have time to solve this case as long as Jiggs keeps sending Pinkerton positive input about the progress we're making."

Dubois answered before knocking back a shot of bourbon. "William wants me to travel with Balfour into Assiniboia to link up with the North-West Mounted Police and clue them in on our investigation."

"Well, heaven help you," Filbert said.

"What the hell does that mean?"

"First of all, you won't have success bringing up the investigation with any of the officers or sergeants at their outposts. Those fellows are hard-core army who follow orders. They are busy patrolling, not policing. Sure, you can ask them an obvious question like, 'Have you seen a lone horseman travelling through this country on a cloud of dust in the past few months?' or 'Anybody you talk to recently drop a big bag of American greenbacks in front of you?' Other than that, what are you going to ask them? They're not investigators, they're soldier boys looking for wayward Indians, rum runners and hoss rustlers. Most of 'em are

Brit boys on parade, looking for adventures they can write home about. The rest are bored farm boys, just in it for the wages."

"Balfour and I will mosey up to the North-West Mounted Police headquarters in Regina and make contact with the higher ups there. We'll see if we can exchange information, maybe put our hands on a list of deserters and malcontents," Dubois answered.

"That'll be a hell of a trip! Lucky you can do part of it by train," Filbert said, devouring a herring fillet on a slice of rye bread. "I wouldn't leave it too late because, when the weather turns, winter's going to come down like a white tornado. You don't want to be caught out moseying on horseback across the open prairie."

"Yeah, well, I guess we'll be taking off up north as soon as we can get away. Anything else you can think of that might help us in dealing with the Mountie brass?"

"They have some good men in that force," Filbert answered. "But, like I said, they're really a military outfit, not a police force. The old boys at the top are generally hard-assed, by the book, military officers. They're fair when it suits them and they're pretty shrewd. They're not used to sharing information. If you were a U.S. Marshal or an official with the American government, you might receive a decent reception. But even that seems unlikely to me. Remember, you're a Pinkerton and we're a private policing agency. That doesn't carry the same weight north of the border as it does down here. Their men are used to going through channels and following protocol. It's not clear to me if they will cooperate fully with you or, in fact, they will cooperate with you at all. You must keep in touch with William by telegram and by sending him those biweekly letters. If you run into trouble there is always the possibility he can pull some strings for you with Canadian government officials in Ottawa. Not so many years ago the Pinkerton Detective Agency did work for the Canadian government in investigating the Fenians. I know that William has some personal contacts in Ottawa at the highest levels."

"What if we're all wrong?" Smith asked. "Maybe the fugitive turned back and he's walking around among us, right now, on these muddy streets, or in Grand Forks or Fargo, or maybe he went west into Montana. It's a possibility."

Roger Filbert interrupted to say that Flumerfelt had returned from his rounds.

"Sorry for keeping you gents on ice, haw haw," Bill Flumerfelt guffawed as he sat down and poured himself a half pint of bourbon and shoveled a pile of mountain oysters onto his plate.

"I run the wildest bar in the meanest town in this part of North Dakota. I am also the chief of police. I keep this back room for gentlemen like you who don't want to sit and drink with the dregs of society. When they become boisterous and kill one another I'm prepared to deal with them in a no-nonsense manner, thus protecting the interests of the town. I run a direct service from here to the city jail. My deputies tour the streets on a nightly basis and also roust bad actors from the other joints in town. You have to pardon my recent absence. I just kicked some arse down the street."

"You ain't seen a tall feller riding a chestnut with three white socks and a groove in its rump, have ya?" Balfour Smith laughed.

"I wish. I would have let him spend some of that loot in my saloon before I closed him down," Flumerfelt answered, with a twinkle in his watery blue eyes.

The eyes of a gunman, Smith thought to himself. He'd seen pale blue eyes like Flumerfelt's once a few years back in Deadwood when he passed Wild Bill Hickok on the wooden sidewalk outside Nuttal & Mann's saloon.

"When I received a telegram from Bismarck I alerted the boys to be on the lookout," the sheriff said, "but nobody of the robber's description passed through Minot to my knowledge. Course, I sleep mostly in the day and work late into the night. Didn't see him. My boys didn't see him. If we had, he'd most likely have ended up on a slab of ice at the undertakers, waiting for you fellows to come in and take him away."

"The money, I dunno," Flumerfelt continued. "Might have been spent before you arrived here. Haw haw. Hard to say. There's a murder here every week. Why hell, some months there's a murder here every night of the week, some times twice or thrice a night. Money don't mean much here. It don't go very far and it disappears in the blink of an eye," he said, twirling his moustache and inhaling a pickled herring fillet after two cursory bites.

"Well, give us your considered opinion on our robber/killer," Filbert inquired of Flumerfelt.

"Amateur. No professional rides into town alone and ties his horse up unattended in front of the bank. Never mind shoots the bank manager when a yappy little dog spooks his horse. Jeez, must have been a hell of a rider to stay on."

"Just what I think," Dubois said. "Robber had training in horsemanship."

"Yeah, with any luck that twelve-year-old with his Springfield musket shoots the chestnut in the guts and that murderer would have been hanged by now," Smith remarked.

"And if pigs had wings they'd fly," Dubois interjected.

"A pro would have had somebody on lookout outside the bank, handling his horse. Can't think of a bank robbed in recent memory by a lone gunman. If you ask me, it seems a prescription for disaster. It would have been different if he had hit the bank in Minot. If he had struck here, my deputies would have been up in the saddle and after him like ugly on an ape within fifteen minutes of the robbery. They'd have run him to ground while I took half an hour longer to raise a posse with saddlebags full of booze from my bar. By the time the advance boys on the trail tuckered out, that half-drunk posse would be closing like a pack of hounds after a worn-out, panicking fox – a fox that made a serious mistake by attacking the wrong chickens. He would have seen the cloud of dust behind him growing taller and taller in the sky until he finally decided to make a last stand in a pile of brush or behind a big rock in a gully. By then the boys would have been tying the hangman's knot on somebody's lariat. When he emptied his pea shooter we would have moved on him in a flash. Then we would have tied him up and taken our time to find a really dramatic tree to have ourselves a leisurely hanging while we imbibed some more."

"Jeez, that's a harsh but efficient way of keeping law and order. Isn't stringing him up without a trial a lynching?" Smith asked.

"That way no cost to the city fathers, no loss for the bank. Save the expenses of a judge. No need to bother the hangman unless, of course, he happened to be in the posse. We'd all have our names on slips of paper in a hat. The winner would be the proud new owner of a chestnut gelding with three white socks and an impaired right buttock. That's the way it would've transpired around here," Flumerfelt said, staring at Smith while he wiped his big yellow moustache with the back of his hand.

"You certainly run a tidy operation, with solid town backing," Balfour Smith replied.

"Course that lawman in Bismarck is an old guy afflicted with hemorrhoids and gout and he hates climbing into the saddle. He's living high on his reputation. His boys are a bunch of soft drunks who prefer boozing rather than man hunting. On the other hand, I employ a pack of drunks myself, but they're hard and hungry. They're just itching for somebody to give them an excuse for a necktie party."

"We'll have to include you in the hunt," Filbert remarked, almost in admiration.

"What are you talking about?" answered Flumerfelt. "I ain't the least bit interested in what goes on in Bismarck. It's up to them birds down there to take care of themselves. Seems to me they're doing a mighty poor job of it. If you don't catch the fox in the first few hours it becomes tougher and tougher then, all of a sudden, while you're out on the trail, another fox slips in and grabs some more of your chickens. Nope. You fellows are on a dead trail. Maybe you win, maybe you lose."

"I agree with you. This killer needs to be rousted before long or he's gonna disappear under a rock," Dubois said.

"If this feller escapes detection, in a few years he just becomes another rich rancher with a fine herd of cattle who marries some wealthy dude's daughter and lives happily ever after. Before he goes to meet his maker he'll donate money to build a new church or give a donation to orphans to cover his feelings of guilt for committing murder. And, take it from my personal observation, the longer he gets away with it, the more pious he'll become."

"When you received the telegram, did you watch the roads or send out a patrol to scan the countryside?" Dubois knew it was the wrong question to ask before the words came out of his mouth.

"Hell no. You fellows are book learners and schoolboys when it comes to the law in these parts." Flumerfelt burped profusely as he downed another half-pint of bourbon. "I don't pay much attention to telegrams. I don't watch any roads. My boys are paid to patrol the city streets of Minot. They ain't paid to traipse about the country in search of desperadoes. We have a pile of 'em here already and more moving into town all the time. We figure, let 'em spend their money on the local economy before we do our best work with a lead slug and put 'em where they belong, pushing up weeds on Boot Hill. I tell some of 'em, when they arrive for a booze-up in my bar, that I have a cheap room in the ground on a well-drained sidehill on the edge of town. Lot of 'em laugh and think I'm a joker. I don't know how many of those have become permanent residents of Minot."

The next morning, Filbert, Smith and Dubois had a breakfast of steak and eggs in the Morning Room at the Leland Hotel. Filbert once again urged the boys to use tact when dealing with the Mounties.

"If I was you fellows, I'd take the commissioner a few good bottles of hooch.

They have a ban on alcohol up there, but I hear tell that the top brass in the Force enjoy a good shot of the finer stuff whenever they can acquire it. Remember not to play all your cards at one time. If there is any resistance, relax and send a telegram to William Pinkerton. Let him grease the skids with their eastern politicians."

Filbert promised he would keep in touch with Harold Moss, who had travelled down to Bismarck where he was personally attending to the reward campaign. Smith and Dubois said they would take a few days to put their gear together before they left town on the long trek northwest to Regina. They vowed to stop along the way at various communities and North-West Mounted detachments just to pick up on the local customs.

"Police work is the answer," Filbert advised. "See if you can obtain the names of the deserters, malcontents, slackers and those who have been given the boot. By all accounts our man is young, tall, lean and fit. He can't have been in the service very long if, in fact we are looking for a North-West Mounted Police suspect as being the perpetrator of this heinous crime. I want to give you one last bit of information that may become invaluable to you: I have written on this piece of paper the names of two people who work for us in Regina. As you know, we have had a complex Indian problem that has been a thorn in the side for governments on both sides of the border. The Pinkerton Agency has been advising the U.S. government by providing insider knowledge gleaned from prime sources in Regina. These two are spies who work for the Pinkerton National Detective Agency on a retainer from my office. That is all I can tell you about the matter. I suggest you contact them shortly after your arrival and allow them to help you. I think you will be surprised at how efficient they are at producing results."

11

"ABOUT TIME YOU GUYS WERE OUT OF BED," Charlie Parmer griped as he led his horse onto the ferry. "Didn't you hear us calling you last night to bring the ferry over and pick us up?"

"We don't 'a take in travellers, so either 'a way you were 'a spending the night out in that hellacious rain! We 'a work for no man on this 'a river in the dark," the Swede answered.

Frenchie, resembling a wilted rooster, slipped and fell on his bony ass on the slick gangway that had been dropped onto the bank. He picked himself up, in a snarly mood, looking for someone to blame.

"It's 'a those fancy Mexican fruit boots you're 'a wearing," the Swede said.

"How would you like me to carve my initials in your liver?" Frenchie sneered, hocking a greenie into the river.

The Swede, tired of sparring with Frenchie, turned to Parmer. "That'll 'a be two bucks in advance," he said, rolling up his sleeves in case he was forced to throw Frenchie overboard before the trip started. "I'll 'a give my brother the signal to 'a move the mules when you're 'a paid up."

When they had crossed over the Mouse River, Charlie Parmer and Frenchie were still grumbling about the weather. Both of them were wet and cold from a night out in a series of thunderstorms that came one after the other, with big bangers and walls of rain that turned the earth under their feet into a slurry. No matter that the weather had cleared and bright sunshine was shimmering on the river now.

"Just like the last time we came into this country," Frenchie sneered again. "Let's ride into Bottineau where we can dry out our gear and see how tough that tin-plated constable really is."

"Naw, come on Frenchie. We didn't travel all the way up here from Bismarck to be derailed in a dumpy town," Parmer said. "We have business to take care of. You want to make some money, dontcha?"

"That's a fact," Frenchie agreed.

The two of them were enjoying some rest and relaxation in Bismarck, waiting for orders from Jiggs Dubois. They were booked in at the Northwest Hotel. For entertainment they had taken to visiting the local whorehouses on a daily basis. However, their money was starting to run out. The telegram from Jiggs they were sure would summon them back to work was actually a message to say their services were no longer required. They could pick up their back pay at the First National Bank. They had no choice but to grab their money, check out of the hotel and head for cheaper lodgings while they figured out a new way of making a living.

After a day without booze, they sobered up. Frenchie came up with an idea. He proposed that he and Charlie head north, cross the border into the wild, unpopulated area and make a visit to that "Old Coot" who had insulted them when they went up to his place with Dubois.

For weeks they had listened to Dubois exclaiming around the campfire every night how he was certain that the bank robber had exchanged horses at that Quigley's place. Dubois was a man who never ran out of theories. He was convinced that the robber had paid Quigley a good fee for a getaway horse. The remoteness of his locale and the way he conducted his business led Dubois to believe that Quigley was undoubtedly in league with horse thieves. It was well-known that both sides of the border were rampant with them. This intrigued Frenchie, to think that maybe Quigley had a pile of greenbacks. It didn't take him long to persuade Charlie that they could easily slip unnoticed across the border. He was confident he could convince the old wrangler to turn his money over to them.

"Why hell, Charlie, who would he complain to? There ain't no law up there and besides, his money is ill-gotten, so tough beans if we take it."

"He's a cranky old man. We'd have to be careful with him."

"Come on, he's a geezer. We'll surprise him with his pants down. It'll be easy pickings."

Charlie had to agree it was a better idea than any he had. The fact it was over the border meant that they could go in quickly, do the job, then return to the U.S. before anybody was the wiser. On the final few miles into Bottineau, Frenchie agreed he'd turn the other cheek no matter how rude that foolish rube lawman, Gerry, became. They'd kiss up to the foreign barkeep too, so they could drink undisturbed and have a dry place to sleep that night.

"Well, if it ain't the Buckaroo Boys," Gerry said when he saw them sitting over a glass of rotgut at the Bohunk's bar. "Surprised to see you fellows are still alive."

"We learned our lesson the last time we was through here," Charlie said. "You'll have no trouble from us." Frenchie bit his tongue and sat without uttering a sound.

The Bohunk served them up a big bowl of pig's ear soup and they ate it up, slurping and belching from the gas they got from the booze.

"What are you fellows doing up here?" Gerry asked.

"Things didn't pan out with that Pinkerton so we're out of a job. Do you have any ideas?"

"I hear there's work on the railway at Devil's Lake," the Bohunk said.

"Yeah, and they're looking for cowpunchers over there too," Gerry added.

"Well thanks for the suggestion," said Charlie, in keeping with his vow to stay polite and focused. "That second suggestion is more suited to us than breaking our backs with pick and shovel work."

"Long as you two can handle your booze, you're welcome to hang out in town," Gerry said, on his way out to the Widow Murphy's place.

The boys went down to Yip Hong's boiled laundry establishment, where they sat starkers, drinking from a cheap bottle of whisky. Yip Hong loaned each of them a rough grey blanket to wrap themselves in. Then they staggered over to the Bohunk's bunkhouse, where they finished their liquor and passed out. In the morning, Yip Hong brought them their duds, freshly laundered, folded, and lavendered. On the way out of town they stopped at the Bohunk's to pay for the night's lodging.

"On the house, to make up for your last trip to Bottineau," the Bohunk told them. "And I'll throw in this joint of leftover mutton for your lunch."

When Gerry came by for his breakfast of two eggs cracked in a tall glass of beer he asked the Bohunk if he thought those two ex-Pinkerton flunkies had turned over a new page. The Bohunk just said, "Good riddance." He didn't think skunks changed their stripes so easily. The Bohunk figured they were up to some bad business somewhere. He assumed they were play-acting when they stopped in Bottineau. Gerry laughed and said he didn't suppose they were capable of hard work. He doubted they would stay on the good side of the law for long.

When the pair were in the vicinity of Bud Quigley's horse ranch, they decided to camp and put together a plan to make sure they had the draw on Quigley before he knew what was going on.

"He's a tough old bird, we have to be certain he doesn't have a gun around when we move in," Charlie Parmer said.

"It won't make no difference if we have the drop on him. You attract his attention, I'll move behind him," Frenchie replied.

"Thanks for nothing. I get shot up while you sneak in and disarm him. Some plan. No thanks."

It didn't turn out to be much of a problem. Bud Quigley wasn't used to seeing visitors very often. When trouble went away for a long time he grew complacent. His Parker and revolver were in his shack, the derringer was still in his shirt pocket, hanging on the hook behind the door. When Charlie and Frenchie circled and came in from behind his yard, they stopped in the brush and observed Quigley digging up his potatoes with a rig being pulled by Old Joe, his Belgian-Clyde cross.

"Don't that beat all," said Charlie. "Easy peasy pickings."

They rode boldly out from the bush and came on Quigley together.

"Well, well, who do we have here?" Frenchie joked as he reined in his ride.

"How's it going?" Charlie Parmer said as he slid off his dappled gray. "Still keep the coffee pot on?"

"Reckon I do," said Bud. "You boys are welcome to a cup as soon as I ease Old Joe off."

When they reached the firepit he squatted down to give the coals a stir. There was still coffee in the blackened pot. Bud poured each of them a cup. Nobody said anything for a while as they eyed one another.

"What can I do for you fellas?"

"Use your imagination," Frenchie answered.

"Look, it's this way," Charlie began. "Frenchie and me figure you made some money off that robber who came through here when you sold him a good horse. Since he was loaded with cash he must have been a generous, not to mention grateful, customer. Not only that, but you, living in this here wild country all by yourself, have to be making deals with other men on the run from the law. Now to get to the sharp end of the stick. If you know what's good for you, you'll show us where you keep your money. Just hand it over to us and we'll be on our way."

"You figure it's that easy," said Bud, looking at them from between his yellow eyelids.

"No, I don't think it will be easy at all," answered Frenchie, whipping a blade out from the case hanging under his shirt. "But we'll have your money by the time I finish operating on you with my skinning knife and your hide is piled on the ground."

"Wouldn't be worth it, would it?" The words had barely escaped from Charlie's mouth when Bud hurled the steaming coffee pot at Frenchie's chest, knocking him flat on his ass as he broke for the cabin. Before he made it, Charlie pistol-whipped Bud across the side of his head with his Colt.

"That bastard," Frenchie screamed as he jumped to his feet and buried the toe of his boot into Bud a number of times before Charlie could pull him back.

"Stop, you're gonna kick him to death and then we'll have nothing."

When Bud regained consciousness, his arms were pinned behind his back on a stout length of sapling. He found himself propped up against a log.

"Smart bastard," Frenchie screamed over and over again. "Look at this, Charlie. Not only was I burnt, but the bastard ruined my freshly laundered shirt!"

"Jeez, Frenchie, when we find his money you can buy a dozen new shirts."

"You like burning people, eh?" Frenchie said to Bud. "I'll keep that in mind."

"Now listen," Charlie said. "I'm a reasonable man who doesn't like violence, but Frenchie here doesn't understand much else. So either you cooperate or Frenchie has his way and you're a flayed, burnt-to-the-crisp, poor bastard who'll be no use to anybody, never mind yourself."

"Can't win." Bud grimaced at the pain in his ribs. "You'll kill me either way."

"Not at all." Charlie softened his voice and reasoned with Bud to give up his savings. "We want your money, not your life. Why should we add murder to the bill and make our lives more difficult?"

All the time Charlie was talking, Bud was eyeing Frenchie, thinking, *There's no way Frenchie's not going to kill me.*

"Do your best. I ain't giving you nothing. You're gonna murder me anyway, might as well get it over with. You can do to me what you want, but I ain't talking."

"We don't want to see you shed any blood," Charlie said.

"Oh Charlie, shut up, " Frenchie exploded. "You talk too much. This bastard's giving us a lot of lip because you like the sound of your own voice." He turned to Bud. "Now listen shithead, I'm going to cut you down inch by inch until you're screaming for your life. Your God damn money is gonna be ours. But first I'm going to empty your corral of your favourite friends. Then I'm gonna carve some of them with my knife and hatchet and gut-shoot the rest. They'll be dying all over the place because you love your money more than anything else, even your miserable life. You stupid old fool. I haven't even started."

"Frenchie, if I was you I'd stop yammering and take a look around," Charlie said as he dropped his iron onto the ground.

Frenchie, completely absorbed by his own rage, suddenly stopped yelling. Circling them were Alphonse Pointed Stick and ten other men on their ponies.

"Jeezuz, how can this be?" Frenchie said as dropped his knife.

Within minutes Bud was cut free and helped to his feet. Soon Charlie and Frenchie looked like two muskrats on stretchers waiting for the fur buyer to drop by.

"Glad to see you fellows," Bud said, slapping Alphonse Pointed Stick on the back. Alphonse introduced everyone in turn. Bud shook hands all around.

"Leave these rats to rot in the sun while we sit in the shade and have a smoke and talk a little," Bud said as he rubbed the circulation back into his arms

"What's been going on here?" Alphonse asked, sitting down on the chopping block.

"These two showed up here to rob me," Bud said, lighting a rollie. "If you hadn't arrived here today I think I was breathing my last few breaths."

"What do you have that's more valuable than your horses?" Alphonse asked.

"Don't rightly know. They think I have a hidden supply of money."

"These men are dangerous, I can tell by the look of them. They have crazy eyes, like the whites who steal from my people."

"They're both bad, but that skinny bastard with the hawk-face and lovely hair is an evil one. He was proceeding to cut up the horses to get my attention. He had blood on his mind. The other one is just a weak man with no ambition but to live off other people."

"I have a question."

"Well?"

"Why didn't you just give them your money? You can't eat it in the winter when you're hungry. When it's gone it will not make any difference to your horses. When I have money I just spend it for what I need. You white people are always hiding it. You even construct buildings to hide it."

"I didn't give them my money. I figured if I did Frenchie would have killed me on the spot. I was hoping for a miracle. I received one when you and your friends showed up."

"It's your lucky day," Alphonse answered, standing up, facing west and raising one arm. Soon Bud saw a herd of ponies and riders coming from that direction. He couldn't help but notice the riders were kids who were each leading a pony behind the one they were riding.

"These are our sons," Alphonse said. "Here are the horses you asked me to bring to trade with you. We brought the young boys with us to teach them. Now they will see the meanness in the eyes of these two men who worship money."

In the next few hours Quigley made a deal with Alphonse and his people for four additional appaloosa yearlings to match the three he was coddling in the corral. They agreed that Bud would pay with the trade goods that he would authorize Mac to release from his store in Bottineau. After they had dickered for a while, Bud wrote out the details on a scrap of paper he scrounged from the cabin.

"Now I need a big favour from you, Alphonse, that I cannot put a price on. There is no law available in this part of the country to deal with these men. I cannot release them and let them live around here or they will be back to hound me."

"How do you want us to help you?"

"I want you to take these men with you for a long ride, two hundred miles from here. Drop them off in an unpopulated area with a hatchet, a knife and some fishing line and hooks. Then let them go free on foot. Either that or I have to kill them here on the spot and bury them somewhere."

"We can do that much for you," Alphonse answered after half an hour of palaver with his friends. "Now, we want you to put some coffee on the fire so we can have a drink while we're visiting with you."

"Consider it done," Bud said.

After they had completed their business, Bud walked over to where Charlie and Frenchie were sitting.

"Listen, you two are in for a treat. Alphonse and his pals have agreed to take you on a long ride into a part of the country you probably have never seen. I have decided to make their trip more pleasurable by giving them a keg of the Bohunk's potato whisky. When you arrive at a location in the wilderness where they decide to stop and camp for a few days, they're going to have a party with you boys. They'll drink up that keg of booze and you fellows will provide the entertainment. How does that grab you,

Frenchie? Oh, just to let you know about the deal I made. Every man here gets a new skinning knife from the store in Bottineau. When they are all boozed up and decide to have some sport, they can practice on you with their new blades, just like you were planning with me."

"You can't mean that," said Charlie in a whining voice.

"Come on, you know I was just threatening you," Frenchie added. "I would never have gone through with it."

"That's not what your partner thinks, eh Charlie? When I told Alphonse you were going to cut up the horses, he wasn't too pleased. In fact, he thinks you're an unnatural pair of losers who might be better off as coyote food."

When he was finished talking, Alphonse motioned that Bud should speak with him out of earshot of the two desperadoes.

"What are you saying?" Alphonse asked. "We don't drink! We have no intention of cutting anybody up or killing them. We're peaceful people. I agree these men are dangerous and need a lesson. We'll be happy to drop them off and let them survive if they can, but that's it."

"I appreciate that, Alphonse. I'll owe you big-time for that favour. I just wanted to scare the devil out of these boys, letting them think they're going to be the main attraction at a big Indian debauch. While they're travelling with you, it will teach them what comes around goes around. When you let them go in the middle of nowhere, they'll find out the truth."

In the morning, when they were ready to leave, Bud said, "Don't forget to load up that keg that's in my cabin." Two men went in the cabin and came out with the small keg of molasses that Bud had thrown in as part of the trade.

"Now, listen to me closely. I only have one more thing to tell you two," he said, addressing Charlie Parmer and Frenchie Who-Only-Goes-by-One-Name. "If, by some intervention of God, you two survive and I see you around here again, I'll shoot you both on sight."

Before they left, Bud told Alphonse and his brothers that he owed them for their timely arrival. He invited them to return in the winter months and camp at his place. They could butcher his cows for the benefit of their families and friends.

"Alphonse, when you give my note to that haggis-lover, MacGregor, you tell him I'll be down soon enough to settle my account."

In the afternoon, when the sun was warm against his forehead, Bud Quigley pinched the skin on his bruised arm to see if he was still alive. He was leaning against the corral looking at seven snowflake Appaloosas; two colts and five fillies. Alphonse Pointed Stick had come through with one additional colt and three more fillies on this second trip to Bud's place. Now, he had the stock he needed to make a deal with James J. Hill. *More than enough money to set me up for life. Along with the money in my hiding place.*

Bud's head reeled with thoughts of strange lands and unusual sights. He was too old to hustle horses much longer. He was growing tired of living alone in such an isolated place. Bud knew he had been saved by a slim chance from a slow, savage death at the hands of a sadist.

The arrival of the Pinkerton's sleazy henchmen had given him food for thought. Momentarily, he envisioned the shark-faced Jiggs Dubois coming back into his life. He was still lamenting his foolish decision to let his soft heart prevail when he should have executed the chestnut gelding. It was time to make a deal with Hill, sell the rest of his stock, pull up stakes and head for new adventures with what was left of his final years.

12

October, 1889
Assiniboia District, North-West Territory, Canada

WHEN LES FIRST ARRIVED IN REGINA in the fall to start his training, the frost was already burrowing underground. The howling wind was a powerful force sweeping down over the prairie. Regina was an over-governed town that in no way could be described as picturesque. In the spring it was a mud wallow, in the summer a dusty, fly-specked gulch. There followed a blip of fall and then a long, frigid winter that almost defied description.

Les knew enough to do what he was told and keep his mouth shut. It took a little getting used to, being blown out of bed by reveille at 6 a.m. every morning. When Les wasn't looking after his kit or paying attention to an array of housekeeping and stable duties, he was absorbed in drilling, riding, and rifle and small-arms practice. This was followed by numerous lectures on how to react in certain situations as well as lessons on processing the North-West Mounted Police forms and reports that had to be filled out in triplicate.

He particularly thrived under the attention of the riding master, Staff Sergeant William D. Bruce, who pushed the recruits hard to become decent horsemen.

On a bitter October morning, Les rode his Mountie-issue

horse, Ballantyne, around the obstacle course in a spectacular display of man and beast in harmony that some fellow recruits considered daring.

"Simpson, I'm glad you were wise enough to give him his head in the final stages," Bruce said. "You're showing me guts, effort and real talent for bringing out the best from your mount. You're a natural. I want to use you in demonstrating for your fellow recruits."

"Be happy to," Les replied, wondering if his peers might think he was brown-nosing the staff sergeant. In the end he had nothing to worry about. Most of the trainees were black and blue from falling off on the obstacle course or being bucked off on the parade ground. They were grateful for any help they could get.

The main differences from his former home life were that, in the service, Les ate three square meals a day, with benefits, and his time was strictly managed by his employer. He put on weight and grew an inch, to six-foot-three, during his first six months in Regina. His first year, he earned fifty cents per day for work or training done from dawn until the sun mercifully went down behind the horizon and Lights Out sounded at 10:15 p.m.

Initially, Les spent most of his time with the other younger recruits. As the weeks passed, they were gradually accepted by the older members of the Force, although Les soon grew tired of being ordered about by plummy-throated British muldoons who couldn't stop talking about the old days in India or some other colonial outpost, or constantly reliving this or that cavalry charge.

"Alcott, did you ever lop a head off on one of those gallops?"

"Many times, Ellis, many times. I dare say barrels-full."

"What did you do with them?" Corporal Ellis asked.

"Like everything left on the battlefield – claimed by the birds and the jackals."

"You young chaps will never see the like of it." Ellis directed his comments at the rookie table. "The brass has gone soft. I tell you, it would improve morale around this part of the world if we chopped off a few heads, instead of coddling the savages."

"Hey laddie," Alcott said to Les. "Hear you're touted to be a shit-hot rider. That so?"

"I wouldn't say that," Les answered.

"Don't be modest, lad. Bruce says he'd bet on you riding against anybody in the service. That's quite a compliment from a stick-in-the-mud like him. But jumping over hedges and riding on the parade ground is child's play compared to a full charge with sabres set in the ready position. I can't explain the thrill when the swishing blade cuts through meat like butter and the thundering chargers' hooves are kicking up mud and blood. It's enough to make a rookie fill his pants. By the look of you, you'd be one of those," Alcott said, with the vein in his neck bulging.

"You tell him, Alcott," Ellis said.

Corporals Alcott and Ellis spent their off-time visiting an Indian woman who had set up a tipi on the edge of town and started her own business.

"Cheap prices because she has hardly any overhead," Ellis said. "On slow days we've negotiated her down to two for the price of one. How's that for a bargain?"

Alcott and Ellis talked incessantly about old regiments and eccentric superior officers from the past. They spent hours regaling one another with one tall tale after another. When they weren't doing that they were busy playing pranks on the rookies or prattling on about old wives' remedies for curing social diseases.

On April 5th, after four hard months of training and two more in the stables as an orderly, with more ups and downs than he cared remember, Leslie R. Simpson received his first posting. He was to join a group that included a sergeant and six constables. They assembled a pile of gear to be loaded on the train, including two wagons, to travel down to Fort Qu'Appelle, then to Broadview and on to Moosomin. There, they would unload and head eighty miles south to Carlyle. The wagons had to be disassembled and reassembled whenever they were loaded onto, or unloaded from, a train car.

After a brief respite, they continued another thirty-five miles southeast before reaching their destination on the 16th of July. Alameda, the largest post in the region, was not much more than a few log cabins, a stable and a post office. It was situated on the prairie overlooking the Souris River valley.

When Les and his fellow reinforcements arrived in the south, they joined a weekly patrol that linked Willow Bunch with Wood End and Alameda. The route was roughly parallel to the border. Not only were the Mounted Police showing a Canadian presence to combat the growing population that was moving into the border states, but they were also keeping track of Indians who were freely crossing the line.

The Mounties also had a mandate to deal with the outlaws who plied both sides, rustling livestock, robbing settlers and selling liquor in a region where it was banned.

There were few settlers on the Canadian side. Patrols seldom encountered a living soul as they traversed the country. When they were called into action, it was usually to run down horse thieves or whisky traders. The latter were often so liquored-up they could hardly drive their wagons in a straight line.

That first year they went south, Les and his fellows were hit by a freak snowstorm in mid-September. The next morning the prairie seemed a pristine white blanket in the sunshine. Near Alameda, they came upon wagon tracks that they happily followed until they finally caught up with two grizzled individuals on a seat behind a team of four horses.

"How do?" the driver said as he reined in his charges.

"Where you fellows bound for?" Inspector Pepper asked.

"Here and there," the driver answered. "Here and there."

"Where you from?" Pepper asked.

"Why, from down south," the second man answered.

"What's in the wagon?" Pepper motioned at Sergeant Michaels to look under the canvas.

"Just trade goods."

"More like barrels of whisky," Michaels said as he and Les rolled the kegs from the back of the wagon and dropped them onto the snow.

"You know this is a dry territory," Pepper said.

"No idea about that," the driver replied.

Inspector Pepper ordered the men to chop into the barrels until the whisky ran out onto the snow.

"Tell you what, I'm giving you twenty-four hours to clear out of this country. If I catch you on this side of the border with liquor, I'll seize your horses and wagon and put the pair of you into the lock-up."

Late that afternoon, Sergeant Michaels asked Les and another constable to scrounge a couple of buckets and to saddle their horses. The three then rode out to the site where the whisky kegs had been destroyed.

"I had a talk with the Inspector," Michaels told them. "He figures we've been at it pretty hard and we ought to have a party. You fellows dismount and shovel that whisky snow into your buckets and we'll go back to camp. See that you pack those buckets to the brim. Tamp them down good."

That evening the men at Alameda became inebriated on some very rough booze thanks to two grotty-looking Yanks who, by now, were most likely back across the line.

A few weeks later, the patrol followed wagon tracks down a boggy trail and apprehended the same two whisky traders, back with another load of despicable firewater.

The formal military life of drill and duty, from dusk till dawn, continued at the distant posts without fail, although it eased up somewhat when the weather was bad. Nevertheless, there was a camaraderie on the road and at the posts that Les failed to discover during the long winters in Regina when he was back under the thumb of the strict military regime. Day-to-day life in the barracks demanded respect for a certain kind of conduct and social ethic that left him cold and feeling somewhat of an outsider.

The majority of the constables from the border posts wintered in Regina. That became a problem for Les Simpson. He went stir-crazy in the barracks during the bitter months. The endless routine bent him out of shape. He was appalled by the Mountie circus and its perpetual mood of self-importance and false pride.

Les wasn't in a police force, he was in the bloody army! He grew to despise the army barracks life of parades, pomp and circumstance, spit and polish, and constant drilling, but he had no choice: fifty cents a day beat making fifteen cents a day watering horses for railway crews.

He needed to make money to send home to keep his family afloat. Les found no glory in the service. He endured it for the pay. The longer he was in, the more he despised the leadership of stiff old boys who walked around with swagger sticks and, most of the time, had only a vague idea about what was going on. These were largely impractical men without vision who piled on the busy work to keep their men occupied. They marched them about the country, over some of the most rugged terrain in existence, to keep the machine functioning in an approved manner.

It was during the winters that Les hatched his plan to apply for a leave in spring and then make a lightning strike on a bank across the border. He figured just before the first of the month there would be a payroll waiting to be paid out.

More than four years of following instructions and toeing the line without question had convinced him that a life like his was hardly worth living. He knew his mother, never a robust woman, was living on borrowed time and that sooner or later she would wear out, emotionally and physically, from the awful workload she carried to support her family.

Les decided to make one roll of the dice. If he failed, he would be fulfilling the sense of tragic destiny that seemed to be haunting his family after his father's early death. Could it turn much worse? If he succeeded, he banked on the chance of setting both himself and his family up for a better life.

Back in September, while out on the trail, Les's patrol had encountered a bunch of American drovers pushing a big herd of cattle. The boss asked Inspector Pepper if he would care to stop and
join them in their midday meal of beefsteak, beans and biscuits.

A young cowboy struck up a conversation with Les. "Been on
the trail a long time. We drove these critters all the way up here
from Devil's Lake. Boss has a big deal going on further north."

"I've never been to the United States," Les said.

"Not much different than here," the cowboy answered, "although I guess it's wilder. There's a lot of folks packing iron across
the line."

"Which way did you travel?" Les asked.

"Followed the grass up through Manitoba. Now, that's an isolated place."

"Is it?" Les mused.

"Yeah, we had to keep watch all the time. It's bad country for
losing cows if you're not careful. We travelled wary, armed to the
teeth. There's little law enforcement in that border region. We
felt safer when we headed west into Assiniboia. You Mounties
are always patrolling."

"In your dreams," Les said. "There are thieves every place that
raises cattle. We have our share of them. Rustling is the oldest
profession."

"I've heard that there's only twenty-five men in the whole
Manitoba Provincial Police Force and most of them are in Winnipeg. They're rumoured to be a collection of tough hombres.
They've got all they can handle with robberies and killing sprees
from the dregs that spill over from Fargo. It's said they send out
officers to patrol the rest of the territory, but I've never encountered one of their men"

The cattle puncher told Les about a mysterious wrangler
who ran a small horse operation doing business on both sides
of the line.

"Ran into him once on the trail when we were looking for

strays. He camped with us one night. Talkative fellow, for a wrangler. Quigley's his name. He has a reputation for raising good stock. They say he wheels and deals nags with the best of them. I've heard talk of him in Devil's Lake. There's a rancher there with a champion stud that was bred by this Quigley. You need a horse that can run all day, every day, then this guy's supposed to be the magic ticket. And apparently they can short haul as well. Thought it was kind of funny though."

"What's funny?" Les asked.

"Well, the legend rides a pretty little mare."

"That so?" Les said. "You expectin' he'd be astride a thunderbolt?"

"Not that exactly," the cowboy said. "Men in his business usually display the trappings, and he don't."

"I see," Les said.

"Some people think he's fast and loose but who isn't, doing business in that border country. It's one of those don't-ask-questions kind of places," the cowboy said.

Les kept all this filed in his clutter of interesting facts. He'd need the right horse and a stopover place going down and coming back. When his leave came through, he'd set his plan in motion. He'd purchase a horse and a saddle in Regina and hustle himself down into this isolated area and sniff out the scene. He'd drop in on Quigley and look over his horses and size him up. He thought it would be foolish to pass on meeting a "legend." Les knew that cowboy gossip was more reliable than most. Horses were what they were about. After that, he'd make a final decision about whether he would go through with his plan to rob a bank in North Dakota.

13

October, 1894
Assiniboia District, North-West Territory, Canada

"ARE YOU PACKING, MR. DUBOIS? Or are those candlestick hold-
ers under your armpits? Let's have 'em. Oh, as nice a pair of Merwin-Hulberts as I have seen. A fine weapon. It's out of the
question that you be permitted to walk around Regina with these
attention-getters," Commissioner Lawrence W. Herchmer at
North-West Mounted Police headquarters in Regina looked
straight at Jiggs Dubois.

"How about you, Mr. Smith, what are you carrying? Aha! A
Webley Bulldog. Do considerable damage from about twenty feet
away. That would put a big hole in somebody, wouldn't it Mr.
Smith? Your barroom blaster is a bit extreme for Regina, don't you
think? I'll have the sergeant major lock these up and you can
collect them before you return home. I see by this letter of introduction you have presented that you are Pinkerton Detective
Agency men from south of the border who want to talk to us
about a robbery and murder that was committed in May, in Bismarck, North Dakota. Is that the gist of it Mr., ah, Mr. Dubois?"

"You have it pegged, sir," Dubois answered.

"Oh, I say, we are on the same page then," the commissioner
commented.

"You see, sir, we have been in pursuit of a robber who not only knocked over a bank, but killed the bank manager."

"What's that have to do with me?" Commissioner Herchmer asked.

"The robber was an extremely competent horseman. He robbed the bank in Bismarck and headed for the border in real haste. We have witnesses that say he crossed the Mouse River, well, the Souris River to you, at a crossing known as Swedes' Ferry and then travelled across the border into western Manitoba. There he probably traded horses and hauled further north. Now, the thing is, this robber stopped on the road outside Bismarck. He reloaded his weapon, leaving this cartridge casing for a Enfield Mark II revolver on the ground. Isn't this one of yours, sir?"

"Might be, but I doubt it."

"Why do you say that so convincingly?" asked Balfour Smith.

"The facts, gentlemen. We have imported that weapon several times in the past five years. There are several thousand out there. Some of them have our stamp and a registration number, but others don't. We have men who leave the service and take their weapons with them. We have the occasional deserter who leaves with his weapon. We have had some stolen. The Indians are in possession of some of the older models. You see – Mr. Biggs is it? – this is a very common piece-and-bullet that is found all over the place. You're jumping to conclusions if you think one of our constables has robbed a bank in Bismarck. Sounds like a fairy tale to me, sir. I suggest you give it up."

Herchmer was growing impatient with the conversation.

"Now, what is it I can do for you?" the commissioner asked, looking at his pocket watch.

"We were hoping you could give us a list of your members who have deserted in the past two years. In addition, we wondered if you would be good enough to supply us with a list of men who were granted leave in the past few months. It would be helpful if you could identify how long those leaves of absence were for and the dates, as well as what post the person was at before he took leave," Dubois replied.

"My God, is that all?" asked the commissioner in astonishment. "Sir, put your queries into writing. Have them sent to my office. I will have my investigative team on it at once, to thoroughly analyze the facts and circumstances you point out. I am not at liberty to give you any list of anything from the information that our Force has gathered and maintains. I cannot even tell you how many pounds of turnips we put through the barracks in the winter. Good day!"

Dubois and Smith were suddenly being hustled toward the door by a duty officer who seemed to appear from nowhere.

"Oh, I say, about that liquor that you put on the table. I have asked the sergeant major to seize it in the name of the Crown. It will be disposed of in a suitable fashion. Thank you, gentlemen, for your thoughtful gift, but as you probably know, this territory is dry. We must not accept your magnanimous offer of spirits. The duty officer will see you out."

When they were gone, Lawrence William Herchmer retired to his private room for a shot of the good stuff. It was a bit early in the day, but he had put those two strange detectives in their place. When he said the Mounties had an occasional deserter he stretched the truth somewhat because the number of deserters in the past five years had been closer to five hundred men. He was not, however, about to give classified information away to unofficial lawmen from the United States.

A Pinkerton is nothing in Canada, he thought. *Imagine the audacity of these weedy-looking fellows to walk right into headquarters and start asking for lists and records. They could put their application for information in writing and he would file it away in the dead letter department. Pinkertons, that's a new one. I'll have the boys on duty in town keep an eye on those two.* "Yankee riffraff," he told the mess.

"Jeezus," Smith said, before they hit the front door on the way out, "that blowhard got rid of us like we were a pair of turds in the laundry."

"Yes, he was not playing the game with us," Dubois acknowledged.

"Now what do we do?" asked Smith.

"I think it's time I contact William Pinkerton," Dubois announced.

They went down to the telegraph station where Jiggs sent a telegram to Pinkerton at the Chicago headquarters of the company. "NWMP won't cooperate – stop – Jiggs Dubois."

Later in the evening a telegram from Pinkerton was delivered to Dubois at the Windsor Hotel.

"Will speak to Can gov – stop – W Pinkerton."

Smith and Dubois agreed it was time to make contact with Filbert's spies in Regina. They consulted the scrap of paper that Jiggs produced from his watch pocket. It read, "Lily Flett and Bonnie Blondon above Wardell's Restaurant on South Railway Street."

Smith and Dubois managed to hitch a ride on a delivery wagon that was going that way. When the driver stopped they found themselves in the warehouse district, in front of a brick building that housed a restaurant on the ground floor and a private club on the second floor.

"Where can we find these two women, Lilly Flett and Bonnie Blondon?" Dubois asked the Oriental doorman who was sitting on a box outside the door, smoking a long, curving pipe

"Follow me," he said, leading them into the restaurant. A number of members of the local community were feasting on an enormous fish that was arrayed on the table in front of them. Jiggs and Balfour were ushered upstairs into what resembled a parlour, where they were asked to sit on the big, plush couch that ran along the wall. After about five minutes, a bright, red door opened. A large woman in heavy makeup, wearing a Chinese-patterned robe, came out and asked the men what they desired.

"I'm Miranda. I'm your hostess."

"We've come to see Lily and Bonnie," Jiggs said, just then twigging to the fact that he was in the middle of a whorehouse.

"What discerning choices you gentlemen have made. No doubt you have heard advertising about these two from some of their satisfied customers. I'm sure they'll find it exciting when they realize you fellows are wanting a real romp as a foursome. I'll book you into the Emperor's Palace Room. That'll be three dollars in advance, each, for two hours. Let me fill up your glasses and inform you that, after you're done, dinner below is on the house. The clams are very good; they arrive fresh daily on the train from the coast."

Lily, a slightly case-hardened blonde, came out from behind the brightly painted door followed by Bonnie, a tall redhead who towered over Jiggs.

"These gentlemen will be your guests for this afternoon," Miranda stated as the women led Smith and Dubois down the hall to the Emperor's Palace Room, which contained a very large four-poster bed with a canopy of turquoise silk decorated with peacocks. A discreet knock brought a tray with a bottle of whisky and four glasses.

"Jumping mouse tits, this is a harsh bottle of hootch," said Jiggs as he tipped his glass.

"You get what you pay for around here," Lily answered. "Would you like to order the premier stuff?"

"Not so bad," said Jiggs as he drained another shot. "I have something for you girls."

"Oh, I bet you do," the redhead said as she loosened the cord on her silk robe.

"It's my business card. I'm Jiggs Dubois and this is Balfour Smith. We both work for the Pinkerton National Detective Agency, as you can see. We are here on the advice of Roger Filbert, who told us to contact you when we were up this way."

"I see," said Lily, holding the card up to the gas lamp which threw a hot light on the shimmering river of silk that ran down from the top of the four-poster.

"We need some information that we cannot obtain from the North-West Mounted Police brass," Jiggs stated in a blunt manner.

"Not surprising," said Bonnie. "They don't answer to anybody. Getting information out of the Force is very difficult. The top guns are so tight-assed and protective they don't even fart."

"Yet they act like the sun shines from the arses of their boys. Doesn't matter that they have a huge rate of desertion and a disgraceful reputation in dealing with Indians. Especially regarding the Indian women. It's all covered up," Lily said as she blew a note of blue smoke from the small cigar she lit up. "They investigate themselves and do their dirty linen inside their own walls, if they do it at all."

"That going to be a problem?" Balfour asked.

"Yes or no, depending on how sensitive the issues are," Bonnie said, shifting her weight onto the brocade chair with her long, tapered legs pointed directly at Jiggs.

Balfour outlined the nature of the case. He described the robbery and subsequent murder at Bismarck. The women reported that the North-West Mounted record for desertion meant that a number of these men had gone south of the border to take up crime as a way of life.

Jiggs told them why he thought the shooter in this case was not a criminal type, as such.

"Look, he only hit once and bungled it pretty bad when he aced that bank manager," Jiggs said, taking off his jacket. He removed the empty holsters by lifting the crisscross straps over his head. "I don't think he's a hard core criminal. I think he did it that one time figuring he might make a big score. And damn, he did, getting away with forty-four thousand dollars of the Great Northern Railway payroll that had just been deposited in the First National Bank. When he finished the job he headed north as if he was a homing pigeon. If he were a bum or a deserter he would have headed into outlaw country to hide out. I believe he rode north because he had the opportunity to melt back into society. The fact is that he could ride a horse like a pro, run all day and night across the landscape. And that he left a slug in a dead man's forehead, and a cartridge along the roadside, that points to him carrying an Enfield Mark II revolver, which is North-West Mounted Police issue. So let's get some information and see what we can make of it."

"What do you want us to find out?" Lily asked.

"We need a list of all leaves of absence that were granted from, say, last April 1st until the end of May. We are particularly interested in those who were previously stationed down south in the border posts. We also require a list of those members who are about to be mustered out of the Force in the next six months. Finally, I believe our shooter is a tall man in the prime of life who, as I mentioned, has excellent horseman skills. Not an average rider but a standout. I need you to ask some questions of the right people. We need names and physical descriptions. Can you do that much?"

"There's no place information flows like in bed," Bonnie said, eyeing Jiggs, who turned bright red under the bush that covered his mangled face.

"Yes, and the North-West Mounted Police gossip stream runs right through this room." Lily laughed and stubbed out her cigar in the Buddha ashtray on the mother-of-pearl inlaid table.

"I need to confer with my associate for a minute in private," Jiggs said as he ushered Balfour to the back of the room. The girls shed their silk kimonos and started strutting around in their scanties.

"I'm partial to the redhead," Jiggs said.

"Okay by me," answered Balfour.

Later, when Dubois and Smith were downstairs indulging in the free black bean sauce clams and feasting on steamed pickerel and garlic pea tips, they were approached by a young Mounted

Police constable with a ruddy complex. Ginger Newton was what he called himself. Dubois invited him to sit in on their repast, but he declined.

"The brass, that is, Commissioner Herchmer, would like to see you fellows when you have a moment. Now'd be a good time. I have a wagon outside for you to ride on."

On the trip back to the North-West Mounted Police headquarters Dubois speculated with Smith that it was advantageous to have an important man like William Pinkerton on their side. They both were confident that they would soon be receiving the help they had requested.

"I hear you boys have been circulating around town, taking in some of the opportunities for entertainment in our lively community," Commissioner Herchmer said as he looked at them like a wolf about to lick up a duo of tasty rodents. "Those Chinoise certainly know how to put up a good feast in a short amount of time. How did it compare with what you have down south?"

"Nothing quite like that down there," Smith answered.

Dubois already figured the conversation was headed into the tank. *What is Smith playing at with the restaurant review?* he wondered.

"I sent the constable over to Wardell's to fetch you fellows because I figured it was time we had another conversation. You boys are exasperating me in the most trying way. You're like flies around a pile of crap. I want to make something clear to both of you. You can have your Mr. Pinkerton piss all over his boots and try and pull strings by bringing down political pressure, but it will do you no good at all. You see, I couldn't give a horse's twat what the politicians think. They can kiss my red ass. I'll say it one more time: I have taken your information and I have passed it on to my internal investigation bureau. I will wait for them to recommend action, or non-action, on this ludicrous accusation you are making about some mythical member of our honourable Force. You will not be allowed any fishing expeditions into our affairs. If we find wrongdoing we will take appropriate action. Now, I have a piece of advice for you. I would say that it would be better, sooner than later, if you would finish your business in Regina, collect your weapons and clear out of town at the earliest opportunity."

"Is that an order?" Dubois asked, picking his words carefully. His first instinct had been to ask him if they were being threatened.

"Consider it an advisement," the commissioner answered.

"Then, consider the matter closed with us, for now," Jiggs replied. "Your advice has convinced me that Mr. Smith and I have concluded our official business in Regina. Now sir, it's a long trip home. Smith and I have been diligently employed without a break for nearly a year. I wonder, sir, if you would allow us to continue taking in some of the, ah, er, sights, for another week or so since it took so long to travel here. Of course, we'll just be tourists in search of a good time before we have to travel south and cross the border again."

"No objection at all," the commissioner said. "I'll take your word as gentlemen that you have concluded your private police business. That you will be discreet in your behaviour while taking in the ambience of some of our better establishments. Is that the case?"

"Absolutely correct," Dubois said in a loud, clear voice.

"Next time you're at Wardell's, try the Chinoise duck."

Dubois and Smith were registered as commercial travellers at the hotel. They sat in the local cafe in the afternoon, killing time while drinking tea. They had no other choice: the town was officially dry. They entertained the local rubes by claiming they'd been hired by an unidentified employer who sent them out to investigate economic possibilities in Regina. Lily and Bonnie told them to stay away from the whorehouse until they heard from them via messenger. They didn't want Dubois and Smith to scare off military customers who might be leery of their presence. They promised to get back to them within the week.

"Kind of harsh, isn't it?" asked Balfour. "I was looking forward to returning for a second course."

"It's business, pure and simple," replied Jiggs. "You'll have to keep your pecker in your pants, at least until we acquire some information."

Finally, after eight days of interminable waiting, the Oriental man from the whorehouse showed up at their door to give them the high sign. When they arrived back in the establishment's parlour, Miranda was delighted to see them and poured them shots from a prize-winning bottle of whisky. A gift from a Scottish sergeant major admirer.

"Best blast I've had since we hit Regina," said Balfour, licking his lips and accepting a second.

"That'll be three bucks each, up front. Go right on in boys, you know the way."

The girls were giddy. They had some chocolates and candied fruit out on the table and a bottle of liqueur. "Now boys, your dreams have come true!" Lily said.

"Maybe in more ways than one," Bonnie added, twirling a boa.

"There's something important to mention right now," Lily said. "When you see Mr. Filbert, tell him to put another hundred in our account. He knows the details. We'll expect that money to be in our bank within a month of your departure. Got it?"

"I guess we do," said Balfour Smith.

"So what do you know?" Jiggs asked, looking from the lethal side of his face.

"We have a list of the boys on leave of absences in the past six months. Here is an accounting of this year's rosters in the southern border posts. Everybody who has a tick mark is on the tall, thin side. Here is the list of the best riders who passed through training for the past five years. Bonnie heard it right from the horse's mouth, so to speak – she's ridden regularly by the riding master, Staff Sergeant Bruce. Tick marks again on the tall ones. Here are the members whose contracts are close to being up.

Some are close to re-enlisting, others will be leaving. We couldn't obtain the list of deserters. They guard that number for all they're worth. No chance, it's in the vault. It's a dark secret. But I have no doubt it's a high figure. Look how many new recruits they're training all the time. It's obvious they have a high turnover of men who are headed for greener pastures."

"I see what you mean," Jiggs said. "I'll recommend they add another twenty-five dollars to your fee. You've done a hell of a job. I wish I knew how you did it."

"Maybe you want to find out," the redhead said, throwing a shadow from her long, shapely legs on Jiggs from the bright lamp that rushed across the waterfall of colour.

Balfour was already under the silk sheets with the blonde.

14

WHEN ALPHONSE POINTED STICK TURNED UP unexpectedly with the rest of the appaloosas and saved him from being cut by Frenchie, Bud Quigley took it as a sign. It was the middle of September. Bud figured his luck was still holding. He decided to play his hand as strong as he could. He would try and wind up his affairs and clear out of the country before the onset of another long, arduous prairie winter.

He had heard from travellers who stopped at his place on their way north that the railway tracks were bypassing Bottineau, but that telegraph lines had already reached town. Bud had a sudden impulse. He'd ride into Bottineau, take care of some of his business affairs and send a telegraph to James J. Hill in Saint Paul saying that he had acquired the appaloosas.

When Bud and Suzy plodded into town they were a bit surprised by what they found. The town was about to move. The new railway tracks were coming in about a mile from the current town site.

"That's the way the railway works. They don't give a damn." Gerry was holding the floor at the Bohunk's place, ripping the railway for being high-handed. "They say the new location is because of the grades. They don't want to spend extra money. Well

I can tell you they have put a lot of sincere local business people out of luck by this decision. Now, nobody in town is going to make any money selling their land to the railway. Should have known what was going on when those railway executives came through here. They spent a lot of time coddling the ranchers on the outskirts." "Yeah, the railway's always harsh to the workers, so why should they treat anybody else better?" the Bohunk added.

"At least they brought the telegraph lines into town, even if those are going to move when they build the new train station at the other place."

Gerry spied Quigley standing by the bar. "If it ain't old horse-face himself. Can I buy you a beer?"

"Jeez, I just arrived in town. I think I'll celebrate by sending a telegraph to somebody."

"Good for you," said Gerry. "You'll be one of the first."

Early that afternoon, Bud sent a telegram to James J. Hill's travelling secretary, Florence Mouton. It was short and sweet and to the point. It read: "Have horses – stop – Quigley."

The new telegraph operator was thrilled to have Bud's business and he told him if there was a reply, he would deliver it to him at the Bohunk's. After he left the telegraph station Bud went down the street to see MacGregor at his store.

"It's good to see you," MacGregor said when Bud came through his door. "Wondered when you'd be by."

"Here I am. Let's figure out how much I owe you and we can settle up."

"What do you mean?" asked MacGregor. "We don't need to settle up, just leave it where it is. We can adjust the total with trades and future dealings as we always have."

"No. Just for your ears, MacGregor, I'm selling my stock and taking a holiday. So I'll settle up my account."

"You clearing right out of this area? Where the heck are you going to go?"

"Don't rightly know. I'm thinking about visiting my cousin in

Moose Jaw and my sister in Ontario. Then maybe I will travel overseas for a year or so, just to say I went and did something different with my life."

Bud didn't mind stretching the truth to MacGregor. Only the last part of his previous sentence was accurate. He had no intention of visiting anybody. He was bound and determined to head for the West Coast and find passage on a ship headed to some exotic location, maybe to the Orient or the South Seas. It was still an idea hatching in his brain. He already had over fourteen hundred bucks and with the money he would receive from Hill he would have four thousand, four hundred dollars. More than enough for a comfortable retirement.

MacGregor clucked and chuckled when he looked at his ledger. "That last slug of goods I dealt for you to the Indians put you in the hole with me. Before that you were well into the black, but now you're in the red for the princely sum of forty-eight dollars."

"That's a lot of money when you don't have any," Bud said as he took his billfold from his jacket's inside pocket. "Lucky I have it today."

"It's been a pleasure doing business with you, Bud," MacGregor said, lowering his voice as if he was at a funeral.

"Cheer up," Bud replied. "I'm selling my horses to raise some money so I can retire. I'm not dying. Could be in six months I'll be back living in my cabin taking care of me and one horse. Don't really know."

"MacGregor, I have one more thing on my mind. Now you know Suzy is close to my heart. How old is Lucy, now?"

"Och, she's just turned thirteen," McGregor answered.

"Well, I am giving Suzy to Lucy. I want that horse to have the best possible home that she can have. I have a lot of respect for you and your missus. I figure that sweet daughter of yours could use the companionship of a good gentle mare like Suzy. She's easy to ride and docile, no matter the weather. One final thing – I've got a dozen cows, a bull and some heifers up at my place. There's enough hay for them to make it through the winter. If you see Alphonse Pointed Stick this winter, you tell him to go up to my place and help himself to those cows. I'm putting it in writing, MacGregor – you make sure those Indians pick up my cows without nobody bothering them. I'll be back to see you before I leave. I'll drop off Suzy."

MacGregor was somewhat overcome by Bud's news and by his generosity. He promised he'd keep their business and conversation private. Bud told MacGregor he didn't want rumours of his departure to be let out before he had a chance to sell off his stock. That way the buyers wouldn't lowball him.

From MacGregor's store, Bud rode Suzy down the street. He tied her up in front of Armsted's place of business. Bill Armsted was inside his shop fixing some tack. His corral, with a half a dozen big horses in it, was on the edge of town. Armsted had a lifetime of experience looking after the work horses he used to haul heavy loads on his freight wagon. They did their job decked out in Armsted's family harnesses that dated to his grandfather.

"I'll make you a deal, Bill. I'll sell you Old Joe for twenty bucks because he needs a new home."

"He's worth more than that," Armsted said, without looking up from his work.

"Since I got him from your old man when he was a stripling, he might as well go back to a soft heart like you. A man who regards his horses as family. Never mind paying me, Bill. You can have him for nothing. Just do me one favour. When he's too old to work, let him out to graze with your other broken-downs and remember that the twenty dollars you saved is paying for his retirement."

When he landed at the Bohunk's place, Bud decided to have a few beers and eat the blue plate special.

"Antelope that a railway worker shot is what's on the menu tonight," the Bohunk offered.

While Bud was eating, the telegram office man arrived with an answer to his message. It was an effusive document for a telegram: "Hill delighted – stop – Will be private car – stop – Minot Oct 15 – stop – Horses to train corral – stop – F Mouton."

For Bud, the deal was sealed in wax. He'd hang around in Bottineau to clean up his affairs and find a buyer for the horses he had on his pasture. He'd deliver those appaloosas to the train yards in Minot and he'd collect his fee from James Hill. From there, he'd figure out the rest of his life.

In the back of his mind he imagined taking the train to Seattle and booking passage on a sailing ship or steamer heading for unknown adventures. It was always warm and peaceful in his idyllic state of mind. He would travel across an ocean and find a country that could support him in style on the savings he would soon accumulate. He had been lucky living so close to the wind. Now one of his horse deals had become implicated in a murder. Bud had taken in nearly fifteen hundred dollars for his trouble. The money hung uneasily on him like a hair shirt. He was watching his back closely now after his experience with Parmer and Frenchie. Bud expected that it was only a matter of time before the Pinkerton appeared again. He knew all along that he should have disposed of the chestnut gelding when he had the chance. He decided he'd face up to defending himself while his plan unfolded. Now he was forced to pack around his double-barreled Parker as well as his Smith & Wesson.

Bud finished his business in Bottineau with one last stop – Jensen's Livery and Stables. He told Jensen he had some buggy horses and saddle horses for sale if he was interested. He figured the new railway coming in would pick up Jensen's business. Jensen, no fool, told Bud to deliver him four well-trained buggy horses for ten dollars a head and a couple of good young saddle horses for twelve dollars a head. Quigley agreed.

"Jensen, your family is doing well with horses at Devil's Lake. How about you tell your brothers that I'm selling my stud with eight mares and some younger stock for a fair price to a shrewd buyer. They know my horses. I've been told a number of times that the stud I sold McCall is turning out damn good runners. The best. Send somebody up to my place with some money in hand, Jensen, and I'll kick you back ten percent. Send a telegram. You know I have good stock."

"I have someone in mind," he answered, "but I don't have time to talk about it. You staying at the Bohunk's? Let me get back to you."

"A small bird told me you're selling your horses," Gerry said to Bud when he came into the bar and sat down next to him.

"Well, yeah, more or less," Bud offered. "I'm also giving some away."

"Does that mean you'll be moving on?" asked Gerry

"Not really," Bud answered, "I'm taking six months to a year off to visit my family in Ontario. Then I'll wander back here and start over again at my place, maybe with a horse, a few chickens, a dog and a fishing pole."

"A railway fellow about your age dropped dead the other day while he was driving his team down Main Street," Gerry said. "But we wasn't carved out of the same granite as you, Bud."

"Don't wonder," said Bud. "I'm a lot older than you know. My days are armchair from here on in. Hear anything more about that bank robbery and shooting in Bismarck last spring?" For some reason Bud couldn't resist bringing up the robbery.

"There's a rumour going around that the slug that killed that banker came from an Enfield cartridge casing. Heard it from those two blackbirds who used to scout for the Pinkertons. That's what the North-West Mounted Police use and that Dubois fellow suspects the killer is a rogue Mountie."

"Gerry, isn't that a pretty common weapon around here?"

"Ya, I've seen a lot of Enfields over the years."

"So, isn't that a bit of a stretch?" Bud asked.

"It's way out there, all right," Gerry answered

The next day, Bud was sitting on a chair in front the Bohunk's place when Lars Jensen turned up with a man in a tweed jacket, smoking a cigar.

"Quigley I want you to meet my friend, Mr. Ross. He buys horses for the railway," said Jensen.

"And I have horses for sale," Bud replied. "But maybe not the kind of horses somebody building a railway would need."

"On the other hand," Ross said, cutting in, "I'm looking for really top notch breeding stock. I'm not buying horses to work for the railway. I'm always on the look-out for good horses for my employer who has one of the finest horse ranches on the continent."

"Who would that be?" Bud asked.

"I'm the engineering superintendent for the Great Northern Railway."

"How lucky for you," said Bud. "This is your day."

"What does that mean?"

"I'm currently in the middle of a business deal with your owner. He is purchasing from me a half dozen of the finest snowflake appaloosas in the land for a premium price. I'll be meeting him in Minot in mid-October."

"You're a friend of Mr. Hill?"

"No, only met the man once for a few days. Put me down as an acquaintance he's eager to see. I suggest you may choose to contact my dear friend, Florence Mouton, Mr. James's go-to-it ass-kicker when he's on the road. Here's your opportunity to shine."

"I have had some dealings with Florence Mouton," said Ross. "She's a firecracker nobody wants to go off."

"Not to me," Bud said, "I'm a horny matchstick. I'd like to see her go off."

"What can we do about it?" Ross asked.

"Either way you want it sliced. You can have Lars here tell you how good my horses are, or do yourself a favour and look them over yourself. Line them up for the boss. Flo told me he has a mansion full of eligible daughters. When he hears what a shrewd operator you are you'll be dancing with one of them. Make up your mind soon, because I'll be in Minot on the appointed day and I'll cut my own deal."

"One way or the other, you'll hear from me before then," Ross said.

I can't understand my luck, Bud thought. *Of course! James is an all-round horse connoisseur and I have another significant asset in my pasture. If I act wisely, maybe I can score another grand.*

Suddenly he had a twinge of regret. It was the damn chestnut gelding that kept popping up in his mind like a reminder that nobody's perfect.

"One more thing, Lars," Bud said, "I need a couple of hands to help me move six horses from my place to Minot. I want them to arrive on the 11th. We'll drive the horses down on the 12th and the 13th. I'm paying a dollar a day plus food and a hotel in Minot and two bucks for the return trip to Bottineau."

"How about my son, Lars Jr., and Kenny, the Wilson kid? They work with me all the time and they're good with horses," Lars said.

"Okay," Bud told him, "I trust you'll make it happen."

Bud was certain most of his loose ends had been tied off when he lit out of Bottineau on Suzy's back for the long ride home. The weather was still good and he was beginning to think they were having an Indian summer. The leaves were only half-turned and there hadn't been any cold weather of note, although it was frosty some nights.

On the 11th of the month, young Lars Jr. and his friend Kenny turned up just as Lars Jensen promised. Bud took them out to look in his corral.

"Wow, handsome horses," Lars Jr. said. "I've never seen a group of appaloosas as choice as these. I've seen Indians riding them sometimes, but nothing like these beauties"

"Listen young fellows, I have a deal for you two. I'm pulling out next month and I have need of a couple of employees who will work for me when I'm away from this territory. I have twenty bucks apiece for you fellows if you come stay at my place and feed and water the cattle I pasture a few miles from my cabin. I need you to look after them until the Indians I promised them to show up. It might be a month or two before they arrive. After that job is done I'd appreciate it if you'd ride up from Bottineau from time to time and keep an eye on my joint. It's a good place to go moose hunting if you have a hankering. Certain months you can shoot 'em from my cabin door."

Bud said he'd be away the better part of a year. In truth, he didn't know if he was ever going to return. At least with these two looking in on his cabin there'd be something to return to. Besides it was good policy to let people think he was only taking a trip.

The two boys were adept at handling the stock and without much bother they helped him deliver the seven snowflake appaloosas to the Minot stockyards at the new railway station early on the 14th of October, 1894. Bud and the boys checked into the Leland Hotel where Bud treated them to a steak and egg breakfast at the Morning Room in the middle of the afternoon.

"That's the beauty about a wide-open town," he said. "Breakfast is twenty-four hours a day and so's everything else."

Bud had promised Jensen that he'd keep Lars Jr. and Kenny out of trouble in the bright, tempting lights of downtown Minot. True to his word, the next morning he paid them off and watched them ride out of town.

Late that afternoon, the desk clerk at the Leland Hotel called out to Bud when he walked through the lobby. "I have a message for you, sir, from a Miss Mouton. She wants you to go right over to Mr. James's private car on the siding in the rail yards. They arrived this afternoon."

When he climbed up the step onto the Manitoba, Bud was greeted by the steward who offered to take his coat and hat.

"Sir, go right in. Miss Mouton and Mr. Hill are waiting for you and are hopeful you will be able to stay for dinner."

143

"Well, sir, a pleasure," Hill said as he stood up from the table when Bud entered. "Of course you know Florence, my angel on the road."

Florence, with her hair up into the clouds, was wearing an absolutely stunning low-cut, pink dress with pearl earrings and two strands of pearls around her neck. She bussed Bud on both cheeks.

"You, sir, have turned out to be a gem. I must apologize for my skepticism when we first met. Obviously, I made a mistake, dear fellow, in doubting your veracity. I will make it up to you, I assure you," she said, smiling at him.

"I, too, must offer my congratulations at your straight-ahead way of doing business, Mr. Quigley, is it? You've delivered the goods. I have examined the horses – they are a splendid group of animals. Not only that, but you brought me a lucky seventh pony and he is a magnificent stud. Bud, if I may call you by your first name – you must call me Jim as all my close friends do – you're welcome to bunk here in the Manitoba with Flo and myself while our business deal is completed. You're a friend of the firm. I have taken the liberty of paying your hotel bill and having your goods delivered to my private car from your room at the Leland. Now, if you've a mind, we'll adjourn to the lounge and enjoy some aperitifs before dinner is served. I hope you like East Coast lobsters. They're a passion of mine. I believe we'll also be dining on a saddle of venison with juniper berries and on some butterflied quail that will be prepared in an out-of-this-world Cuban sauce."

"Never had a lobster before," Bud replied.

"Well now is the time," Hill answered as his steward poured Bud a double of Manitoba moonshine on the rocks. "Let me introduce you to my chef, Henry Lafleur. Henry, I would like to present tonight's other diner, Bud Quigley – a horse expert and a rather interesting raconteur about that subject."

Chef Lafleur bowed a little to Bud and chuckled that he always enjoyed meeting and cooking for Mr. Hill's friends.

To lead off, they had a bowl of turtle soup, then an appetizer of oysters on the half shell followed by a chili-pepper-infused spot-prawn salad served on a bed of shaved ice. The steward used a sword to slash the cork from a champagne bottle. They toasted as the precious liquid spilled over their glasses onto the floor. No matter, towels appeared and the steward opened several additional bottles. Bud was captivated by the delicious flavour of the lobsters. Florence instructed him as how to pry the meat away from the shells. He polished off three two-pounders while ignoring most of the other entrees.

"You have the hearty appetite of the outdoors man, that's for sure," Florence said, as she urged Bud to try the crispy quail in their "divine Latin sauce."

When they had finished the entire repast, they decided to hold dessert for a later hour.

Hill called for more whisky. "Let's get stinking drunk. This is a banner day. These horses you have brought me, Quigley, are going to be a present to the future King of England. The man who has always wanted everything will soon have it," Hill said with a long hearty laugh while cigar smoke was expelled from his nostrils in two great streams.

"We'll talk about business tomorrow – nothing tawdry to spoil the ambience of the evening. I have a delight for us – I brought along a quartet of European musicians. They will perform for us while we are having our dessert, cheese plate and liquors, and then coffee and cigars. I will break the rules a little and enjoy my cigar all the time. With Miss Mouton's approval."

"Why, yes, James," Florence answered. "I would be delighted if you would smoke. I adore the ambience of the Cuban leaf."

I must have died and gone to heaven, Bud thought.

Before the music started, Florence had Lamont, the steward, and his assistant pull the shades down on the windows and turn the gas lamps low, so that the room took on the ambience of a theatre. The steward then arrived with Miss Mouton's hookah, which he set up on the table in front of the couch she and Bud were sitting on.

"Bud, you're going to love smoking a bowl of Mexican tobacco. James and I find it a delight in the evenings while we are listening to these exquisite musicians."

She and Bud and James indulged themselves and the evening mellowed while the chamber music played under a clear sky full of stars over the Manitoba, parked on a siding in Minot, North Dakota.

Late in the evening, Hill passed out and was helped into his bedroom by Lamont and his assistant. The musicians retired from the room.

"You may consider yourselves off duty now," Florence said to the two servers in white coats. "I will be looking after Mr. Quigley myself."

Bud sat up drinking liquor with Flo Mouton and smoking from her deluxe hookah that made his head swim with lovely fish. He couldn't stop smiling until his cheeks hurt. Soon they were cuddling under the silk sheets in her private boudoir at the back of the car.

Somewhere in the night Bud told Florence about his dream of travelling to an exotic land where he could vanish for a year or two finding new adventures. He told her about how he dreamed of going to sea, how he longed for new shores to explore before he grew too old. He was tired of living alone. He wanted to find a new purpose for life.

"I conjure up white sand with palm trees, turquoise water and the billowing sails on the ships that pass by. There's nobody to stop me from doing just what I like, which is nothing. Once in a while I catch some fish or spear a pig and throw a party for the locals, who go stiff on my home-brewed beer. Is that too crazy an ambition? I'm a simple man."

She understood completely. "Bud, I don't see why it can't happen. But now let's get down to it while we have the chance." She slipped the pink silk over her head and pulled Bud to her more than ample bosom.

The next morning, Bud and Flo ate croissants and wild strawberries and drank coffee while they waited for Henry Lafleur to prepare their poached eggs and kippers. Jim, as Bud took to calling Mr. Hill, had taken a quick trip into Minot to meet some business associates for breakfast at the Leland House. In the afternoon he was back, dressed in a smart suit and a top hat. He excused himself and asked Flo Mouton if she could confer with him privately for a moment in his office at the far end of the Manitoba.

When they returned, Hill said, "Bud, let's talk about our deal. I offered you five hundred bucks a piece for six prime appaloosa horses. You gave me a discourse on the breed. A few months later you returned with seven horses, each one a magnificent animal. To my reckoning, in an often disappointing world that makes you an astute businessman, a man after my own heart. I have instructed Florence to pay you the tidy sum of three thousand five hundred dollars from my private safe. We have also received a rather detailed report from our Mr. Ross who is engineering superintendent for this section of the railway. He tells me that his experts, the Jensens from Devil's Lake, say that you are a champion horse breeder. To that end he has put a value of an additional fifteen hundred dollars on your herd, which we would be pleased to acquire for our ranching operation in Minnesota. If that is agreeable to you, I will have my employee send some wranglers out to your place to round up the horses.

"Bud, that ups your total to five thousand dollars. Miss Mouton has suggested another reward that I am considering granting. However, you must stay one more night with us and I will see what morning brings in the way of information. In the meantime, we are having a small soirée this evening with some of the local nobs and the staff who work for me in Minot. You are welcome to continue celebrating with us. Tomorrow morning, your choice herd of appaloosas will be in a livestock car on their way to Saint Paul. Shortly thereafter, my private car will be hooked on to a train and Flo and I will be headed to Seattle. We have important business there."

Guests began to arrive late in the afternoon and Bud joined the party, making the acquaintance of several of Mr. James's friends and associates. Ross arrived, already three sheets to the wind. Hill was pretty wound up about his railway's soon-to-come one-year anniversary of linking Seattle by rail to Saint Paul. He waxed on effusively about the numerous new business enterprises he was opening in the Pacific Northwest and the robust economic atmosphere that was evident there.

"Now that my railway has reached the West Coast, I am bound and determined to build a seafaring empire. The next step is to build a far-reaching trading network that will connect my Great Lakes shipping ventures with my railway and a fleet of steamers travelling to the Orient."

When he was tired of listening to his own voice, Hill turned his attention to his guests. Henry Lafleur's food lived up to his reputation, to which Hill referred after every course. Champagne flowed over a tall pyramid of glasses in the sumptuous surroundings. Hill was joined by two athletic blondes from the bordello in Minot who spent the evening fawning over him. Just before midnight, when Hill shooed the last of his guests away, he took to his private boudoir with the golden-haired ones while Bud and Florence sat naked on the bed in her boudoir and smoked the hookah until long after dawn.

In the late morning Jim, fresh as a daisy in his silk bathrobe, invited Bud to sit down with him for a cup of Indonesian coffee. "I have a surprise," he said. "In this envelope I'm holding I have a pass for you which allows you to travel on my railway without charge in perpetuity. It also holds a letter of passage which entitles the bearer, Bud Quigley, to return passage on any Empress ship bound for the Orient from Vancouver. You just have to show it to the shipping authorities a few days before the ship sails. I am also including a schedule of the next three months' sailings. Bud, I have extensive business contacts in the Orient. I have given you a letter of introduction and some important names and addresses in various seaports and capitals. I have asked my friends and associates to treat you as they would one of my family members."

"Here's your money," Florence said as she handed Bud a small valise. "A couple of railway guards will ensure that you leave Minot untroubled by any thugs."

"No thanks," Bud answered. "I don't relish the attention. I'm riding home with Mr. Parker across my saddle."

"Bud," Hill said, "you have given me the means to woo a future king with a priceless gift that is so stunning it can't help but astonish him and win his friendship. In return, I'm giving you the adventure and freedom you desire. One man does for another. Now get the hell out of here, so Flo and I can leave for Seattle. There's going to be a brass band waiting for me there."

15

BY THE TIME HE HAD TAKEN THE TRAIN from Brandon to report for duty back in Regina at the North-West Mounted Police barracks on July 15th, 1894, Les had spent enough solitary hours of thinking to help him clarify his situation. He would go back to work and deal with the sensitive issue of having completed his leave and then declining to re-enlist after all.

He expected the brass would be annoyed and that his last few months in the Force would become a drudgery of harsh duty and estrangement. He prepared for the encounter by staying in good cheer and remaining in a positive mood. His terms of enlistment were up on the 15th of November, which meant he had only four months to go before he was a free man.

Les was worried about timing. He replayed the robbery and the awful memory of the killing in his mind until the only way he could handle it was by remembering he left a sack of money buried in a shallow hole in the ground under a pile of rocks. Upon reflection, he had trouble understanding the decision he made when he buried the money. The problem was that on his run back to Canada, the bulky sacks of cash tied across his horse's withers had weighed on his mind. The chestnut had been wounded and he was uncertain how far it would travel before it broke down. His packhorse had come up lame. He had fretted that before long he might be making his way on shanks' pony.

Les panicked under the pressure. He kept imagining himself on foot, sinking out of sight under the load he was carrying. In the grip of trepidation, he made the decision to bury the money and fly for the border.

Les had been rattled, and had made a rash decision that was to weigh heavily on his future. A gnawing in his being had convinced him that although he couldn't see it, danger was lurking in every shadow. That sense of anticipation prickled on his skin. He persuaded himself that, after recovering the money, it would be wise to travel overseas as quickly as possible.

Murder, he thought, *is something they never give up on.*

Another sense of foreboding occurred as the weather started to change and he realized winter would soon be showing up on the plains. Not just any winter either, but the winter of howling winds and minus-forty-degree weather when travel was difficult as well as being wickedly dangerous. He figured that he would have to dig up his money before the end of November or he might as well wait until spring turned again on the prairies.

All the instincts he possessed warned him that waiting for spring would be a gamble that would increase the odds he would be caught. He was driven by the thought that, if it worked out, he might be free and easy with forty-four thousand dollars – enough for any man. He decided that, without fail, he would pluck his money from that hole in the ground before it was locked in by the concrete frost. By the coming of spring he expected to be five thousand miles away and still travelling.

Les was greatly relieved when crusty Sergeant Major Robert Belcher called him in to his office.

"Laddie, you're in luck. You're to report to Staff Sergeant Bruce and work with him and his horses while he puts the lads through their paces. At least that's where you're going until further notice."

For the next four weeks Les immersed himself in his duties in the stables, helping Bruce. He watched the new recruits around the horses. Before long he had a pretty good idea as to their characters as they improved their skills.

Bruce was a master who wanted everything done by the book.

"When you find yourself in an emergency, doing things automatically because you have the training miles under your belt, you'll be thanking me for driving you. You better take care of that which is currently between your legs, if you know what's good for you," Bruce said in his own sarcastic manner to the recruits who were mounted in front of him. "Otherwise you're liable to find yourself alone in the wilderness without a friend. Depending on the circumstance, if you give your horse his head he'll lead you to water or carry you to safety in a storm. If you treat him well, he'll stand by you if you're injured. Otherwise, he'll take off and leave you to fend for yourself. At the end of the day you must put your horse's needs before your own."

One afternoon after lunch, Les was ordered to the commissioner's office.

"Simpson, yes, come right in. I won't beat about it, Simpson. We're rather surprised to find that you have changed your mind. Now, you don't intend to re-enlist for a further three-year extension? This is not what we expected when we granted you your previous leave."

"Yes sir," Les replied. "Then, I fully intended to re-enlist. Unfortunately, my widowed mother is failing badly and is unable to attend properly to my five younger siblings in Brandon. My trip home has only proven to me that I must return as quickly as possible to take over the day-to-day care of my family. My mother is in need of rest. I'm afraid my brothers are turning hard without me there to bring them up. I've seen serious signs, sir. I will be leaving the Force and going into business in Brandon so that I can devote myself to supporting my family."

"I see," said Commissioner Herchmer. "If it's any consolation to you, Simpson, we regard you as a very decent bloke and proficient member of the Force. On your re-enlistment we were going to promote you to corporal. Staff Sergeant Bruce has a high opinion of your riding skills and the talent you have with horses. He requested we put you under his auspices to take advantage of your gifts. He thought it a way for you to move ahead in the Force."

"Thank you, sir, for all your considerations," Les said.

"Now that we fully comprehend your situation I commend you for your devotion to your family. It must be hard to be here full-time when the home front is threatened. Here's an idea for you. Should your mother's health improve, and your circumstances change, and should you desire to re-enlist again, you will be welcomed back. I can guarantee that you will be returned in the rank of corporal. Is that understood? Further to that, I will recommend that you be transferred into the equine section."

"Yes sir. Very decent of you, sir."

"Not at all constable. I'll add your mother's name...what is it?"

"Mary, sir."

"I'll add your mother's name to my prayer list," Herchmer said, marking it down on a sheet of paper.

When he left the commissioner's office, Les was shaking like a leaf in the wind. He could not understand why. The dressing down he was dreading had not happened. The sergeant major had chirped at him in his Scottish brogue and made a few disparaging comments, but Les knew that was the man's way of saying everything was in order. He reported to Staff Sergeant Bruce, who put him back on duty as "stable orderly." He made sure the stalls were cleaned out, horses fed and watered, and that each received a nosebag morning and afternoon. He supervised the recruits in caring for the horses until it was time to go off duty when the night guard turned out.

On September 1st, Les was called to the sergeant major's office, where he was ordered to spend the rest of his enlistment policing in Regina. He would work out of the smallish frame station that was located two miles from the barracks, but was connected by a telephone wire. Les and two other constables, under the direction of a corporal, would greet important passengers coming in on the train, and convey telegrams and packages to headquarters. Their presence on the streets was meant to convince the locals that they were being protected.

Les knew he was being shunted out of the way. When he returned from leave he had expected to be transferred down south to finish his service in one of the out-of-the-way border posts. Not many constables relished the post in the middle of Regina. It was largely a thankless job. However, there was one benefit. At least he could stretch his legs there, free of being ordered about when he made the rounds. The town was dry. With the massive presence of the North-West Mounted Police headquarters in its midst, it was hardly a wild atmosphere.

Late in September, Les and another constable, named Jimmy Scoggin, were ordered to meet two government officials who were coming in on the afternoon train. They were advised to have these important men picked up by wagon at the station and have them driven to the Windsor Hotel at Broad and Tenth.

After completing this duty, Les noticed two tough-looking men standing on the boardwalk talking with Charlie Howson, who owned the hotel. There was a lot of guffawing and laughing coming out of Charlie, who seemed to be half-cut most of the time. The other two were so focused in their intensity that they attracted Les's attention. The peculiar-shaped man wearing a bowler hat had a long body and short legs that were draped in a enormous, grey full-length coat that touched the ground. When the man turned and looked in Les's direction, in an unfocused stare at the general activity in the street, Les shivered. He could not escape noticing the cold-blooded eyes and the somewhat lopsided, damaged face that was evident, even under the bristly beard. The other man was tall and thick as tree trunk under a wild thatch of grey hair that stuck out from under a stylish, tweed deerstalker cap. He had the look of a man in his middle spread who could still take care of himself. A teddy bear of a man with an iron core.

When Howson saw Les and Scoggin, he left his friends on the boardwalk and invited them into the hotel for a few minutes because he wanted to report some thieving that had been going on. The wagon had yet to leave.

"The gentlemen I was talking with are looking for a lift over to Wardell's," he said to the driver. "Do you mind dropping them off on South Railway Street and then coming back for these two constables I am going to be having a coffee with?"

Les and Jimmy walked into the hotel lobby while Howson helped the two men up onto the wagon seat behind the driver. When he walked back in, he asked Ed the desk man to go and fetch three cups of java.

"A pair of Yankee dudes," he said, "trying to pass themselves off as business travellers. First thing is there's no business around here for anybody to travel to. Secondly, they were armed to the teeth when they arrived. Rumour says they're Pinkerton detectives up here to talk to your bosses. I have nothing against them; their money is as good as the next man's. Which reminds me. Somebody stole the cigar store Indian right off my front doorstep. Now maybe you boys making your rounds will recover it for me. It was a real fine piece of artwork I bought from a drummer from Toronto who came through here three months ago. My customers are used to Wooden Head, and are wondering where he went. I have a hankering to get him back."

When the wagon returned, Scoggin and Les climbed back up for the ride to the station. By now, Les's mind was working overtime. He had been badly spooked when Howson shot off his mouth about the two men on the boardwalk.

Scoggin looked at Les and lit the hand-rolled cigarette between his lips.

"They're probably up here on railway business. I saw a couple that could have been mates to that pair up here a few years back, investigating crooked railway workers. Real hard cases they were, rather settle things with brass knuckles than talk about it. If you ask me, they're going over to Wardell's now, to have a workout in the cathouse upstairs. Did you see the hands on that grey bloke? They were as big as hams."

Les said nothing.

They're on a fishing trip, he thought. Now he was certain it was imperative he bide his time carefully and make a quick move when his duty to the Mounted Police was up. The rest of the day he played a number of scenarios over again until finally he decided Scoggin was right. However, in the middle of a night of tossing and turning, Les suddenly sat up in bed. They were after him, he was certain. They had travelled all the way to Regina from below the border. It was only a matter of time before he would run into them under different circumstances.

Murder, he thought. *They will never quit.* In a moment of panic he briefly considered making a run for it, but reason won out. *How could they know? There were no witnesses at the bank. My face was completely covered when I made that wild ride out of Bismarck. The horse? Maybe Quigley became soft in the head and failed to eliminate the chestnut and it turned up somewhere. And even if Quigley had ratted me out, he didn't even know my name or where I came from. They're guessing.*

A week later, when he and Scoggin were patrolling in Howson's neighbourhood, Howson told them that, by magic, his cigar store Indian had returned on its own.

"Maybe he went to a powwow!" Scoggin said, convulsing in fits of laughter.

"All's well that ends well," Howson answered.

"Still have your beefy detectives on the premises?" Les asked.

"No, those fellows cleared off. They hung around like deep shadows for ten days and then they left in a big hurry. Guess maybe they had business elsewhere."

"Bet that big cigar store Indian of yours could have kicked their asses," Les said for no particular reason.

On his rounds with Scoggin, Les talked about what he was

going to do in the last few weeks of duty. He told Scoggin he was looking to buy a saddle and some gear and a good solid horse to ride home to Brandon, if he could find the right deal. The livery stable had some nags and there were a few horses for sale around town, but nothing to write home about.

"I know a fellow you might want to meet," Scoggin said when he came on the afternoon shift. "I met him at the train station last night when I was on duty there. He seems a decent fellow but he's in a bind. He's staying over at the Lansdown Hotel. This afternoon, when we're out on South Railway, we should go over and have a chat with him."

It was just as Jimmy said it would be. The man's name was Garth Templeton, a cowboy. He suggested they accompany him down the street to the stable where he was boarding his horse. Templeton had ridden to Regina from Moose Jaw. He was in a rush to catch the train to Vancouver. He was willing to sell the horse, a six-year-old bay gelding that he swore by, plus his saddle, tack, saddle bags and a Martini-Henry .450 rifle, for the right price.

"What do you think is fair?" Les asked.

"Well, you have me in a bind, that's for sure. I'm eager to travel to the coast, not certain I'm coming back."

"Twenty-five bucks," Les said.

"I'm in love," the guy blurted out. "My sweetheart has moved to Victoria to look after her ailing grandmother. I miss her so much."

"Sorry," Les answered.

"What about the rest? I also own a packhorse and winter camping gear."

"Thirty-five for the whole shooting match."

"Done."

Afterwards, Les spoke with the stable owner about boarding the horses and taking care of his gear until he left the Force. Les and Jimmy continued on their rounds. Jimmy thought Les had made a good deal. Les thanked him and said that he needed to make a profit when he resold the horses in Brandon when he returned home. That was pretty well the end of it.

In the ensuing days, Les made a few careful purchases in the general store, buying some cartridges for the Martini-Henry, a small pick, a double-bladed axe and a folding shovel. Down the street on another day he bought boots, mittens, gloves and a hat with earflaps. He also purchased two large, waterproof canvas bags. He delivered these items to the stable and added them to his collection. When his contract was up, Les would load everything on the pack animal with some food, saddle the bay and reclaim the money he now regretted burying over the U.S. border.

On the 1st of November, two weeks before his date of departure from the service, he was called back to the barracks to take up his former position as stable orderly. Les was leaving the Force. Men who were departing because their term was over often felt something slip in the face of group politics. Perhaps the men who were remaining caused the feeling of disinterest that settled into former long-term relationships which were now quietly falling apart as new alliances were being formed. Les was leaving, he wasn't planning to stay in touch with any of his colleagues. Unlike some who loved the camaraderie and friendships they found in the North-West Mounted Police and called it the greatest days of their lives, Les considered it a job and not much more.

He calmed himself in the final days with the thought that soon he would be difficult to find. Not so much different than many of the others before him who had served their contracts and now wanted their lives back for a different purpose. Just the same, he was different and he knew it. He looked over his shoulder, wondering if anybody was on to him. He still had the twenty-second reminder of the murder he committed lurking from time-to-time in his psyche. The sight of Pinkertons standing on the boardwalk in Regina had taken him by surprise and scared him.

16

WHEN THEY ARRIVED IN MINOT from their arduous trail rides to Regina and back, Smith and Dubois were elated by the news that greeted them. The campaign to find the chestnut gelding had returned positive results. A telegraph had been sent from Helena, Montana, where a man claimed to have information about the wanted chestnut gelding with three white socks and a wound on its right buttock. He was anxious to find out how much the reward was going to be. Harold Moss, with enough cash in his pocket to pay the hundred-dollar reward and buy the horse, had travelled to Helena to interview the reward claimant.

Moss reported that the claimant was a gospel-reciting card sharp by the name of Reverend Jeremiah Bigalow, who had sold the chestnut to a local horse dealer. When Moss reached the dealer's corral to examine the horse he realized it was a perfect match to the description of the getaway horse.

What was even more interesting was the story that Bigalow spun about how he acquired the animal. He claimed to have purchased the horse from a man named Quigley who resided over the Canadian border. Bigalow had arrived in Bottineau with a pair of wagon horses that were in pretty bad shape. Some locals there directed him north to Quigley, who they claimed had well-trained wagon-pulling stock. They also intimated that Quigley was far easier to deal with than the local horse flesh peddler.

Moss went on to relate more of the story. Bigalow claimed to have acquired the chestnut by making the services of one of two chippies he was travelling with available. These women left him when they hit the environs of Helena and went to work for Big Mike Hammond in his whorehouse in the middle of town. Bigalow said that, at first, the chestnut was one solid colour but, as the miles began to pass and the longer it splashed through puddles and creeks, the more obvious it became that the animal was developing three white socks above its hooves. Later he noticed a scar on the rump that was also becoming more distinct as time went on.

Moss took Bigalow's statement in writing and had him sign it. He paid Bigalow, who was down on his luck, fifty dollars – half the reward money the First National Bank had offered. He used five dollars of the money left over to acquire the animal from the livery stable that had purchased the horse from Bigalow. The owner wanted no trouble. He reacted in a distressed fashion when Moss went as far as suggesting that the horse had been stolen in the first place and wondering if anybody had a bill of sale. Moss assured the stable owner that, if he provided the horse to the Pinkertons at a decent price, the matter of him buying a questionable horse would be forgotten. Thus, Moss made himself a tidy profit on both deals before he turned up in Minot, where he stabled the chestnut and waited for Jiggs Dubois and Balfour Smith's return.

The chestnut was skittish around Dubois, who was tracing the bullet wound on the animal's rump with his gloved fingers.

"See how the bullet just grooved his ass, Balfour," Dubois commented.

Just then the horse backed up, sidled to the right and squeezed Dubois into the side of the stall.

"Son of a bitch," he said as he extricated himself. "There's no doubt this is the nag. You've done a good job, Moss. Now we'll see what that lying bastard Quigley has to say for himself."

Dubois and Smith had studied the information gleaned by the Regina agents and had put together a list of ten possible robbery suspects which they sent on to Roger Filbert. Filbert would analyze the data with his experts and arrive in Minot on the train from the West Coast in four days. In addition, Filbert had promised to have somebody from the U.S. Marshal's office on hand to view the progress they were making on the case. Before the meeting, Dubois decided that he, Smith and Moss had time to take a trip to Quigley's place to confront him with their findings.

"Maybe when we put the bastard under pressure he'll fold and just give us the name," Smith suggested.

"And we'll have a suspect gold-plated for Filbert," Dubois said.

"What's this Quigley like?" Moss asked.

"Well, he's no gunman, that's for sure. I'd say he can handle himself, but he's a wrangler, not a gunslinger. He has a stubborn side, though, and he jumps on his high horse pretty fast."

"Do we need reinforcements?"

"Jeez, Balfour, there's three of us and we're all probably twenty years younger than him. If it takes more than the three of us I'd say we should resign from this occupation. Let's gather our gear together and hit the road. We'll surprise him when he sets eyes on the chestnut and knows the game is up."

"Yeah, he'll save his own skin and give up the shooter." Moss figured. "But what's he really done wrong, except play around in a shady manner in the horse business? That's a huge pastime for a lot of people in this territory. My guess is he'll hand over a name as long as it stops his ox from being gored."

"Well said," Smith offered.

Smith, Moss and Dubois were in a good mood on the trip up to the northern border country. When they arrived at Swedes' Ferry, they found the twins to be rather uncommunicative. They showed them the chestnut but neither brother could remember if that was the particular horse they spotted in spring when the gunman crossed the Mouse River on their ferry. They decided it would be a waste of time to bother cutting Gerry, the law in Bottineau, in on their adventure.

"He ain't wearing a pair of balls when it comes to police work," Jiggs sneered in disgust. "We'll bypass Bottineau on the way up and stop there on the return trip. Then we can fill Gerry Do Nothing in on our investigation and let him know the U.S. Marshal might be headed his way in the near future.

⁕

When Quigley returned from his eventful meeting with James Hill, he was higher than a kite. His tidy fourteen-hundred-dollar nest egg had now grown to over six thousand dollars, more than enough money for him to live on for the rest of his life. He also had the train pass and the letter that authorized his travel by ship to the Orient. He had studied the sailing schedule he was given by Hill and made up his mind that he would be in Vancouver at the end of November so he could ship out on the *Empress of Japan*, scheduled to depart on December 4th. He took a final ride down to Bottineau, where he left Suzy with MacGregor, dropped off Old Joe at Armsted's and delivered the horses Jensen bought for his stable. Jensen was happy to see Bud when he received the one-hundred-and-fifty-dollar fee for being the middleman in his horse deal with Hill.

On the ride back to his cabin he decided he would not leave until Ross's men showed up to round up his mares and the stud and the young horses that were still up in his pasture. Once that was done, he was free of his obligations. He would saddle up the last horse he had on the place – a dun that he kept in the corral beside his cabin – and ride to Minot and catch the train to Seattle. He'd park the nag at the stables in Minot for the afternoon, then leave him there when he boarded the train for the coast. Now all he had to do was guard his money and prepare himself for the new world he was about to enter.

Bud saw them in his mind before he set his eyes on them. It

was mid-morning and the sun was burning the mist off the fields beside his cabin, as it often did this time of year. He was trying to concentrate on the details of his final trip out of this country. For some reason, Bud felt uneasy about the way the morning was unfolding. When he saw the tiny, dark, insect-like figures far in the distance approaching his place, Bud felt some relief. It was undoubtedly Ross's men who had come for Hill's horses. However, when they reached a certain distance, he recoiled in shock. He had seen that same shape astride a horse, once, a few months before. It was the unmistakable figure of the hunched-up Pinkerton, badly riding his Hanover over the uneven ground. He was accompanied by two other riders.

Bud hustled into his cabin and grabbed the Smith & Wesson and tucked it under his belt. Then he opened a box of shells for the Parker and spread them around in the pockets of his jacket and pants so they were handy to reach. Finally, he bolted out the door and jogged around to the back so he could get the drop on the men who were approaching. They were bunched in a small knot, moving almost imperceptibly closer as the minutes passed by. He checked the bushline all around in case there were out-riders, like the last time the Pinkerton arrived at his abode. This time they were coming straight in.

They stopped when they were within about forty feet of Bud's cabin. Dubois and Smith climbed down off their horses. Moss, who was leading the chestnut, stayed aboard his ride.

"Quigley, are you home?" Dubois bellowed.

Silence echoed in the yard. Everything was still as stone.

Finally, Moss punctuated the air by unloosing his own voice. "It's obvious he's not here," he said, loud enough for the others to hear.

"Yes he is," said Bud, stepping out from behind the cabin holding Mr. Parker in the ready position.

"Well, well," said Jiggs, "not in a very friendly mood, are we?"

"Not hardly," said Bud. "Might have something to do with

those two scum you brought up here in the summer. After you left, they came back and behaved in a disgusting manner. In fact their behavior was so bad it put me off Pinkertons forever – including you, Dubois. You'll have to pardon Mr. Parker, he has two barrels loaded for bear. I'll keep him handy with an eye on you three fellas while you state your business. If I was you, I wouldn't make any quick motions on account of Mr. Parker's hair-trigger personality and my twitchy fingers."

"Sorry to hear about that Quigley. I had to terminate Parmer and Frenchie because of their bad manners and unsavoury characters. I had no knowledge of their activities after they left my employ. So I can hardly be held responsible for them."

"On the contrary, Dubois. I hold you responsible for their very existence. You invented them and empowered them to do your bidding so they are your responsibility. Fortunately, I was able to send them on a long trip into unfamiliar country. It's a story that will have to wait for another time."

"As I said, I am sorry if they were obnoxious," Dubois answered.

"You there on the dandy grey. I would advise you to carefully dismount in Mr. Parker's presence. Join your friends here on the ground where I can keep an eye on you."

"Listen, we have something to show you," Dubois interjected as Moss carefully dismounted.

Moss took a step away from the grey. He led the chestnut forward toward Bud. He tied the halter rope on the hitching rail in front of the cabin and walked slowly back to join Dubois and Smith.

"So, here's the famous chestnut gelding with three white socks and shot up rump that you claimed to have no knowledge of," Dubois said. "Seems a reverend card sharp in Helena, Montana, purchased this animal from you, Quigley, in July when he was headed west with a couple of young ladies. Moss here travelled down to Helena and took his sworn statement, which will soon be handed over to the U.S. Marshal's North Dakota office."

"As far as we know, the worst thing you done was buy a wounded horse without a bill of sale and sell it to someone else without a bill of sale," Balfour Smith added. "If you were to give us the name of whoever you acquired the chestnut from, why we might just forget the rest of it."

Then Jiggs Dubois made one of the most unfortunate statements he would utter in his entire history as a Pinkerton detective. He tweaked his moustache and sniffed his own hand that was covered by a greasy glovelet.

"You must be a rich man, Quigley. Only a rich man would sell a horse for a piece of ass!"

Bud, brandishing his Parker, walked over to the chestnut, put the business end of the gun to its head, calmly cocked one hammer and pulled the trigger, blowing away its brain. The horse went down like a tub of shit in a thunderstorm. The sound of the Parker frightened the three men, who were totally taken by surprise. They stood with their mouths gaping like fish starving for water. The gelding's hind legs made a circular motion in the dust, just like a wounded frog, for about thirty seconds, until it became still. The thirsty dust quietly absorbed the pool of blood.

"Now the first one of you fellows who even twitches will be joining old hay bags here on his last ride. I have one barrel left. If you ask for it, you'll all die a most horrible slow gut-shot death."

"You, Jiggsy boy," Bud said, with his eyes narrowed into slits aimed at the bristling face. "You take your coat off and then you carefully, with your fingertips, drop those Merwin-Hulberts into the dust and kick them gently in my direction. Then sit down with your hands behind your head."

After that was accomplished, he invited Moss and Smith to undertake the same procedure. When they were all seated on the ground, unarmed, with their hands behind their heads, Bud broke the Parker in half, ejected the spent shell and reloaded the empty barrel.

"Now, gentlemen," he said, "you're all detectives and I assume you would not leave home without your handcuffs. So, one by one, starting with you Dubois, I want you to fetch your handcuffs with one hand. After you hook up the man next to you, I want you to drop the keys onto the ground."

He watched while all three men were cuffed with their hands in front of them.

Dubois looked for the yellow in Bud's eyes to see if he could find some recognition of the man he encountered before, but it was nowhere in sight.

"You're for it now," Dubois said. "That's evidence you just offed."

"All we want is a name," Smith repeated.

"I want you boys to listen real close," Bud said as he lowered the Parker. "You fellas can go screw yourselves, for all I care. You run down across the line and find your U.S. Marshal. You can bring him up the border and spin his badge until it shines up your asses. No U.S. Marshal has jurisdiction in Canada. Now, you can also ride west of here and talk to the North-West Mounted Police at Alameda, but I think you're going to find yourself plumb out of luck. The men there have a mandate to patrol between posts in Assiniboia. If you haven't noticed, I'll let you know now. You're in Manitoba! Manitoba has its own police force. However, I doubt if, at the present time, there is a Manitoba policeman within two hundred and fifty miles of here. If there was one I doubt he'd have time to deal with something as insignificant as a gut pile. For that is all this deceased horse is going to be within a few days. Because, gentlemen, after you leave here I am going to hook a chain around that dead nag's hind leg and drag it out to the bushline. The pack of coyotes that's howling near here every night is going to have a banquet. I reckon within a few days nobody will be able to tell what kind of horse that gelding was, never mind its colour or the nature of its socks. By the time you boys have your crap together, it will likely be longer than the coyotes and birds will need. You can bring all the law you like here to analyse and inspect the gut pile. What's left of it will be waiting for you."

"You'll never get away with this," Dubois told him. "There's a little matter of a forty-four-thousand-dollar payroll that was heisted from the bank in Bismarck."

"Get away with what?" Bud replied. "You know I haven't robbed any bank! Your smarter friend, the big bastard, has already pointed out that the worst I done was trade somebody a horse. I don't know nothing about any bank robbery. I have no name to hand out. The man who dropped the chestnut here was in a hurry. He had no name. He was moving so fast he left behind no description of himself beyond what you probably already have. So I say, boys, you are a sad lot of detectives who couldn't find your own dung if it was dropping out your bottoms. Now I recommend you climb on those oat burners you're riding and head back down to the U.S. border. Stop harassing citizens in this land with your petty claims and your unreasonable attitudes. I don't want to hear another word from any of you."

After the three Pinkertons had ridden away, he gathered up their weapons and dropped them into the well. He hooked up the dun and dragged the chestnut's bloating carcass out to the treeline.

Forty-four thousand dollars! Bud thought. *Tall Bob wasn't carrying that kind of money when he pulled into my place, all worn out on a half-dead nag.* By the end of the afternoon he had it well plotted out. Tall Bob had kept him in the dark about the take from the robbery. Bud in turn had been distracted by Tall Bob's unfortunate tale of murder. He had just assumed the money in Tall Bob's possession when he rode into his yard was all the loot from the robbery. Now he realized why the Pinkertons were so wound up. Bud remembered Dubois's cold, deliberate speech about getting the money back at any cost. Dubois and his men still didn't have a suspect. The Pinkertons seemed to be trolling in a very deep lake with bare hooks. Now they were back fishing in his lake, so to speak. It wasn't surprising to him. Pinkertons were famous at exacting revenge when they couldn't arrange justice.

When Quigley identified Dubois and his burly companions coming across his field he quickly made up his mind to go on the offensive. He knew that Pinkertons often made their own rules. He was afraid Dubois and his henchmen would try to grab him and drag him across the border to face some kind of trumped-up horse stealing charge. When he saw the chestnut standing there in the midday doldrums, he impulsively decided to do what he had promised to do in the first place. Now Dubois could return to Canada and bring his precious chestnut gelding, the pride of his police work, a fancy bouquet of flowers.

"Well, what's this?" Gerry, the lawman, said from the chair on the boardwalk in front of his office as he watched Dubois and his mates plodding down the front street of Bottineau. "You fellas look like escapees," he said when he saw the handcuffs.

When they were dismounted, the three of them walked over to the Bohunk's for a drink with Gerry trailing along behind. When they had liquor in their glasses they told Gerry and the Bohunk their sheepish story.

"Dubois, you have all the easy answers. I warned you that the border was a dog's breakfast, but you continue to proclaim that you know the laws without rightly knowing what country you're in. You have no chance operating over the border without the law on that side in your pocket. What would possess you men to handle this situation in such a manner?" Gerry asked, suppressing a laugh at their expense.

Dubois asked Gerry if he had any handcuff keys that might unlock the metal bracelets that held their wrists.

"No, I'm an old-fashioned lawman. I just use an axe handle and they wake up the next morning in the cell. I don't use any aids like handcuffs or leg irons. Too much trouble; I'm always losing keys. Why don't you fellows have a bowl of the Bohunk's prairie chicken stew while I go and see if the blacksmith is handy."

"What did you do to make Quigley so mad at you that he made you wear your own handcuffs?" the Bohunk kept asking.

When Gerry came back he told Dubois that Henderson, the blacksmith, was busy shoeing two dozen big horses that the railway boys had brought into town. There was a priority on him finishing their work. He advised them that Henderson suggested coming over to his shop the next afternoon when he would endeavour to free them.

"You're joshing me," said Dubois.

"No, that's the plain truth of it. You Pinkertons come second to the railway. If I was you I wouldn't bitch about it since, if you do, there's a likelihood you'll be wearing those charm bracelets on your wrists when you next set eyes on Minot. Henderson has a bone to pick with you fellows from a long time back when he worked in coal mining."

"The bounder got the drop on us and took our weapons," Smith said.

"Don't look at me. I have no jurisdiction up there," Gerry said. "It's not like you fellows to let somebody embarrass you. Frankly, he's right about that former four-legged piece of evidence you dragged up there. In a week it'll be unrecognizable."

"Quigley is going to pay dearly for this!" Dubois said. "That scoundrel is nothing but a bloody horse thief. You people in Bottineau all know it."

"Deals in four-legged stolen goods," Smith added.

"I'm sorry you feel that way," said the Bohunk. "Bud's been a friend of mine for a long time. I'm so offended at your accusations that I am closing my establishment to Pinkertons. Furthermore, the bunkhouse is booked solid tonight. You fellows are out of luck."

"Jeezuz, Gerry, talk some sense into this hunky knothead," Dubois replied.

"Sorry boys, but the manager has asked me to clear you fellows off the premises. According to the bylaws in Bottineau, I have no choice but to follow the rule of law."

"Where are we going to go?" asked Moss.

"That's your problem," Gerry said. "Big mouths cause big wrecks."

"Come on, Gerry, give us a break." Dubois was whining.

"Sorry, no vacancy. The last time you needed a place to crash, I had an empty jail. This time I'm full-up with bad-tempered, overworked railway men who took the town apart last night. You boys should practice not being obnoxious. All I can suggest to you is that, like Joseph and Mary, you see if there's room for you over at the stables. It takes plenty to rile Old Man Wilts. The last time you were in town, if you remember, your personal thugs were booted from Wilts's place. He was worried about his livestock being molested. Hard to blame him considering the company you were keeping. This time, if I was you, I'd keep your coats over those handcuffs and ask him politely."

17

"It wasn't your finest hour."

"I have to admit that," Jiggs Dubois answered.

"After all the good work you and Smith pulled off in Regina, you return to Minot to make an impulsive, poorly-thought-out decision and go off half-cocked and get your asses spanked like little boys. Then you return here, unarmed, looking like amateurs. Bungling like that besmirches the Pinkerton name. I know how it goes. Now you'll have to go and brutalize somebody to prove you're not a bunch of pansies!"

The speaker admonishing Jiggs Dubois and his two experienced colleagues in a private room at the Leland Hotel in Minot was Roger Filbert, with a spray of white-hot syllables that seemed to dart like sparks from his teeth. Dubois was instantly forming a new opinion about Filbert, a man he formerly thought was a bit of a fop. His opinion, perhaps, had been clouded by Filbert's appearance. His slick hair parted down the middle, three-piece blue suit with a large gold nugget watch fob and his fine, nervous, manicured hands left the impression he was something of a dandy.

Filbert took off his suit jacket and carefully folded it over the back of a chair. It was obvious he had a nickel-plated Tranter in a carved-leather shoulder holster under his right arm. With his jacket off, wearing a bright white, high-collared, starched shirt, Filbert, in full flight, gave off a dangerous, excited aura.

During that memorable night of boozing with the police chief of Minot, William Flumerfelt, Dubois had begun to regard Filbert as a lightweight. He wondered how such a dapper little dude could hold down a high-level job with the Pinkertons. Unknown to Dubois, Filbert had made his reputation several years before, doing clandestine work in labour disputes with a length of piano wire. Size had nothing on the weasel-like ferocity Filbert had learned to unleash with controlled accuracy, greatly to the enhancement of his career.

"A bunch of deadbeats with scat for brains. I can't believe you let an old man kick your fat, stupid asses. You walk right up to Quigley and he says 'hello boys' and he drops that chestnut into its grave while you boys stand around. Then you go to Bottineau and show the locals there that you are a trio of prize-winning numbskulls. To make it worse, you show up in Minot wearing your own handcuffs. Now that sets you apart. Nobody is afraid of you flat-footed pussycats, therefore you earn no respect. That's not the Pinkerton way. The next time you go up to the border country you have to cut somebody's goat. You understand?"

"Jeez," Jiggs said, "we thought he'd fold his hand and give us a name."

"Well, it seems he raised the bet, called your hand and flopped aces," Filbert mused while he gobbled a few Concord grapes from a bowl on the table.

"Fortunately, I returned here before you idiots came back from your bungling adventures in ridiculous behaviour. I've had a chance to look at the data you brought back from Regina."

"If I may interrupt," Jiggs said.

"Interrupting me is never a good policy," Filbert stated.

"I just want to alert you to the fact that our agents in Regina want to be paid as soon as possible."

"Yes, those two do more on their backs in an hour than you three men can accomplish in a month."

Jiggs decided to wait out the fireworks and, when things grew less intense, he would make his move. He told Filbert that he and Smith had examined the North-West Mounted Police records and they had come up with twenty possibles. They had written the names of the ten top candidates on the file and put them into the documentation sent to Filbert.

Filbert had previously ordered lunch. They retired for drinks to the mezzanine which, Filbert pointed out, was decorated with the taxidermy of John Delbert Allen. Specimens included an enormous bison killed on the Little Heart River, as well as a plains grizzly shot by Theodore Roosevelt near Medora. Lunch was served in the Dakota Room. Filbert waxed on eloquently about Allen's artistic talents between shots of whisky. The room was filled with the artist's oil paintings of notable Indians from the state's troubled past.

"Didn't know you were a fancy gent," Jiggs said.

"Enjoy your surroundings, gentlemen, life can't be exclusively reserved for the endless details of work. They do a credible baron of beef here. Let's wash it down with some imported India pale ale that the manager assures me he keeps on ice. Now, I have a surprise for you fellows. I have decided to reimburse the loss of your weapons. Stop in at the gunsmith downtown. He'll replace what you surrendered to that old wrangler. It will be charged to the company account."

Dubois, Smith and Moss were totally confused. The tirade that had poured out of Roger Filbert's tiny mouth had given them fits.

"Another thing. I am going to omit from my report the fact that you three were disarmed like schoolgirls and might have been executed on the spot if our wrangler had been a professional killer. I am doing this because, while I think you are careless, I commend you for the police work you have done in turning up the robber's horse and helping us zero-in on a candidate. Now we can take steps to recover the bank's money and solve this bloody murder."

Dubois saw it as a good time to again press his point that he and Smith had compiled a list of ten likely suspects from the data they received in Regina.

"Keep it under your hat," Filbert told him. "We already know the identity of the man who robbed the First National Bank on May 28th." Filbert poured more beer into his glass. "Furthermore he hasn't picked up his money yet. When he does I want to make sure that you three comics will be there to end his brief crime spree and thereby redeem yourselves."

The three of them sat mute.

"His name is Leslie Robert Simpson," Filbert stated.

"How do you know that?" asked Dubois.

"When we examined the lists he kept showing up and we were able to see that he served in the border posts during his tour of duty. He took a leave of absence on May 15th, which gave him lots of time to travel to Bismarck. He came back on duty on July 15th. Once we compiled a list of suspects, we started investigating until they put themselves out of suspicion. The kicker was when the riding master told our lovely agent in silk about a tall lad who could eat up a horse in jig time. Had to be the kind of man we were looking for. After that it was easy. He's a loner; nobody in the Force calls him a close friend. He has a mundane service record, but he stands out as a horseman. At the present time, he's a constable on duty in Regina. On the 15th of November he's a free man. Another of our agents in Regina happens to be a constable in the Mounted Police who is operating under the alias of Scoggin. This man, far cleverer than you three doughheads, befriended the suspect in his last weeks of duty. In this capacity he helped the suspect put together the kind of outfit a man would need if he was planning to take a long trip out onto the prairie to dig something up. He did this by introducing our suspect to another of our agents who posed as a desperate cowboy eager to part with his stock and his gear. Simpson, who claims he is pining to return home to take care of his ailing mother, has purchased a sound horse, a pack animal and a load of supplies with digging tools. If he was really concerned about returning home quickly, he'd take the train to Brandon. We think he has something else on his mind. Undoubtedly, on his retirement from the North-West Mounted Police, our suspect will be making a final trip to dig up the money – God only knows where."

"You did all that while Smith and I were being stonewalled at headquarters?" Jiggs asked.

"We figured you two would receive the runaround by the top brass, but that news of your arrival in Regina might help flush our quarry. The fact that you two look like a pair of pirates at a nuns' picnic didn't do our plan any harm. You boldly made enquiries while our agents working undercover filled in the gaps. Now, when this man finishes his last day in Regina and makes a run for the money, our cowboy plant, who is an expert tracker, will be on his tail. We have a dozen Pinkertons arriving in Minot later this week. Dubois, it will be your job to deploy them. We will spin a web of men in the country we expect him to travel through. Eventually we will close in on our suspect and, hopefully, catch him with his saddlebags bulging with bank loot. Then, we'll arrest him for murder, as well, if he survives the interview."

"What if you're wrong?" Dubois asked.

"That's already an incorrect assumption," Filbert answered. "It's more like what if *we're* wrong. From the beginning you spun the notion our killer was an active member in the North-West Mounted Police. Nobody believed that at the start but you. Eventually we followed your logic, with some weak clues, and here we are today on the verge of success or spectacular failure. I'm afraid we'll all have to live with the result either way. Now Smith and Moss, you are free to go while I discuss a few details with Jiggs."

After the two men left the room, Filbert held his hand out to Dubois.

"Look Jiggs, no hard feelings. I admit I was peeved at your recent activities. Your rash action in confronting that Quigley fellow with the gelding was ill-advised. However, the Pinkerton organization, in general, has confidence in you for your loyal service in the past. Not to forget your enthusiasm in taking up the detective calling in a most vigorous manner. You're a go-getter Dubois. If this case breaks our way it will be because of your tenacity. Now, there's someone in a room nearby who we must see at once. I caution you Dubois, mark your words well: your future in the organization depends upon it."

"Yes sir," Dubois answered. His dream of replacing Filbert, or rising above him in the Pinkerton hierarchy, had turned into a dull memory. He would fall into line and regard Filbert as his mentor. What choice did he have? The sad tale of him losing his pride and joy, the Merwin-Hulbert matched set, was one story he hoped would remain untold.

They walked down the corridor to the final room at the end of the hall. Filbert knocked twice on the door. It slowly swung open. A man ushered them into the room where William Pinkerton, dressed as a Catholic priest, sat at a gaily-decorated round table drinking tea.

"Gentlemen, it's been a while."

"Yes sir," they both admitted.

Pinkerton introduced the other man in the room, who was also wearing prelate's garb.

"Gentlemen, this is my trusted assistant and bodyguard, Edgar Haines. We are headed to Seattle to brief James J. Hill on the progress of this case and some other matters. I arrived by train this morning. I'll be climbing on another this evening. You'll have to excuse our garb. Unfortunately, these days I can't be too careful. Our people have been hearing persistent rumours that there are plotters in the land who have been hired to assassinate both myself and my brother, so I have taken to travelling in disguise. Hopefully the good Lord will protect me," Pinkerton said. "Dubois, thanks for your detailed reports. Both of you men have done very well in executing your duties for the Pinkerton National Detective

Agency. When I last saw you we were grasping at straws and I was being seriously gored by one of our most important clients. In a very short time we have pulled this case together. Now we are on the forefront of something more important than either of you men can possibly understand without being briefed. That's why I stopped here to meet with you today."

"Thank you sir," Filbert answered. "We appreciate your confidence."

"When Dubois and Smith received the runaround from the Mounted Police brass, I had occasion to try and pull some strings behind the scenes. You may or may not know we have had a presence in Canada for some time in helping combat the threat from the Fenians. To that end, we have the ears of the most important politicians in the land. However, the pressure that was exerted by these esteemed men did no good at all."

"Yes sir," Dubois said. "It only seemed to make the Mounted Police commissioner more uncooperative."

"From the attitude shown in this case, it is apparent the top brass in the North-West Mounted Police are running a closed shop that may or may not bear scrutiny. Subsequently, positive forces in eastern Canada have decided that the Pinkerton Agency might be an appropriate agency to hire to investigate the internal policies and behaviour of the Mounted Police administration. That organization seems to see itself as a sacred cow that defies accountability."

"Why not?" said Filbert. "We have already infiltrated them."

"I'm sure I don't have to tweak your imaginations too much for you to understand that such a commission would enhance our international prestige. It would also greatly increase the Pinkerton National Detective Agency's influence on the North American continent," Pinkerton stated.

"How, then, shall we proceed?" asked Filbert, while Dubois stood by looking dutiful.

"When this killer makes his run for glory I want you to make something happen without fail. I don't want you to spook him again – he'll already be fragile in his misgivings about killing a man. This is not a professional killer but an adventurer. He's the worst thing a man can be. He's a policeman who has lost his way and joined the other side. He has probably done it for noble reasons but, alas, a man can rationalize anything if it suits him. The facts are, he's a robber and a killer. I don't want you to make a move on him until he has the swag in his possession. That's the only way we can prove for sure that this Simpson has blood on his hands. When you do catch him, if you can take him alive, so much the better. I want you to haul him straight across the border so we can keep him on ice in the United States. Now, if it turns out this suspect has held up a U.S. bank and killed a man while on leave as a member of the Mounted Police, then we are in luck in two ways."

Suddenly, there was a clattering sound in the hallway outside the room. Edgar Haines made a sign with his hands that everyone should remain silent while he hauled his Volcanic Repeater out from under his cassock and stood listening at the door. After a short time the fuss outside the room ceased and Edgar relaxed, putting his dog's leg back under its black shroud.

"You can see, gentlemen, Edgar is very good at his job," Pinkerton said as he sipped from his bone china teacup. "Where was I? Oh yes. We will be able to lay the facts of this case out to the Canadian government in orderly fashion. It will be obvious that superior policing methods, as espoused by Pinkertons, solved this case, despite the fact that we were totally rebuffed by the North-West Mounted Police. Not only will we make a case for being hired to investigate the policies and usefulness of the Mounted Police, but we will offer to bring our new policing methods to Canada. Naturally, with a considerable amount of remuneration for our efforts. Who knows where that might lead to in the future? Our efforts will certainly show that the North-West Mounted Police is nothing more than a military operation with limited capability in taking on criminal investigations."

"Sir, I've already spoken at length about our activities with high-up officials in North Dakota who have promised total co-operation from Marshal Albert Price's office. Marshal Price is presently understaffed, but he's agreed that two of his deputies will be standing by to take custody when our Pinkerton force apprehends this man. They've made it clear they will not cross the border," Filbert said, ending his report.

"When you catch him red-handed with the money, under no circumstances are you to turn him over to the Canadian authorities," Pinkerton said. "If they find him first it's unclear to us as to what might happen. They might confuse the issue and hide behind some British mumbo jumbo about diplomacy and how gentlemen behave. We feel the best result would be for you to catch him, then quickly haul him across the line into U.S. territory so he can be charged in a timely manner. That way we can make political hay and further put the boots to Mounted Police credibility. It's going to give them a big, black eye if we show up with one of their boys in good standing and he turns out to be a bank robbing murderer. We'll have a field day of publicity, at least until the trapdoor springs open. There's nothing like a little dose of law and order to motivate politicians to make wise choices when they spend their money."

"You have a way with words," Dubois said.

"That's why I'm the boss," Pinkerton answered.

"That's why he's the boss," Filbert reiterated.

"Now, on to Seattle. I trust that I can tell James J. that justice is about to prevail?"

"Sir, we'll do our best," Filbert said.

"It's in the bag sir," Dubois assured.

"One last thing," Pinkerton said as he adjusted the large crucifix hanging around his neck. "Warn the green deputies Price is sending up here that they should watch out. It's easy to catch a stray slug in this part of the world."

"Very good sir," Dubois and Filbert answered at the same time.

179

18

A FEW DAYS BEFORE HIS ENGAGEMENT with the North-West Mounted Police was to be severed permanently, Les was called to a routine meeting of the Board of Officers at headquarters. The officers there were chatting amiably while they shuffled a few papers on the table. In front of them was a summary of Leslie Robert Simpson's career, when he entered the service, divisional postings, his promotions and conduct record. The reverse side of the form contained his physical description and the location of his future intended place of residence, as well as notes on when and where the Board of Officers meeting had occurred.

After a spirited discussion about the merits of eating certain kinds of cheese, they called Les into their presence and handed him his discharge certificate. His departure from his engagement in the North-West Mounted Police would be as low-key as his arrival. None of the people in the room addressed him with any words or formal goodbyes. They merely handed him the document and continued talking about cheese without missing a beat, just as they had done before Les appeared in front of them.

The lack of recognition in their eyes allowed Les to relax. These men were oblivious to Les and his self-conscious state of uneasiness. If they were on to him, one of them would have given him the hard-eyed stare. But there was nothing but twinkling eyes, laughter and silly puns about cheese.

The sergeant major spoke to Les in a gentler manner than usual. He told him he expected him to pull his weight during the final week, but suggested that nobody would be looking closely if he needed to take a few hours off to take care of personal errands during his final days.

The next afternoon, Sergeant Major Belcher asked Les for a favour.

"Laddie, when you're out and about, do you mind picking up my dress jacket? It's being let out by the seamstress above the laundry on Broad Street."

The weather had turned colder toward the end of October. A storm brought a night of wet snow that only hung around for a week. On many mornings, fog stayed for most of the day before it burned off. Les managed to ride out of town a few times on his new mount, each time taking the Martini-Henry. He sighted it in at a dumpsite about two miles south of town. He had already made up his mind he was going to use the gun, so he might as well be able to shoot straight with it.

Les had only four more days to go, until the 15th of the month. There were still a few items on his list that he wanted to add to his outfit while he had the chance. He knew he was going to be in the elements for extended periods of time. He needed to take precautions to keep himself and his horses going. Les purchased two nosebags, a sack of oats, a canvas bucket and jar of horse liniment. He walked along in the fog on Broad Street, thinking about how cold the nights were soon going to become. The multicoloured framed buildings were barely visible through the thick fog. When he came to the laundry, which had a bright orange door, the fog seemed to magically lift. Les found himself looking at a patch of blue sky as he climbed the outside wooden staircase to the second floor, where he found the seamstress and her assistant.

The seamstress was not quite finished with the sergeant major's jacket. She asked Les if he had time to wait for half an hour until she could complete the job. She suggested that the sergeant major had been eating too many desserts. Les agreed that Belcher had a sweet tooth. He wasn't in a hurry and sat down at the table in front of the window while the seamstress brought him a cup of tea. When he glanced down at the road from between the gauzy curtains that hid him from view, Les suffered an intense moment of self-discovery. It was such a shocking sight he felt as if his entrails were hovering in the balance.

Across the street, in front of a nondescript, unpainted storefront, Constable Jimmy Scoggin was in deep conversation with a cowboy holding the reins on a handsome black gelding. Within a few seconds it dawned on Les that it was Templeton, the cowboy who sold him the horses and other gear he was keeping at the stables. Templeton, he remembered, had been in a lather to catch the train to the West Coast.

Not in such a hurry now. Maybe he's not in love after all, Les thought.

After a short conversation the two men disappeared inside the unmarked building. Before the seamstress was finished with the sergeant major's jacket, Scoggin and Templeton had returned to the street. The delivery wagon stopped to pick up Scoggin. Templeton went back inside. A few minutes later he came out wearing a duster. He walked over to the black parked on the hitching rail. When he climbed aboard Les saw the glint of cold steel that gripped his belt.

Now his mind was racing like a runner who was headed for the horizon. His whole being, every pore, every follicle, every cell in his body, was frantic with the realization he had been set up. A thousand flashes rushed through Les's psyche. The big picture had come clear just about the time the fog lifted entirely from the muddy Regina street.

A gunman on a fast horse. Les thought. *That's not the way the North-West Mounted Police does business. The Pinkerton's are on to me. Scoggin is moonlighting.*

Back at headquarters, Sergeant Major Belcher was thrilled by the way his jacket fit. He offered Les a jolt from his personal flask. "Those ladies are gems."

"Sergeant Major, I'm a little concerned by what I saw across the street from their place. I think there's a booze can in the joint across the street. Saw a fellow emerge who looked like he was packing. To be perfectly honest, those sweeties on the second floor said that one of our boys in uniform spends a lot of time inside."

"That so? Thanks for the tip. Is nothing sacred? Those women will be hounded out of there. Can't have that. I need my repairs and I enjoy a scone and a cup of tea with the ladies. The home cooking up there is out of this world. Have another shot of brandy."

"Don't mind if I do," Les said. "Put somebody from headquarters up in the seamstress's place and you'll soon know who goes in across the street."

"Packing, you say?"

"Unmistakable. I can tell every time. It's the training."

"Bless you lad, we're going to miss you around here. I'll have eyes on that joint in the morning."

Les knew that the sergeant major would not tolerate such an affront as an illicit booze joint. Sergeant Major Belcher was a ramrod who prided himself on knowing the lay of the land and performing well. He was much more than just a member of the Force. He was a committed citizen who valued the quality of life in Regina and took part in many social activities. He was a proud Freemason who had worked diligently behind the scenes on the proposal to house a Masonic Lodge within the North-West Mounted Police headquarters in Regina

For several months he had supervised the diligence of Constable Phillips, who was busy working full-time in the barracks on the altar, pedestals and columns that he was building for North-West Mounted Police Lodge No. 11. These were painted white and trimmed with the Mounted Police colours of blue and gold.

Sergeant Major Belcher had the energy of three men and knew how to lead his charges into battle. Now, his attention was focused on the new construction project.

"Lads, it was a proud day when the word came down from the brass that the powers that be in Ottawa had granted permission for us to found a lodge within headquarters. So now we'll build it double-quick."

Les knew nothing about Freemasonry but he was living in close quarters to it in the barracks. It was impossible not to see the daily progress that was being made in the workshop. Fourteen Masons, all Mounties of different ranks, were already meeting in the building. The go-ahead on the new lodge had seen a sudden shift of attention from routine police work to what could only be described as Masonic husbandry.

Les thought it unlikely they would tolerate anybody setting up an illegal drinking establishment under their very noses. Sergeant Major Belcher would ensure that the old boys' network took matters in their own hands to clean up the problem. Anybody trying to run an illegal operation in Regina under the jurisdiction of the North-West Mounted Police, as well as their Freemasonry chapter, was daft. Certain social opportunities that passed under the blanket, so to speak, operated only under the auspices of both organizations.

Les knew that Scoggin would be observed going into the premises and that his days in the Force were likely to be fraught with peril from that time forward. He could not help but think back to Sergeant Major Belcher's colourful way of speaking when he got his dander up. "I'll have his balls for a necktie," was his favourite saying.

The next morning, Les went out to the butcher's and bought sausages, a slab of bacon and five pounds of jerky. At the general store, he purchased tea, lard, oatmeal and a bag of dried apples. He picked up a bottle of medicinal hootch from the Force-approved bootlegger. He spent most of the day over at the stable packing his gear. He cleaned the Martini-Henry and put a half-dozen cartridges in his coat pocket.

I'll take him for a leisurely ride out into countryside, he thought. *When he's far enough from town, I'll derail the pest. Then I'll head south as far as he's concerned, while I work my way back to Regina.* It was the plan his mind was churning over. With the money he had a chance to get away, without it he'd be riding in circles – a marked man who would eventually come to a bad end.

In his heart he knew it was a sure thing that Templeton would cruise out of the gate behind him, following along until he was joined by more of his brethren. If they had a choice, or if it worked out to their advantage, they'd tail him all the way to the money, and the scaffold a short time later.

Then it dawned on him – a plan to do what he did best, better than ever. He'd make them think he was taking his time. He hoped he had set them up by behaving like he was going on a long expedition, while he regarded his trip down south as an all-out sprint for the cash. He'd give them the slip and then throw in a few tricks.

In the middle of the morning on November 16th, Leslie Robert Simpson began reverting back into Tall Bob again as he rode out of Regina on what he figured was a Pinkerton horse. He was headed roughly northwest of the city. It was late in the afternoon when he picked up the rider. Looking back, he caught a glimpse of him on the bushline. He pushed along until about an hour before darkness set in. It was coming on a clear night and he was wishing for a glorious ceiling of stars.

Finally, he found a good spot. He rode the cowboy's nag into the bush. Les tied him and the packhorse to a couple of saplings. Walking back, he set up behind a windfall that he'd noticed beside the trail. When the man on the black horse glided into view, Les let his breath out, took careful aim with the Martini-Henry and shot the black horse in the chest. The horse screamed and took off across the open field between fingers of bush. It ran full-out for fifty yards, with Templeton hanging on like a circus rider, before it fell stone dead.

Les made his way back to his horses, untied them, mounted up and rode away, leading the packhorse, without looking back. He knew that Templeton, or whatever his name was, had lost interest in the game. If he walked away from that wreck he was going to be mighty stiff. Les thought he might stay down for a long time. He figured he'd put plenty of hoof beats between them by dawn, when Templeton, if he was smart, started heading back toward Regina.

Early the next morning Les plodded into Regina. Now the easy part. He'd feed and water his horses and load them in the late morning on the train bound for Fort Qu'Appelle and ultimately headed to Moosomin.

Bobby Allison, a pal from Brandon, was employed by the railway, in charge of transporting livestock. When he first came back from Brandon, Les had run into Bobby in the Regina train station. He told him his time was up on November 15th and that he had lined up a job down south wrangling horses. Bobby told him he could arrange a train ride on November 16th as far as Moosomin. Les was taking him up on his offer. From Moosomin he'd travel south to Carlyle, where he'd dump his winter camping gear, keeping only the essentials, carry as much hay as he could comfortably pack and make a run for his money. If it looked bad, or if he ran out of energy, he could always change direction and head east.

It turned out that he'd made the right decision. Les's pal was a straight shooter. At the railroad yards, Les was directed to where his animals could easily be loaded onto a livestock car. The train left for Fort Qu'Appelle on time. None of the watchers in Regina noticed who was catching up on his sleep in the hay beside his horses.

The man called Garth Templeton had spent a very bad night out on the prairie. The wild fifty-yard sprint had nearly frightened him to death, but it was nothing compared to the fall. When he came fully conscious several minutes later, the sun had already almost completely left the sky. The pack animal he was leading had taken off, bucking all of his gear into the bush. At first he figured his back was broken, but then he thought maybe it was both legs. In the end, it was his right ankle. He had the good sense to make a fire, hopping around locating wood before it turned full dark. He sat in front of that fire, tending it, for two days before a hunter happened by and hauled him into Regina. He had tried calling the pack animal back to him but it remained a small, black figure far out on the treeline, grazing on the withered, yellow grass. Templeton was in a bad way but, when he arrived back in Regina, he managed to send a telegram to warn Filbert and Dubois who were waiting in Minot.

"Gave me the slip – stop – Suspect headed south – stop – GT."

"Well there's a poke in the eye!" Jiggs said.

"He's recognized as the best long-distance cover man in the business," Filbert remarked. "I can't believe he's already out of commission."

"At least he warned us that the suspect has left Regina," Smith remarked.

"When?" asked Roger Filbert. "If it's a timely warning we can figure out when to expect him, then deploy the men you have in place, Dubois. Wire Templeton back and ask him when the suspect left Regina."

An hour later, Dubois came back into the room clutching a handful of telegrams.

"The diabolic bastard lured our man out on the trail for nearly a day's ride. Then, just before dark, he shot his horse out from under him. Our boy was in the wilderness for two whole days with a broken ankle until a hunter found him and hauled him into Regina."

"You mean he's been on the loose for two or more days than we knew? Have you put your men in place, Dubois?

"Well, mostly, sir, but I will be sending the rest out tonight."

Something was starting to dawn on Dubois.

"I would say that he's two or three days ride south of Regina," Smith said.

"What do you base that opinion on?" Filbert asked.

"Logic says he's headed south, and the only thing in doubt is how long he's been on the trail."

"He's a real smart ass," Dubois said. "He's playing a game with us. The only predictable thing about him is that he's unpredictable."

"I still think he has a formidable ride ahead of him, over harsh terrain in iffy weather. Can't see him arriving down here for a few days yet," Smith said.

"How do we know he's coming all the way by horse?" Dubois asked. "He might've bumped off our man's ride then doubled back and caught the train down south."

"Do you really think he's that clever?" Smith asked.

"Don't bet against it," Dubois said. "He's a crafty man with a notion. He knew what he was doing when he derailed Templeton. Simpson altered the game for a reason. He let us know he's onto us in dramatic fashion. I wouldn't put anything past him."

"Then he's already close at hand." Filbert said.

"What do our spies in Regina say?" asked Smith.

Filbert, lighting a wicked little black cigar, said, "I've just read all these communiqués. Our office there was raided by some half-cut Scottish sergeant major in charge of the morality squad. He found a .44 calibre Colt on our Mr. Templeton while he was being treated there by a doctor. They also lifted the twenty cases of whisky we had stored there for the whorehouse. Alias Garth Templeton is on his own. We don't allow clandestine agents to compromise the organization in a foreign country for minor charges like liquor or gun violations. If he's lucky he'll end up with a big fine and a month on the rock pile. I don't know what they'll do with the booze."

"Drink it! Those soldier boys will drink every damn bottle of it. That's how they do things up there. They pretend they don't, but that's how they acquire their booze. There's a retired commissioner for the Mounted Police who they've turned into a cranky judge. He'll assess the damages and collect his pound of flesh. In this case it will be drink. The sergeants' mess will kick him back a few cases," Dubois said.

"Maybe if we put it in the hands of Lily and Bonnie they'll get Templeton off on their backs. Remind me to send them a bonus!" Filbert mused aloud.

"Send them a bonus!" Dubois said. "There, I reminded you."

"Dubois, let's move out on the roads and motivate our men to cover the trails. Contact our various communications points. Let's see if we can have this bastard run down."

"He's coming over the border," Dubois had finally woken up. "Yes, he's fooled us and given himself a real head start in picking up his goods. I think he's crossing the border because he foolishly buried the money somewhere between Minot and Swedes' Ferry. Originally, when I interviewed the Swede on the ferry, he told me he was a tall man riding a chestnut gelding and that he was travelling pretty light. There was a tarp on the back of the horse but no sack or large bag. We'll let him go to Quigley's, if that's what he wants. I'll be surprised if he goes there. He's in a hurry. We'll let him over the border. I'm betting he'll ride to Swedes' Ferry, cross the river and head straight for the cash. When he digs up the money and turns north again we'll have him trapped between Minot and the ferry crossing."

Later the same day, while Dubois was gathering his things together before hitting the trail, Filbert knocked on his hotel room door.

"I just received a telegram from William Pinkerton. He's communicated with his connections in Ottawa. Pinkerton has the green light to cross the border and arrest Simpson and bring him back to the United States to be charged. It will be the story of cooperation between two enlightened police forces – the North Dakota Marshals and the North-West Mounted Police," Filbert said.

"Do they admit he's one of their finest?"

"They admit nothing until they see who we catch red-handed with the cash."

"Bloodstained money will tell the tale. Better to swing in the wind than die in poverty," said Dubois. "That's what he's decided."

"Profound," answered Filbert.

"The killer has known we were on to him for some time."

"You're insightful Dubois. If I was the suspect, I wouldn't like a blunt, savage thinker like you chasing me," Filbert said, peering through his squinty eyes.

"No, I'm sure you wouldn't," Dubois answered.

19

November, 1894
Province of Manitoba, Canada

ON THE 18TH OF NOVEMBER, 1894, four of Ross's men arrived at Bud's place to collect the horse herd that now belonged to James J. Hill. The following day, they left Bud's with the intention of driving the herd down to the railway yards in Minot and loading them onto livestock cars bound for Minnesota. That left Bud with exactly one horse, the dun, in the corral beside his cabin.

Bud made sure the cattle meant for Alphonse Pointed Stick and his people were taken care of before he shut them out of his mind. He had hired the boys who were looking after his cabin, Lars Jensen Jr. and Kenny Wilson, to feed and water them. If Alphonse failed to show up in the winter, then Lars Jr. and Kenny were free to sell the cattle in the spring and split the money.

The weather was close to turning. The sky was a bank of grey cloud that looked like snow was in the offing if it got any colder. Bud had a plan – the next morning he would retrieve his money from where he had hidden it, fill his saddlebags, mount up the dun and ride to Minot, where he would dispose of the horse and saddle. Then he would board the Seattle-bound train using the pass he received from Hill. That would allow him plenty of time to make it to the coast, cross the Canadian border by stagecoach and travel ninety miles to Vancouver. He planned to arrive on December 4th, five days before the Empress of Japan was scheduled to sail. Long enough to prepare before he presented Hill's letter at the shipping office and claimed his ticket to the Orient.

Bud knew he was running out of good weather. If it started to snow in earnest he would have to alter his plan. He would sit it out in Bottineau for a few days or with his friends the Swedes at the river crossing. However, if he got lucky and the first winter snows were only a cursory warning, he would press on. He would pack his beaver hat, wolverine-fur gloves and full-length bison winter coat to aid his survival on the trail. At night he would build a lean-to of evergreen boughs and sit up in his winter gear beside a fire. He was sure he would have no problem travelling to Minot. If a blizzard happened to interrupt his schedule, he had the option of arriving later in Vancouver to catch another ship that was due to depart near the end of the month.

The only possible snag was that he might stumble into the Pinkertons along the way. If they were in Bottineau, he was sure that Gerry would not get involved in the matter of the chestnut gelding. He also was aware that Minot was a bustling frontier community with a police chief who minded his own town's business. Any action the Pinkertons might take against him on the trail would depend on the moment. However, since they were largely tenderfoots who rode badly, he was sure he could outmanoeuvre and outrun them.

There was a slow curl of smoke ascending from the cabin stovepipe. Only during the past month had Bud started burning a fire in the cast iron stove inside the building. For most of the year, he employed a summer kitchen and cooked outside. In the late fall and winter, he used the stove in the cabin to cook his food and provide heat.

The afternoon was waning. Bud was sitting outside on his chopping block with the Parker next to him as he drank the dregs of his second pot of coffee. He felt peaceful, but strangely out of sync, now that he had no responsibilities left. The horses were gone. He would soon be on his way to new destinations. In his imagination, he kept conjuring the same vision of ocean waves on a long white beach bordered by a fringe of palm trees. He knew he was never coming back to this place. He was savouring his last few hours of being free of his former encumbrances.

Bud was distracted by something at the distant treeline for a third time. He thought he saw movement, a glimpse of a horse's tail swishing as the animal grazed. For a second he wondered if Ross's men had dropped an animal along the trail and it had now worked its way back home. He stood up. It was his habit to cup his hand around his eyes. He peered far into the distance.

The noise knocked him off his feet as convincingly as the slug that tore into the right side of his chest, four inches below his collar bone. When Bud hit the ground he knew that somebody had put a bead on him with a rifle sight while he had been trying to work out the reason for that horse grazing on the treeline. He put his hand on his chest and felt the gush of blood. He knew that if he tried to stand up, the shooter, who was probably resting his rifle on a rock or a hump of ground, would zero in and put another slug into him.

Adrenaline took over. Although the pain was intense, Bud decided that he would try to cross the bare ground and make it inside the cabin. He knew this had to be done quickly before the shooter rode down on him and finished the job. The thirty-foot crawl seemed to take agonizing minutes as Bud scuttled like a crab as best he could across the sandy ground and reached the door.

He made the trip to safety in well under a minute, but now his energy was nearly all used up. Bud stuffed an empty flower sack between his shirt and the big, bloody hole in his chest. He had enough wood to stoke the fire if he needed to hold out and a bucket of water he had brought inside to wash with.

When he had accumulated another well of energy he struggled to his feet. He took the loaded derringer out of the shirt hanging on the back of the cabin door and put it into his pocket. Then he picked up his Smith & Wesson and a box of cartridges. He staggered across the small cabin, sinking down on the floor directly opposite the cabin door. Bud propped himself up on some horse blankets beside the bucket of water. All he could think about was the need for survival. He was still alive.

After the better part of an hour of sitting quietly, barely breathing, he took personal inventory and made a solemn decision. If he had to die like this he would do his utmost to make sure that his attacker also died. His first job would be to lure the shooter into his range for a good opportunity at returning the favour. Once he disposed of the shooter he would set about summoning enough energy and courage to somehow climb on a horse and ride to Bottineau for help.

In a gambit, he expended much of his energy in opening the stove and pushing in a slab of the firewood from the stack against the inner wall. At least he would stay warm while he waited for his assailant to show himself. He wet his parched lips from water he dipped with his tin cup. As he hunched his body against the wall under a heavy piece of canvas he heard the sound of someone moving around outside the cabin.

"Hey Big Shot, guess who has come to visit?" a voice asked.

He knew who it was the second he heard the words.

"Quigley, you're some joker," the voice said, "but let me tell you, I had a hard job surviving your little prank. I crawled across the wilderness living on berries. Every mile I thought about the day I'd put a bullet in your mangy hide. And guess what? Today is the day!"

In his dire state Bud knew he was listening to the depraved voice of Frenchie Who-Only-Goes-By-One-Name. He realized then that he had made a huge error in letting Frenchie live when he had the Indians transport him out to the middle of nowhere. Men like Frenchie didn't give up. They endured until they destroyed what small dose of humanity they possessed in their beings. He began to wonder if Charlie Parmer was outside as well, waiting for the opportunity to finish him off.

"Jeezuz mother, you sure left a lot of your self in globs out here. I just wanted to wing you so you'd be eager to show me your money. Guess maybe my shootin's a bit off these days. Looks like I hit pay dirt with one shot. Now doncha go dyin' on me until I have your money," he said, with a choking laugh.

By the carnage of blood that Bud left behind before he scrambled into his cabin, Frenchie was of the mind that he had shot Bud through the lungs and that it would be just a matter of time before he succumbed to the awful wound in his chest. He would have to proceed carefully if he was going to pry the location of Bud's money from him before he died. If that happened he'd achieve nothing but the satisfaction of gunning down the old fool. Revenge may have been sweet to Frenchie, but it was not a tangible commodity that would provide him with the rewards that would ensue if he came away with Bud's savings. He'd have to proceed quickly and carefully if he wanted to succeed. If Bud died before he put his hands on him then he would have committed murder for nothing more than settling a grudge.

Bud stayed silent. He surmised that maybe Frenchie would grow impatient and open the cabin door when he decided that Bud had probably died.

"Guess I'll build up the fire out here and warm myself up. You know a hunter lets the game stiffen up before he sets off to finish the job. If you can hear me, I promise you all I want is your money. So I put a bullet in you – that's fair payment for what you put me through with those gawd-damned Indians. If you think Charlie Parmer's out here with me, forget that notion. When he came back to life after that long walk, he scrammed up north toward Saskatoon. That left me to settle the score. Now I consider it done. You give me your money and I'll ride away without another word. I feel a man of your mettle could make it to help in Bottineau if you start on that trip in time. Otherwise you're going to die in there like a cornered rat."

With his mind focused on survival, Bud decided to wait until darkness had settled in around the cabin. He could see the light was diminishing quickly through the oilskin that covered the small excuse for a window high on the far wall. When it had gone black outside Bud made his move.

"Wa----ter! Wa----ter!" he cried out in a desperate voice.

"Well, well. Guess who's still alive and in need of a drink? Water is one thing there's plenty of out here. Why there's a whole rain barrel full of drinking water."

"Waaaaa----ter! Waaaaa----ter!" Bud cried, over and over again.

"You don't expect me to give you water for nothing, do ya? First I gave you a bullet for nothing. Now, you want me to give you a drink of water for nothing. Well, think again, sucker. Everything in the world has a price. This water I'm splashing about is no exception. It's costly stuff. You have to pay the bill I demand or it stays here spilling out of this bucket."

"W-a-a-ter! W-a-a-ter!" Bud repeated, the only words he uttered the whole time.

"Jeez, your starting to wear on my nerves, I have your damned water right here. It's just what you need. Here's how you get it. You just open that door and toss your piece out. I already own your Parker. When I hear the gun hit the ground I'll come in and give you that drink of water you desperately need. Do you hear me?"

"Wa-a-ater! Wa-a-ater," Bud croaked at half the volume as his previous cries.

"Look, you're fading fast, maybe there's a chance for you to live if you put some water into your poor, shot-up body. You're not doing that with me sitting out here with all the fresh water in the world running down the sides of this here bucket. You might as well be pushing up daisies. That's what you'll be doing real soon if you don't have some water."

"Wa-a-a-ter! W-a-a-a-ter! W-a-a-a-ter," Bud repeated.

"I'll make you a deal," Frenchie said. "You throw the revolver out the door. I'll come in with a pail of water and help you out. I won't bother to bring a gun with me. I want your money. I don't want to kill you. Now look, I was aiming to wing you a little so I could persuade you to hear my way of thinking. Maybe I did shoot a little low and caught you in the chest. That doesn't mean we can't ride out of here together. I'll just take your money, drop you off in Bottineau and head for the hills. If you can't ride I'll send somebody up here to help you."

"W-a-a-a-ter! W-a-a-a-ter," Bud gasped out of his throat like some kind of oath.

While Frenchie was stoking up the fire under Bud's coffee pot, the door to the cabin came ajar a few inches. Bud tossed the handgun out from the opening. It landed with a thud in the dust.

"Finally, you've come to your senses!" Frenchie exclaimed loudly as he walked over to the cabin door and swept the gun toward the fire with the side of his foot. Now that he had Bud's Smith & Wesson, he figured it would be easy to push open the door and manhandle Bud by his wound until he screamed out the location of his cash. If he had to, Frenchie would use his knife on Bud to make him talk. Once he had the money, he'd put a finishing shot into Bud and wind up the whole business.

"Here I am bringing you some water," Frenchie called as he made splashing noises with the bucket. He took out his skinning knife. Holding it in his right hand, he walked forward from the flickering light of the bonfire into the darker area in the front of the cabin. He slowly opened the door and stood in the doorway, peering into the darkness, trying to adjust his eyes so he could quickly locate Bud.

Bud, sitting on the floor with his back propped against the wall, rubbed the fog from his eyes before he held his hand out pointing in the darkness, and squeezed both derringer triggers. The first shot hit Frenchie in the right eye, the second caught him in the throat. Both killing shots. In his new state of death,

Frenchie wavered briefly in the cool night air before falling backwards out the doorway. He had gone down without even a perfunctory gurgle.

The adrenaline rush provided the impetus Bud needed to rise and pull the door shut. He dropped another slab of wood into the stove and wet his lips with small sips of water from the tin cup. He lit the candle on the table so that he had enough light to examine his wound. He couldn't see the bullet hole clearly but he could touch it with his fingers. The wound was only seeping now but his whole chest shuddered in pain whenever he tried to move. Even in his state of peril, he had felt relief when Frenchie hit the ground and was no more. He was still operating on the high from that fading moment. Bud used the last of his energy to crawl onto his bunk and cover himself with blankets.

I'll stay here until morning, he thought, falling back into an unconscious state, into a dream. He was a young boy running along a wide, white sand beach in front of waves that rushed against the shore. It was a place he'd never been before.

20

On November 18th, the two deputies from Albert F. Price's U.S. Marshal's office, Boswell and Hogg, arrived in Minot and checked into the Leland Hotel. They informed Robert Filbert that they were ready to take charge of a prisoner should the Pinkerton Detective Agency prove successful in apprehending the man responsible for the Bismarck bank robbery and subsequent murder of the bank manager. The deputies told Filbert they expected the Pinkertons would be supplying evidence to link the suspect to the crimes. They had been warned by Marshal Price not to interfere with the Pinkerton operation. As Price put it, "Too many cooks in the kitchen are a pain in the arse."

Under no circumstances were his deputies to cross the border or participate in any kidnapping operation. They were to stay in Minot, collect the prisoner and the evidence from the Pinkertons, and escort the criminal back to Bismarck for trial.

Filbert and Dubois had established a command centre in a meeting room on the mezzanine at the Leland. Dubois had long before convinced himself that Les Simpson had stashed the money somewhere between Minot and Swedes' Ferry. With this in mind, he dispatched Harold Moss plus two additional Pinkerton detectives to Swedes' Ferry to set up a watching station on the south side of the river. Under no circumstances were the watchers to reveal themselves to the ferry operators or to the suspect, if or when he crossed the river. Their job was to let the subject pass, then to come out from hiding and wait on the south side of the river. Three additional groups of three Pinkertons each were already camped out on sections of the trail between Minot and Bottineau. The main group would act like one of Flumerfelt's relentless posses.

Dubois's plan was a simple one. He hoped to advance on Simpson with the main group of men under his direction on the trail north of Minot and drive him back to the Mouse River ferry, where Moss and his men would be waiting. Dubois reasoned that, once they had him trapped between the main posse and the men at Swedes' Ferry, the game would be up.

Earlier in the week, Dubois had gathered all his agents together and issued some simple orders before they were sent off.

"The suspect is on the move. You must follow my orders to the letter if we are to have success in bringing down this guttersnipe. We must give him time and space to dig up the money from the bank robbery before we close the trap. Be careful, he has already shot an unarmed man in cold blood. The agents on the road will leave the suspect alone until it is obvious he has already picked up the money. The main posse will run the bugger to ground. Once the criminal possesses the bank loot and is making a run for it, it's open season. Go ahead and shoot him if that's what it takes. Remember, he took out one of our agents by shooting his horse, so feel free to return the favour. We want this man dead or alive but he must have the money in his possession. How will you know? The rogue Mountie is travelling with a pack animal. Once he grabs the payroll he'll abandon the packhorse and make tracks for freedom. No doubt he'll have a big sack or a bag on the back of his horse. Forty-four thousand dollars in small bills is going to be a bulky package no matter which way he tries to pack it. If we can corner him and catch him alive without any of us dying in the process, then so much the better. Once he has the money, shoot him down. He knows we're on his trail. He's already given us the slip. He has nothing to lose. He knows that if we catch him, he's going to hang. If he gets the chance, it's likely he'll kill you before he'll say hello. If, by some fluke, he avoids the trap and makes it back across the border, we will pursue him into Canada until he is apprehended." ·

Filbert was a little alarmed by Dubois' speech.

"Dubois, I think you went a little over the top with that *shoot him at the first opportunity* speech you gave the boys. Didn't Pinkerton tell us there was political hay to be made if we could capture this guy and keep him alive? William wants us to catch him so he can use a long, drawn-out trial and hanging to convince the Canadians they need our services to keep their Queen's cowboys under control."

"He didn't clearly specify dead or alive. This Simpson's a jackrabbit on a horse. They run for him like nobody I've ever dealt with before. It will be damn embarrassing if he outruns us and takes a powder with the forty-four thousand dollars. Can you imagine the outcome? We'll be reduced in rank and probably end up guarding shithouses. We don't want to disappoint William Pinkerton. I'm speculating that a bullet might be the only thing that'll bring him down."

"Yeah, maybe you've made a point there," Filbert answered.

The Pinkerton posse, headed up by Balfour Smith and Jiggs Dubois, along with five experienced operatives, set off from Minot on the morning of the 18th of November and established a station on the trail about twenty miles north of there. The next day, after a lunch of sliced meat and beans, Smith and Dubois were sitting on folding chairs in the large tent the Pinkertons had set up beside the trail. They were avoiding the wind while anticipating the hunt they were sure was about to take place. The five men they brought with them, experienced Pinkerton agents called in from various locations, were warming themselves around a fire. It had turned colder. An occasional stray snowflake danced around in the gunmetal sky.

On the morning of the 18th of November, Les unloaded his horses from the train in Moosomin. He provided them with oats in their nosebags and let them water. He was concerned there might be Pinkertons in Carlyle. When he arrived there after a long hard ride, the way seemed clear. His manoeuvre out of Regina had thrown his tracker off. Now he was hoping that his ploy of boarding the train and gaining as many miles as he could travelling south would save his horses and give him a decent opportunity to dash across the line.

When he cleared Carlyle without acquiring another follower he was certain that all his problems would be in front of him. Les guessed that, sooner or later, the Pinkertons would deduce that he was well on his way south. His edge would be the fact that he had gained many hours by taking the train as far as Moosomin. If they overlooked the possibility he had boarded the train, they wouldn't be expecting him for a few days. His plan was to head south until he was a few miles north of the border. After he reached his destination he would find a coulee, hide his horses and rest up for a big push the following day.

Once he had secured the money, Les was not quite as clear about how he would engineer his escape. He knew he would need a stopover on his way back into Canada. Depending on the circumstances and the weather, he would decide on one of two options when he had the cash and was on the run. The condition of his stock would dictate his actions. He'd either head for Quigley's place or cut in a westerly direction and lay up at one of the North-West Mounted Police posts in southern Assiniboia.

By then, the Mounties along the border would have packed up their horses and gear and headed to Regina to sit out the winter. That was their normal winter routine. He was confident that the posts would not be manned. They were potential resources that could provide him with shelter, wood and feed for his horse. If he managed to hole up somewhere and rest for a day, he could continue working his way across the southern part of the country. Ideally, he'd use the vacated Mounted Police posts until he had the opportunity to head north and catch the CPR train to the coast. In principal, it wasn't a bad strategy because he knew the territory, and the stations, while devoid of humanity, would be stocked up. If he ran into a Mountie patrol he could bluff his way through by claiming he was headed to work at a ranch. He spoke the Mountie lingo so he figured he would have no trouble on that account. There was a good possibility he would know the men on patrol. He was certain they'd be eager to help a former member who had just left the Force.

Les knew that escaping was a long shot. Now that he had been identified, it would only be a matter of time before news spread. Then the law on both sides of the border would be after him. His only chance was to pick up the payroll and find his way to another part of the world. They'd have to kill him to stop him. He had decided that being captured was not an option he could endure. He knew the shark-faced man and his burly companion he had spied in Regina would be on his trail like bloodhounds. Fretting over the bank manager's death had worn a groove in his mind. No matter how many times it occurred, it always ended with a hangman's noose dangling in the wind.

Early in the morning on the 20th of November, Les crossed the border. He followed an Indian trail about ten miles west of Bottineau. He intended to avoid all contact with Bottineau and travel across the grasslands over to Swedes' Ferry. He speculated that, if the ferry was being watched, he would be let through. He knew that the Pinkertons were obsessed with getting back the payroll. They would never have gone to the trouble of conning him in Regina by setting him up with a good horse and an outfit unless they were eager to catch him recovering the cash. Les figured the deeper he rode down into North Dakota, the more numerous the Pinkertons would be watching the roads and trails. If he managed to dig up the money he would have a surprise in store for them on his return journey.

By the time he reached the ferry the weather was shifting. A cold wind was blowing from the southwest. The river was filled with large patches of skim ice. He dismounted and stood between his two animals in order to cut down his visibility in the event that someone hidden might be taking aim at him. He was certain he was being watched. He stood on the bank for twenty minutes, waiting for the Swedes to spot him and bring the ferry over to transport him and his horses across the river. When the Swede arrived with the ferry, Les noticed he didn't seem nervous or agitated.

"Hell of a day," the Swede said as he dropped the landing ramp onto the shore. "Smell snow a' coming some time tonight, for sure."

The Swede's demeanor convinced Les the brothers had no inkling that the drama unfolding around them was even going on. When he reached the far bank he felt the sharp blade of the wind cut across his face and stab right through the front of his buttoned coat.

After Les left Swedes' Ferry and proceeded along the trail, Harold Moss and his two Pinkerton colleagues emerged from the brush on the south side of the river, behind Les, to make sure his return trip to the ferry would be greeted by a hail of lead. Moss was no hero. Taking Simpson alive was not an option he cared to contemplate. He and his fellow Pinkertons had already decided they would dig in on the riverbank and gun Simpson down on his return trip. Dubois' speech had been taken to heart.

While there was a well-defined road from Bismarck to Minot, the stretch north from Swedes' Ferry up to Bottineau was no more than a glorified path. Les managed to avoid one group of watchers, about two hours ride from where he buried the money. He saw smoke from a campfire gusting up from a clump of aspens in the distance. This forced him to make a wide circle around the trouble and come out about two miles further down the trail.

The three men at this watching place were defying Dubois' orders about remaining vigilant. They were cooking a couple of rabbits they had shot the night before on the trail. Les made a mental note to avoid this spot on his way back with the money. The fact that these men were visible on the trail heightened Les's awareness that more watchers and hunters were likely arrayed against him in various locations.

Les rode along, skirting the trail whenever he had the chance. He felt relieved when he finally reached the group of tall elms near the place he buried the payroll.

Unknown to Les, a watcher with a telescope in a stand of trees had spotted him. This discovery sent the man scrambling down to where his partners were hunched down out of the wind, playing cards. The watcher alerted his colleagues that Les was in the vicinity, then set off down the trail to warn the posse that the quarry had been sighted. His fellow Pinkertons decided to proceed carefully, now that the suspect was in the area. They spread themselves out and rode slowly in the direction the spotter reported seeing Les. This section of the countryside was filled with patches of bush and large stands of cottonwoods that grew along the banks of several shallow creek beds – plenty of opportunities for a man on horseback to hide.

Despite his confidence that he'd never forget where he hid the money, Les became slightly confused approaching it from the opposite direction. It took several false starts before he decided to search out a landmark that he recognized and then retrace his original route. After a few minutes of contemplation he suddenly had an idea. He decided to go to the base of the tallest elm, which had looked much different in full foliage than it did now, standing like a skeleton in the rising wind. From there it was easy to target the evergreen and locate the exact spot where he had buried the payroll.

Les tied off his horses and moved the rocks so he could pick the earth and dig up his treasure. He pulled the slicker-wrapped potato sack out from the ground. Then he took one of the bags from the back of the packhorses and filled it with the money. He gasped at the considerable volume and weight of the bills that he was stuffing into the bag. After he finished he cinched it shut and tied it securely to the back of his saddle. The second bag that contained his extra clothes, boots and the double-bladed axe was secured with heavy cord on top of the first one behind his saddle. Les knew he had reached the moment of truth. His rations were in his saddlebags. He dumped the load of camping and digging gear from the back of the packhorse, removed its halter and gave the horse a slap on the rump. It jumped away, skittish from the loss of its load, then settled in to grazing. Les pulled the Enfield Mark II from the holster under his coat and checked to make sure it was loaded, something he'd already done twice in the past three hours. Now he had nothing to do but turn his attention to surviving. That meant managing his horse so it had some run in its legs at the appropriate times. He was hoping that his luck was written large on this bitter, windy, November day.

Les had made friends with the horse on the trip down. He knew he was riding a solid animal that would respond to the pressure from his knees should he need his hands for other purposes. This horse would also run like hell for him. He felt confident that it could travel for a long time over a tough course and still have some dash in its limbs. Lastly, he gave the animal a chance to have a good long drink at the creek before they set off.

Half an hour down the trail, the watcher came clattering into the Pinkerton stop, nearly running over Smith and Dubois who were still sitting in their chairs in the tent. The horse had brushed the tent when the rider pulled it up short and jumped off.

"Jeezus, what in hell is goin' on here?" Balfour Smith asked as he picked himself up off the ground.

Dubois was already out the door, climbing on his Hanover that had been tied to a picket line between two trees. "Let's go boys!" he yelled.

They set off at a good clip, following the spotter who was taking them to the quarry. Dubois hoped his partners would be shadowing the suspect by now. Following Flumerfelt's formula, the posse was in full-gear, chasing down the watchers they hoped were keeping the quarry in sight. The program was simple – close ground but keep the suspect on the move until he had run himself to a standstill.

Les was worried about the men who had put up the smoke signal that warned him earlier to depart from the trail. On the return trip, he swung off the route and skirted the area they had inhabited earlier. He gradually worked his way back onto the main path that headed to the northeast. Les figured to make as many miles as he could on even ground until he was forced to improvise again and head overland. Almost simultaneously he heard the sound of a shot and the whine of a bullet passing by his head. He ducked down on the horse's neck and took off in a sprint as several other shots followed before he could disappear into the bush.

In a quick assessment of the situation, he guessed that two men with rifles had decided to take a crack at him from two hundred and fifty yards or more. They were almost directly behind him. Now, he had a buzz saw on his tail that was spewing bullets. He had no alternative but to spur his horse and outrun the problem. He knew he had to do something to discourage the followers, but it was too early in the chase for him to have to expend so much horse for such little gain. Les needed to put some doubt into the mind of his pursuers. He couldn't just continue to ride on and let them take potshots. After twenty minutes of covering ground at a frantic pace, he came to a place on the trail that he figured would work to his advantage. He rode deep into a thicket and secured his horse in a depression out of the wind. Pulling the Martini-Henry from its scabbard, he returned to a location that allowed him a view of his back trail for about a hundred and fifty yards.

Les hunkered down behind an enormous discoloured rock that stuck out of the prairie like an ancient cranium. He warmed his hands in his jacket pockets while he waited for his pursuers to show themselves. They came into view, riding single file, as if sensing an ambush. *They aren't rushing into anything*, he thought as he calmly waited for them to come closer. If they wanted to follow him they were welcome to do so, but soon they'd be doing it on Shanks' pony. They had seen him sprint away, but they weren't too anxious to run fast behind. Now he'd give them good reason to become even more cautious.

He carefully positioned the Martini-Henry on the top of the rock until he had the sights centred on the chest of the first horse. He gently squeezed the trigger. The animal went down to the ground. When the second horse turned sideways from the shock of the lead horse being hit, Les squeezed off a second shot that bored into its hind quarters. It collapsed in a shuddering heap. Both riders were off their respective rides, running for cover. He fired two more shots in their general direction, alerting them to the danger they faced if they slipped up again.

When Les made it back to his horse and mounted up, he heard a muffled shot that sounded like a revolver. He figured one of the riders had crept out to put his wounded mount out of its misery. Now Les and the horse had time to breathe as they picked their way through the bush back onto the trail.

⚜

The sound of so many shots invigorated Dubois and his posse. They were sure the watchers on the trail had entered into a war with the fleeing criminal. The long silence indicated to Dubois that maybe they had succeeded in gunning the runner down. After twenty minutes of hard riding, they arrived at a scene of carnage. The two Pinkertons were desolate. One of them was holding his arm awkwardly against his chest while the other man mopped his own sweating brow with a red bandana. Both of their horses were down, dead on the trail.

"What the hell? This is a mess!" Dubois exclaimed as he climbed down from the Hanover.

"We had a good chance at him," the agent with the broken arm whined. "We had him dead to rights but, damn, both of us missed our chance to bag him."

"Yeah, that's a problem with this fella," Dubois answered. "If you miss, you find your ass eaten up by a whirlwind. This fugitive shoots horses. I gotta admit they do make big targets. Since you two fellas are on foot, you're out of the picture. You can wait here until somebody comes along or you can start walking back to our bivouac."

"Scoundrel!" Balfour Smith exclaimed. "He shot the first horse right through the heart and paralyzed the second one by shooting the poor thing in the hind quarters. He exhibits no honour."

"Honour? Jeezus Keerist, Balfour, this guy's dangerous! If we catch him his neck is stretched for sure. I don't reckon he loves shooting horses. He's giving us notice that we're all going to be walking pretty soon if we keep on crowding him. He's not panicking, he's a very cool customer. While we're sitting around here gaping at his handiwork, he's putting miles on us. Let's mount up and head out. Stay spread apart on the trail. If he tries to ambush us the two back riders have to take off and try to outflank him. Maybe we can catch him making a mistake and line him up in a crossfire."

Smith didn't seem convinced by Dubois's assessment of the situation. He figured the jockey in Simpson was running like hell, racking up the miles, and an ambush was probably the last thing they could expect.

The two men on the ground confirmed that the rider had baggage on the back of the horse up behind the saddle.

"Well, he's retrieved the money so now it's a matter of cat and mouse," Dubois said.

"Like you say, Jiggs, the criminal's dangerous but he's not

dumb. Why is he heading straight for the Swedes' ferry? Surely by now it must have occurred to him that we have men covering the crossing?"

"Maybe not," answered Dubois. "He had no trouble coming down. Perhaps he thinks we're all behind him. If he's going to Quigley's or heading home to Brandon or another place in Canada, he has to cross the river some place. That won't be an easy feat this time of year with the temperature dropping like it is today. I'm guessing he's aiming to reach the ferry before dark. If he does, he's playing right into our hands, because Moss and his men will gun him down in a quick finish to the whole problem. Let's ride."

21

DUBOIS AND HIS POSSE HAD NO TROUBLE following Les's trail. It led them over the half-frozen ground like an inscription written in horseshoe tracks that read "follow me to the ferry." They couldn't believe their luck. The wily Simpson, who had so far defied capture, was now riding swiftly to his death at the hands of three crack-shot Pinkertons who were spread out in the bush in front of the ferry slip.

The two Swedes had refused to listen to Moss's suggestion that they leave the site and head for the hills lest they end up casualties from the action.

"Naah! We a' run the ferry as long as there's light and the a' river's not full of thick ice."

Les was no longer bothered by the fact that he was being pursued in earnest by gunmen who were bound and determined to bring his crime spree to a halt. As he rode along he rehearsed his river crossing just as he had countless times before. By losing the follower near Regina, then taking the train for part of his journey, he had thrown the timing of his arrival south of the border into doubt. He assumed Dubois's men, by now, would be waiting in ambush for him on the south side of the crossing to make sure he stayed on this side of the river.

Two miles from the ferry station, Les stopped to adjust the cinch under the horse's belly, securing the load that was up behind the saddle. He took out his Martini-Henry and fashioned a sling out of a length of cord so that he could carry the rifle across his back. His plan was to ride straight in, within a quarter mile of the ferry station, then make an abrupt left turn and angle away from the crossing site toward the place where the river widened dramatically. The money and the gear he needed were stored in the canvas bags he had tied up behind his saddle. The rifle on his back and the ammunition he put inside his jacket would ride above the waterline when he swam the horse across the river. It was a risky proposition at any time of year, never mind at the beginning of winter when the skim ice was rafting on the surface. He had ridden the horse enough to know that the gelding would willingly do anything he asked, even risk its own life.

Moss, surveying the terrain with his telescope saw Les coming from a long way off. "Load up men, this is it. He's going to come right on in here like a pigeon looking for a roost. Let him ride within fifty yards before we open up on him. I can see from here he has a big sack on the back of his saddle. Now we are going to end the escapades of one soon-to-be-sorry sucker."

Les came on but didn't come close enough for Moss and his men to fire a shot. They waited for the small figure on the horse to become larger, but it didn't happen. Before they could react, he veered off and was headed west toward the winding riverbank. They stayed hidden, too stunned to really comprehend what was happening.

When he reached the edge of the water, downstream from the ferry station, Les urged the horse into the river. The animal responded as he knew it would. They travelled about thirty yards through the shallows until they hit deep water, where the horse began to swim for all it was worth through the thin layers of patchy ice. Although the current carried them off course, Les, clinging to the horse's mane, stayed in the saddle and, after twelve minutes of furious swimming, they were up the bank on the far side of the river.

Moss and the men with him were astonished at the audacity of this action. They watched stunned from the far side of the river as Les quickly dismounted. Soon after he began massaging the horse's legs with some old sacking and the liniment he had obtained in Regina.

Thirty minutes later, Dubois and the posse appeared on the scene. The last few miles they had been listening, waiting to hear the shots that would announce the end of Simpson's crime spree. When they approached the ferry station they saw Moss and his men staring into the distance across the river.

"What in damnation is going on?" Dubois asked as he jumped down from the Hanover.

"Simple," said Moss. "The runner went down the bank to the wide section out of our range and urged that damn nag of his into the icy river and swam him over to the other side. You can see for yourself, he's just finished giving the horse a rub-down before he's about to take off again."

"What the hell are you doing over here?" Dubois thundered. "Why haven't you boarded the ferry and crossed to the other side after him? That's what you're paid to do!"

"To be honest with you, Jiggs, the boys and I were a little hesitant to follow up while he's attending to his horse over there. I mean we'd be sitting ducks on that ferry if he decided to pick us off one by one."

"You're nothing but a bunch of gutless wonders! The way the light is going we have to cross to the other side before darkness sets in. Where are them damned Swedes?"

The Swedes were having a coffee break beside the ferry slip. They weren't much amused by Dubois' bad temper and his threats to have them put out of business. They were already fed up with Moss for trying to boss them around and now Dubois was just making it worse.

"When a' we finish drinking our brew, we'll a' make a' one more trip across the river with a' the ferry before it's a' too dark and we stop a' for the day."

"What the hell are you talking about?" Dubois said. "I have

eight men and horses that need to go across. How many can you take on one trip?"

"Four a' horses and riders," one brother answered.

"I'll give you an extra ten bucks if you make two trips," Dubois said.

Nothing he could say or no amount of bribery would hurry the Swedes or change their minds about making only one last trip for the day. Just fifteen minutes or so before the light was about to leave the sky for the night, the Swedes set their mules to walking in their circle and slowly the ferry began to glide across the river. Dubois, Smith and two of their posse members were onboard, standing at attention beside their horses. When they were halfway across the river, in the deepest part of the channel, they spotted Les standing out in the open on the far bank.

"Look, he's not even running," Balfour said, with stunned shock in his voice.

"Jeezus, that is odd," Dubois answered, straining his eyes.

They watched helplessly as Les took the double-bladed axe out from the sack on the back of his horse and removed the cloth that covered the business end of it. He walked over to the enormous cottonwood tree where the ferry rope was attached to a block and he began chopping the thick fibres until the rope snapped back and fell limp across the water. The ferry careened to the left and began to spin slowly in circles downstream, in the middle of the channel, until it finally came to rest on a long, thin sand bar. The strange action of the current on a craft that was really not much more than a glorified raft upset the horses. They began to fidget and rear up, causing some real commotion.

"The son of a bitch!" Dubois shouted.

"Well, at least he's not shooting at us," Smith said.

Before they had much time to react, darkness had come down on the river like an enormous curtain. The bitter wind off the water grabbed the men by the throat. The horses stamped on the planks in an uneasy peace.

"How do we escape this floating disaster?" Dubois asked.

"We a' wait until a' dawn. It's a' too dangerous in a' the dark," the Swede answered.

"Are you joking or what?" Dubois said.

"You a' go ahead and jump overboard in a' the dark with your a' big horse. The fish in the river won't a' be hungry this a' winter."

"For God's sake, how can this have happened? That bastard is going to pay and pay when I catch up with him!" Dubois screamed.

"Pull yourself together," Smith said. "It's coal black out here. There's no use doing something rash that'll get us all drowned."

Before anybody had a chance to make another comment, a pitch-laden dead evergreen that was covered with dry brown needles on the far riverbank went up in the sky like a torch.

Les had tethered the gelding in the vicinity of the flaming tree to warm him after his swim in the frigid water. Les himself was standing stark naked in front of the blaze. Before long he had put on a change of dry clothes and boots from one of the water-proof bags. Once he was warmed up, he took the saddle off the gelding and rubbed the nag down again with sacking and liniment. He put the nosebag full of oats over its head and sat down beside the burning snag and ate the food he had unwrapped from the oilskins in his saddlebags. Les and the gelding would rest for a couple of hours beside the blaze, then he'd saddle up and head off into the darkness to begin the trek up toward Bottineau.

Dubois and his fellow Pinkertons were resigned to the fact that they were going nowhere until dawn came again and lit up the river so they could figure out how they were going to get off the ferry.

"How could we manage to have men on only one side of the crossing?" Dubois kept asking nobody in particular. "How is it possible? I explained the plan fully to our men at the Leland Hotel."

"Guess you didn't make it clear enough," Smith replied.

"I'm not really asking your opinion," Dubois answered.

To make things worse, sometime after midnight it began to snow. Soon Dubois and his men were covered in the white powder sifting down from the sky.

The Swede was a Swede. Stoic. He was not a man to waste words. Dubois turned sour, then sullen. Balfour Smith and the other Pinkerton men stamped their feet along with the horses and beat their bodies with their muffled arms to promote a little warmth. After a few more hours it grew exceedingly cold and boring out on the sand bar. Dubois was not fit for conversation. The other men were grumbling about the conditions. The Swede, in his big, snug, sheepskin-lined coat and fur hat, was silently regretting that he didn't have a fishing line.

Hours later, the thin orange light of dawn was glimmering around the edges of what seemed like a solid wall of grey cloud. Dubois cheered up. The long cold night was coming to an end. His companions were not nearly as optimistic. When the light became more fully developed it began to illuminate their dilemma. Dubois' speculation that they might make it ashore with only wet feet was a myth of his own spinning.

The Swede on board was eagerly waiting for his brother to harness the mules and bring them down to the south riverbank so they could salvage their crudely constructed ferry. His plan was to fish for the rope, then have his brother row their skiff out to fetch it and take it to the south shore where the mules were grazing. For a while the brothers jawed across the water, trying to formulate a rescue plan. There was a possibility that the horses and men, combined with the weight of the ferry, were too heavy a load to employ the mules to pull it off the bar.

Dubois was fretting how to make it over to the far shore. He knew there was only a slim chance to stay in the race. He was sure that, if the quarry escaped, Filbert would turn on him and blame him for them coming up empty. His mind was working overtime, imagining Simpson escaping with the money. He could envision the stern face of William Pinkerton telling him that he had bungled big-time, and that his services were no longer required. It would be a massacre. Dubois made up his mind. Failure was not a possibility. He and his fellow Pinkertons would drop the ferry ramp on the sand bar. They would swim their horses to the north side of the river. From there they would defy the elements by making the ten miles to Bottineau in their wet clothes. When he informed the others of his decision they were not enthusiastic.

"Look at it this way boys, you either swim your horses for it or consider yourself former Pinkerton employees. I'll let you fellas explain to William Pinkerton why we sat in the middle of a river while a murderer trotted off with forty-four grand of James J. Hill's money. It certainly won't be the Pinkerton National Detective Agency's finest hour. I'll tell you one more thing. None of you unemployed will ever find a job working for the railroad!"

"Lighten up, Jiggs, we've been through too much to give up," Balfour answered.

The other two men, Moss and Finnigan, long-time Pinkerton stalwarts, decided they, too, were in on the gambit. Their decision to risk the river perked Dubois up.

"We'll haul our frozen asses up the trail to Bottineau where we can thaw out and refocus on chasing that bastard over the border."

Dubois decided he'd go first. Since he was the leader he had to provide inspiration for his men. However, unknown to everyone on the ferry, Dubois was undergoing a crisis that challenged his very existence. Jiggs Dubois not only couldn't swim, but he was terrified of water. When he climbed up on the back of the Hanover and the Swede dropped the ramp, the big horse refused to move.

"Maybe this ain't such a great idea," Smith offered.

Dubois slid off the Hanover. He was relieved to feel his feet touching the planks on the ferry deck. After a conference, they decided that, if the three other horses could be induced to swim for the far bank, then maybe the Hanover would follow. Balfour Smith was first up. His horse, named Butter Ball, clattered down the ramp onto the sand bar and went right into the river, making enthusiastically for the other side. Moss followed on his dappled grey beast, making a fuss but moving along. Finnegan, a better rider than the other two, had no problem getting his buckskin lined up and down the ramp onto the sand and into the river. That left Dubois balancing precariously, as usual, on his sturdy Hanover with its crazy eyes. All Dubois could think of as the horse lurched down the ramp onto the sand was that he needed to hang on with both hands if he wished to stay aboard during the trip through the frigid water. It all seemed like a nightmare to the terrified Dubois until his big mount climbed onto the river bank.

Wet and shivering, Dubois said, "Men, the only chance we have is to show some grit. If we can keep these nags moving, maybe we can make it to Bottineau before we freeze to death."

"Jiggs, don't you think we should make a big fire first and warm up?"

"Hell, no." Dubois answered. "He has a head start and if we stop to fool around it will only make it worse for the horses. We gotta keep moving."

A few miles along the trail, Dubois and his henchmen looked as if their lower bodies were constructed of ice. Pant legs were frozen stiff as stovepipes and they were riding glittering horses that sent steam forming into small clouds that drifted off into the bush.

Late in the morning, when they plodded into Bottineau, the locals came out of their homes and businesses to stare at the four strange ice-laden travellers on their mounts, standing like frozen statues in front of the general store.

Gerry was summoned by Adam Mott, the mayor, who sent his son Oliver down to the Widow Murphy's place to drag the constable out of bed. A few of the locals, feeling sorry for the horses, helped the four men. All of them were frozen to the saddle and it took some chipping and hacking to free them and lower them to the ground. After the saddles were off, the horses were led down the street to the local stable. Jensen was horrified when he saw the condition of the Pinkerton horses. He sent his helper around town to ask for volunteers because he knew there was no time to waste if they were going to be saved.

By the time Gerry arrived, the four Pinkertons were huddled up together in the general store, wrapped in blankets in front of the pot-bellied stove with steaming cups of coffee in their hands. They were sitting with their froze-up feet, still in their boots, in buckets of warm water.

"Chancing the river this time of year is a pretty foolish proposition," Gerry said to a complete wall of silence. "Dubois, your tongue must be frozen. I've never known you to be such a stoic."

MacGregor was bustling around the store, gathering together new sets of underwear, socks and pants for the men, while his assistant Tommy was checking their boot sizes. Dubois wanted all four of them outfitted with a complete new set of winter outerwear as well, including wool pants, heavy coats, gloves and fur hats. He also ordered foodstuffs and camp gear necessary to help sustain him and his men when they set off again on the chase. He gave MacGregor instructions that everything would be charged to the Pinkertons and the bill would be paid from the head office.

Half an hour later, Jensen arrived from his stables. He was furious and gave Dubois hell for treating horses in such a cavalier manner. Dubois placated him by telling him he was prepared to pay his price for four new saddle horses. He wanted Jensen to haul their saddles down to his livery and warm them up.

"We'll be here for no more than three or four hours. Then I want the new horses saddled and we'll be off again. Your horses and services will be charged to the Pinkerton National Detective Agency. Do you understand?"

"Yes," Jensen answered, "but you're paying a premium. I don't know if I want to sell horses to people who abuse them."

"The cost doesn't matter," Dubois answered. "This is about something else."

"This is such a bizarre situation, I have no idea what to ask you boys," Gerry said.

"Don't waste your breath," Dubois replied. "It's too long a short story."

22

December, 1894
Province of British Columbia, Canada

HE WAS STANDING ON DECK, looking at the blue mountains on
the north shore of Vancouver's harbour, as the ship slowly made
its way down Burrard Inlet. The snow-topped mountain peaks
of the granite Lions rose like sentinels among whale-backed be-
hemoths. He was onboard the RMS Empress of Japan, one of
the sister ships in the Canadian Pacific Railway fleet of
steamships providing luxury service to the Orient. The letter of
passage obtained from James J. Hill had opened up doors to a
world that Bud Quigley couldn't have imagined existed.

When he disembarked from the Great Northern train in Seattle on November 27th, the weather was mild and it was gently
raining in the bustling city. He checked into the Occidental
Hotel on Pioneer Square and ordered himself a hot bath. For
more than an hour he sat in the near-boiling water and cleansed
himself of many of his past sins and worries. After that, he walked
into the city. He located a haberdashery where he found a gentle
eastern European named Milo who, after a short conversation,
assured him that he was a man with the perfect build to show
off his merchandise. He purchased a frock coat, three vests, a
tuxedo and two tweed jackets that the tailor said were imported

from Scotland. He didn't have time for Milo to craft suits for him, so he took what the tailor had already constructed. In addition, he acquired a deluxe topcoat. Milo told him he could wait there, if he liked, while the tailor and his assistant made quick alterations, or he could use the time to go down the street to the hatter and pick out an appropriate *chapeau*, as he put it. He walked into the Dunlop hat shop and chose a homburg that was packed for him in a deluxe box. Back at Milo's, he picked out underwear, socks, pants, suspenders, shirts, sweaters, shirt collars, cuffs and ties. After paying his bill he asked for his goods to be delivered to him at his hotel.

Later that afternoon at the Bon Marche, not far from the hotel, he purchased a pair of square-toed boots, a pair of dress shoes, spats, a money belt and a steamer trunk that was tricked out with a false bottom.

He was going on a long trip on a steamer to the Orient. A pamphlet, which came attached to the letter of passage signed by James J. Hill, outlined the kind of formal attire passengers in first class were expected to wear onboard ship at dinner and various other occasions. Without this primer in good taste and fashion, he would have stood out like a bruised thumb at a convention of manicurists. Now, with money in his pocket and the salt air in his lungs, he felt like a new man.

Back at the hotel, he set about arranging his travel gear. He opened the trunk and marveled at its clever secret compartment. He stuffed his money belt with cash until it could hold no more. Then he counted out the rest in stacks and secured it in bundles in the false bottom, under his new array of fashionable clothing. He oiled and polished the Smith & Wesson, then loaded it, wrapped it in black bag with a drawstring, and placed it in another secret compartment under the trunk lid. He also cleaned and loaded the derringer, now his constant companion, and tucked it safely into his inside jacket pocket.

He had purposely chosen a high-end hotel so he could observe the clientele and see how they acted in their day-to-day movements. He was also concerned with security. He felt safer with his pile of cash in a better establishment. When he had first checked in, unshaven and scruffy, carrying a couple of canvas bags, he felt out of place. However, after sitting in the lobby in a wing chair reading the newspaper, he noticed that it was not so much the way a person dressed, but how they acted, that set them apart. He realized that, often, the men checking in were rough and ready types, recent arrivals from rural locations where they had been attending to their business. These same men materialized a few hours later in the lobby shaved and dressed to the nines. Their demeanor was no different than formerly, when they had been wearing dungarees and old work boots. They were confident men who used the weight of their own substantial personalities and carried on without hesitation.

He quickly noticed that these men promptly and discreetly tipped the people who served them, as if it were an obligation given to them by God. For two days he went out to restaurants and hung around using the services of the hotel so he could practice tipping waiters, doormen and maids. He soon realized that being a gentlemen meant he didn't carry his own bags or open many doors. He made sure he had a supply of coins and small bills on hand to take care of this new obligation. He felt his new way of acting was part of the disguise he needed to carry off a new life on another continent. He might as well start working on his image from the start.

When he reached Vancouver on the 30th of November, after an uneventful stagecoach ride across the international border into British Columbia, he checked into the Alhambra Hotel in Gastown. When he journeyed to the Empress Line office to show his letter of passage he was overwhelmed by the treatment he received. Initially, he was shaken when the clerk at the wicket took the letter and abruptly turned tail and departed through a door into a back room. For two minutes he fretted in the lobby wondering if the police were being called.

Suddenly, a burnished metal door at the far end of the room opened and a distinguished-looking gentleman with grey mutton-chop whiskers approached briskly, holding out his hand. "Ah, Mr. Quigley, a delight indeed to meet you. I am Arthur Cathcart, Vice President and Manager of Passenger Services, Canadian Pacific Steamship Company. Any friend of J. J. Hill is an honoured guest of the Canadian Pacific Railway. Sir, I will be providing you with a top top-of-the-line stateroom on the Empress of Japan. I must tell you at once that you will be a welcome guest each evening at Captain Henry Pybus's table. Now, if you will tell me the name of your hotel we will send a landau to pick you up on the morning of departure and transport you and your luggage to the ship. No need for you to remain here waiting for the completion of routine paper work. That will be done and in the hands of our staff who will call for you at your hotel."

For a moment he was taken aback. He remained speechless for several seconds, torn, wondering should he or should he not give Arthur Cathcart a tip? Something in Mr. Cathcart's bearing and his attire convinced him that it would be gauche. He made the right decision by smiling at Mr. Cathcart and warmly shaking his hand with both of his own in a gesture of gratefulness for the kindness and consideration. This produced a beaming smile and slight bow from Mr. Cathcart, an action that taught him more about society than any other convention he had previously witnessed.

The day before his ship was to sail, he had two more duties to perform. He wrote a cryptic message on a sheet of hotel stationary and put it in an envelope addressed to Ida Mae Simpson, General Delivery, Brandon, Manitoba.

He then filled a box with linens, cloth napkins and a tablecloth that he purchased at a shop down the street from the hotel. He wrapped the tablecloth around the package of cash he inserted in the middle of the parcel along with a folded sheet of paper that read Last Will and Testament of Bud Quigley. He addressed the box to *Mary Nuttal, RR 4, Elora, Ontario*, and sent for the hotel's concierge.

"I want you to mail this letter for me and also this package." He proffered his hand as discreetly as the rich men he had watched in Seattle did, slipping three folded dollar bills into the concierge's hand. "Can you do that for me today? When you return with the receipt I will repay you the cost of mailing."

"Yes sir," the man said as he tucked the generous offering into his waistcoat pocket.

The look on the concierge's face said it all. He would spend his time on the voyage watching and continuing to learn how the rich interacted with the serving classes and with one another. He had already absorbed the valuable lesson that attitude and money were keys to success. The ship would be filled with the rich and the entitled. Now he had to master the art of feeling comfortable in their presence.

Time and places had passed in a blur in front of his eyes since he had travelled by rail to the coast from the frozen prairies.

In the morning he was ushered to the landau for the trip along the waterfront to the pier where his ship was berthed. He was astonished by the many nationalities he saw crowded together on the cobblestone streets. At the ship's gangway he was greeted and welcomed aboard by a ship's officer resplendent in a formal nautical uniform.

When he reached the deck he was immediately introduced to the valet who would accompany him to his stateroom to unpack his things and lay out his wardrobe. Shortly thereafter, a steward arrived with a glass of champagne on a silver tray. Even in the lap of luxury he was still eager to soak up the local colour. He hurried back out onto the ship's deck. He watched the seamen raise the gangplank and prepare the ship for leaving its berth. Other passengers on deck were waving hankies and shouting last minute instructions to their family members and friends who had come to see them off. A brass band on the quay was playing the music hall songs of the times.

After the ship was underway, he stood at the railing watching the seagulls flying overhead and felt the lush ocean wind, mellow and inviting against his face. He watched sailboats passing in the harbour and heard the clang of the bell buoys that rang out as they passed. He was intoxicated by the sense of freedom he felt on the deck of the immense ship as it made for open water. He tipped his hat to his fellow passengers who had also strolled out on deck to enjoy the departure.

It was a far different world from the countryside of the long, hard winter ride he had just endured. He had taken shelter at vacant Mounted Police posts along the border country until he arrived, half-frozen, in Havre, Montana, and presented his rail pass at the wicket in the railway station. The clerk looked at the pass and issued him a ticket with car and sleeping berth numbers. Something in his heart sank to the level of his boots when a stern-looking man approached. He looked around the station expecting to see Pinkertons coming from every direction. However, to his relief, it was the porter arriving to offer assistance.

"Welcome aboard the Great Northern. Would you like us to put your bags in your sleeper on the train?"

"No, I'll keep them with me. I want to clean up a little before I board the train and my kit is in one of the bags."

"Very good, sir. Your train to the coast will be leaving within the hour. Everything is in order, all the way to Seattle. Hope you enjoy the trip, Mr. Quigley."

Quigley was a mouthful; a name he would have to get used to being called.

At the river, when Leslie Robert Simpson saddled up the horse provided for him by the Pinkerton National Detective Agency, he had no idea where he was bound. All he knew was that, for the time being, he had outsmarted the Pinkertons, who were last seen freezing their asses off in the middle of the Mouse River while he and his mount, reinvigorated by fire and food, headed off into the darkness.

The night was bitterly cold. It snowed off and on but he made careful, steady progress. When dawn came he spurred the horse on. They made good time on the last stretch up to Quigley's, arriving there in the late afternoon.

Les had approached cautiously to see if there were watchers in the vicinity. After checking the area by making slow circles in toward the cabin, he assured himself there was no immediate danger.

He noticed a gentle curl of smoke coming out from the cabin stovepipe. When he was closer he saw the dead man lying on his back outside the cabin door. At first he assumed somebody must have killed Bud. Closer yet, he realized the dead man was a stranger to him. The man had been shot twice. Once in the throat and once in the right eye. Oddly, his left eye, though glassy, had frozen partly open. He could see ice crystals had formed on the dead man's eyelids.

Les spotted the Smith & Wesson lying on the ground. He picked it up and put it into his coat pocket.

"Bud," he yelled, "are you inside?"

At first there was no response, then he heard muffled voice. "Come ahead but keep your hands in sight."

Les carefully opened the door and let a terrible stench out of the room. It was so pungent it grabbed him by the throat. It gave him the dry heaves.

"Jeezus, Bud," he said, "what's going on here?"

"That Frenchie bastard killed me, is all," Bud croaked.

"Appears to me you gave him a headache he's never going to get over," Les replied.

"Tall Bob," Bud said. "Never thought I'd see you again."

He was lying on his bunk in his blankets. He had been in his cabin for three days. Gangrene had set in and his strength was ebbing by the minute. Les put the Smith & Wesson on the table, stoked up the wood stove and fetched a clean bucket of water that he dipped from the frozen-topped rain barrel. Bud's yellow-rimmed eyes were sunk into his cheeks.

Les asked Bud if he could look at his wound. Carefully peeling back shirt and underwear top he was dismayed when he saw the black and brown flesh, the slimy substance that was oozing out from it. The smell was enough to set him back once again.

"He gave you a good one," is all Les could say.

"That greasy dead thing outside my door is a Pinkerton invention."

"I'm sorry about that," Les said lowering his eyes.

"Don't be sorry about it kid, I let you down."

"What do you mean?"

"Remember that chestnut with the three white socks? I let the nag live. Old soft-hearted me, I couldn't do it. Pinkertons followed up here and couldn't let it go."

"Take it easy, Bud, you need to save your strength."

"Never mind. My flesh has gone putrid and I stink like death. That Frenchie blew me up and now I'm a feast for blowflies. Answer a dying man one question – what the hell are you doing here?"

"I'm on the run. I buried some of the cash from the robbery. I came back for it. You might as well know I was in the North-West Mounted Police when I came down here and knocked off that bank."

"I know."

"How?"

"That shark-faced Pinkerton got a hold of the empty from the shot you fired in Bismarck. It was an Enfield cartridge casing, which is Mounted Police issue."

"I slipped up."

"That ugly-faced bastard ain't dumb. He added up the horse coming this way plus the casing and he got stubborn about it," Bud rasped again, trying to sit up.

"Lie back, don't waste your breath."

"I'll make you a deal. Promise to send my money to my sister and I'll give you a way out of your problem."

"What are you saying?"

"What's your name? Your real name."

"Les, Leslie Robert Simpson."

"Not no more," Bud said, falling back and sinking farther into his fever.

When he came alert again Bud motioned for Les to hand him the papers that were on his table. "Listen to me carefully, Tall Bob. From this day your name is Bud Quigley. You take this railway pass, this letter of passage courtesy of James J. Hill and you ride like hell out of this country before they catch you. You are a purveyor of fine horses to a railway magnate. Remember that. Hill looks after his friends. Give me some more water."

"That's a good deal for me. What can I do for you?"

"Fetch my six-thousand-dollar nest egg. You make sure it goes to my sister."

"Where is your nest egg?" Les asked.

"Where a nest egg should be. Why, underneath my chickens, of course."

"That's a good one, Bud."

"You write a note with the money saying: Last Will and Testament of Bud Quigley. You send it with the money to Mary Nuttal, RR 4, Elora, Ontario. Can you remember all that?"

Les nodded his head.

"Good man. Now go scatter those hens off the roost and fetch the money."

When Les came back in carrying the valise full of money he pulled out from under the straw, he found that Bud had lapsed into a shaking delirium.

After an hour of rasping and wheezing, Bud again tried to sit up. He told Les to open his hand. He put the derringer and cartridge box on Les's palm. Bud instructed him to take the Smith & Wesson with him and throw the Enfield Mark II onto the cabin floor.

"Why would I do that?" Les asked.

"When I die, you drag that grease ball in here and lay him on the floor beside that revolver. You stoke up the stove, throw the kerosene from my lamp around the room and you turn this cabin into an inferno. It'll warm me up some and it'll give you a new life. I'll be dead and you'll be the new me. When the Pinkertons arrive they'll figure we both perished in the fire."

"It might work," Les answered.

"Never mind, it will work. One more thing."

"What's that?"

"Put your horse in the corral. Leave on the brown nag the grease ball rode in on. When you take off from here, don't stop for any man."

Les sat up with Bud for the better part of the night.

In his delirium Bud travelled back to his childhood. He had a conversation with his mother, then he started a streak about horses before he faltered and the words fell into being gibberish. Les felt like he was in a cave. He could do nothing but comfort Bud and watch him die. *A good man, maybe one of the best*, he thought. He couldn't think of anyone who outclassed him. Now he was near the end, in the presence of silence and the yawning cold at a godforsaken place.

Sometime in the early hours, Bud began to rasp and wheeze, then the death rattle issued from him and he slumped back, dead.

It was perhaps an hour before dawn and snow was falling gently from the frozen sky. Les went out to the corral to find the still-saddled brown horse. By the shape of its features, it looked to be a game nag. That was usually the case but never the rule. Sometimes the worst-looking scabby cayuse turned out to be a firecracker.

Back inside the cabin he folded the railway pass, shipping pamphlet and Hill's letter and tucked them into his shirt pocket. He slid the Smith & Wesson into his holster and dropped the Enfield onto the cabin floor. Outside, he packed the valise into one of the bags with his money and secured both up behind the saddle. Finally, he dragged Frenchie's stiff body into the cabin.

He had only one more task to perform. He stoked up the stove until it was groaning from the heat then he splashed kerosene around the cabin. He lifted the metal burner from the top of the stove and lit a piece of kindling. He backed out of the doorway and dropped the flame into the cabin. Within seconds there was a whooshing noise. The dry old place was burning with vigour. Something inside him told him to saddle up before first light and be the hell gone. When he left he was wearing Bud's bison coat, beaver hat and wolverine gloves. He rode about fifty yards before he stopped the brown horse. He looked back at the burning cabin. It was starting to snow harder now, greatly reducing visibility.

Good thing, he thought. *It'll cover my tracks.*

He saluted Bud Quigley, turned the horse to the west, and set off.

⁂

Eight hours passed before Dubois and his colleagues were prepared to leave Bottineau. After thawing themselves it was apparent the Pinkertons needed a few hours of sleep to recover from their frantic chase and the all-night river ordeal.

Dubois set them back further when he started a shouting match with Jensen about the cost of the four replacement riding horses and three pack nags he needed to carry supplies he purchased from MacGregor. Jensen insisted on having his price in writing with a substantial down payment, which took all of Dubois' cash. He then demanded Dubois send a telegram to head office to confirm the deal. He further insisted on an answer before he would release the horses.

"What the hell, my word and paper not good enough for you?" Dubois asked, scowling at the room.

"It's not that. I just figure the way you go about your business you have a good chance of getting your ass shot off before this adventure is over. Where does that leave me?" Jensen answered.

Dubois sent a telegram to Roger Filbert at the Leland Hotel. Two hours passed before Filbert answered the wire in the affirmative about paying top dollar for the horses. Jiggs complicated matters by growing sour and fretting about their delay in starting out and then insisting they travel at night.

"Maybe we should wait for first light," Balfour Smith said.

Dubois was livid. "First light! Are you daft? That killer has bolted and you want to sit on your ass humouring the local peasants while he runs plumb away. Am I hearing you right?"

"We can cover ground quicker by daylight and we won't blunder into a bad situation and end up shot. It will be a tough trip up there in the dark. Won't be any picnic if he decides to make a stand somewhere along the route. Shouldn't we ask Filbert to send reinforcements? Maybe we can fan out and catch him making a mistake," Smith reasoned.

"The smug prick had a two-hour nap in front of us while we were stuck on that fff'ing sand bar. Now you want to sleep longer in Dinkville while Simpson scampers away with the railway payroll. I tell ya, that bugger's not sleeping now. He's rested and making tracks while we jack off and talk stupid shit."

"I think it might be you're taking this whole thing personally," said Smith.

"Personally? You've got that right! I've been thinking about trapping this rodent and watching him swing twenty-four hours a day. Any objections?" Dubois asked.

"No, I guess not."

"If you do, stay behind. I'm gonna apprehend the bastard if I have to chase him all the way to hell. When I finally see him I'll put a bullet into his hide to ensure he slows right down. Then he won't be hard to catch. I'll strap him on a four-legged rearend. Then I'll haul him stiff to Bismarck so the sheriff there can see what a beauty he missed out on. Bet Flumerfelt will get a charge out of seeing Jiggsy Dubois traipse through Minot with a trophy Mountie and his filthy sack of lucre slung across a mule's back." Dubois's hands were shaking when he lit a rollie. "Imagine the satisfied look on William Pinkerton's face when he hears the news. Think of the glory when we turn up with James J. Hill's payroll! Sleep is our enemy. Let's saddle up and head out. If we don't move fast the SOB's going to make horses' asses of us all."

They were hampered on their journey to Quigley's place by having set out in pitch darkness. It made the trip a slow meander through harsh country and the cold hours. Several times they inadvertently left the trail, tangling themselves up on rough ground, only to turn around and retrace their path to find the way again. When they were within a few miles they could smell smoke on the prevailing wind. Still, they were careful in approaching, fearing an ambush.

They arrived to find a pile of smouldering ashes. They located the Pinkerton horse Simpson had been riding in the corral, but there was no sign of forty-four thousand dollars. Dubois and Smith sat on their haunches, looking into the vestiges of the fire. There was something peaceful about the glowing embers and the steady heat that pushed against their faces as they leaned over warming their hands.

Hours later, after the pile had cooled down, Smith, having walked around poking in the ashes with a long stick, reported finding two bodies.

"I hate to say it but it looks like Quigley and Simpson perished in the fire."

Smith emerged from the mess with the charred remains of the Enfield Mark II revolver on the end of the stick.

"There's not much doubt that this is the murder weapon."

Dubois was beside himself cursing their luck. "Where's the money?"

"Must have gone up in flames."

"There has to be more to it than that?"

"No," Smith said, "there's nothing more."

The wind picked up. It started to snow with a vengeance. Before long the yard was under a white blanket. Now and then the empty square of ashes hissed and crackled.

NOTES

Many of the characters in this story were real people in their time and place – in the year 1894 on both sides of the border on the American Great Plains and the Canadian Prairies. Two distinct ways of naming landscape in two unique jurisdictions.

I wrote this book for Dolores Reimer who on a lazy summer afternoon asked me to tell her a story. With thanks to Terry Jordan, Geoffrey Ursell, Tania Craan, Robin Thompson, Susan Buck and Nik Burton.

ABOUT THE AUTHOR

ALLAN SAFARIK is a poet, non-fiction writer and novelist. He lives in the historic Jacoby house in Dundurn, Saskatchewan on the Louis Riel Trail. Born and raised in Vancouver, British Columbia, Safarik's work is located in two different regions – the West Coast of Canada and the Canadian prairies.